FROM GIRL TO WOMAN

Delany managed to bring a jaw-cracking blow against the side of the black-bearded man's face. Then suddenly my attacker was running through the trees.

I stood unsteadily as Delany turned to me. "You all right, Anna?"

Suddenly I was in his arms, sobbing and trembling, and pressing my cheek against his chest. His arms cradled me with a gentleness I wouldn't have thought possible. I could feel the rapid rise and fall of his breathing. The strong, firm length of his body pressed against mine was the sweetest warmth that I had ever felt. I seemed to change as he held me, a bewildering metamorphosis from a timid girl into a woman with frightening desires.

"I'm sorry," I whispered. "I should have listened to you."

His lips touched my forehead in a whispery kiss. "It's all right, Tiger," he said. "Everything's all right."

And at the moment, for one brief instant in time, I believed him.

THE WHISPERING WINDS OF BLACKBRIAR BAY

LEE KARR

ZEBRA BOOKS
KENSINGTON PUBLISHING CORP.

ZEBRA BOOKS

are published by

Kensington Publishing Corp.
475 Park Avenue South
New York, NY 10016

First printing: February, 1991

Printed in the United States of America

With thanks to Ann LaFarge,
a talented editor who enriches my life and my work.

Chapter One

One of my earliest memories is sitting on my father's lap while he showed me his gold pocket watch. The memory is a warm one, and only years later I learned the watch held a secret to terror and murder. When he flipped open the lid, I stared fascinated at the bold black numbers and fragile hands of the watch's face. On the opposite side a faded photo fit into the lid like a locket.

"My sister, Minna," he had told me. "Taken when we were fifteen." A sadness always crept into his expression when he looked at the girl's laughing face, and I assumed that she must have died young. The young man looping his arm through hers looked nothing like my care-weary father, who had deep creases in his cheeks and furrows in his brow.

My brother, Davie, who had been born deaf, never had the pleasure of listening to the watch's mesmerizing tick-tock, but he would touch the smooth casing with his fingertips and then smile in a wistful fashion that always tore at my heart.

My mother had died when Davie was eight. I was

7

seventeen years old and had practically raised the boy. My father had little time or energy for looking after the two of us. He was too busy trying to strike it rich in the high Sierras of Nevada. Rocky Gulch was the third camp we had called home in less than two years. Our house was nothing more than a shack built against a wall of rocks. It had an earthen floor, and poorly caulked timbers that let in the rain, wind, and snow.

I didn't understand the furies that drove my father. After my mother's death, Benjamin McKenzie had deserted our Kansas dry land farm and headed west. Moving from place to place, we lived in small frontier towns in Colorado and Idaho, braving the harsh winters and dusty summers. We finally moved on to Nevada two years ago, when tales of mountains filled with silver and gold fired my father's wanderlust.

"After we make our strike, we'll head for San Francisco, Anna. Buy one of them pretty houses," he said in his dreamy fashion. "Dress you up so pretty that every buck in the county will come courting. You'll have plenty of rich men to choose from." My father's choice of a proper husband for me was another of his dreams. He kept saying he was willing to endure all the hardships of prospecting so I could have a better chance at life than the worn, weary women who inhabited the mining camps. My father made it clear to me that I was to have no acquaintance with any young man in the camps, and if one looked sideways at me, he would be in danger of losing one of his front teeth to my father's fists. I was rather amused that he was so protective of me. None of the unshaven, rowdy young men held any attraction for me, and I agreed with my father that there wasn't a decent husband among them. Like most young women

8

my head was filled with foolish fantasies about the man who would one day claim me as his own.

"Should I marry a banker or a sea captain?" I asked, playing the game.

"A banker," my father said without hesitation. "And don't take the first one that asks you, either. Be choosy."

"That I will," I promised with a laugh that had an edge of despair in it. Even though my father thought my McKenzie red hair and brown eyes were pretty, I knew better. He had told me often enough that all the McKenzie women had flaming crowns of titian hair which set us apart. That much was true. I'd never seen another head of red hair as coppery as mine, but I didn't find it to be any kind of a compliment. Even my brother Davie's hair was an attractive shade of deep red, more like my father's before it had darkened and showed slivers of gray at the temples. I thought my father, Benjamin McKenzie, a handsome man, and I was proud of his tall figure and the way he carried himself. He always looked everyone straight in the eye. His honesty was never in question, nor his willingness to help someone less fortunate when he had the chance. I knew there were plenty of widows who would jump at the chance to marry him. When he was teased about them by his men friends, he'd laugh and say that his pretty daughter kept his house as neat as any wife . . . and was a lot less trouble. He promised me that someday I would have a different dress for every day in the week. My appearance was the least of my concerns. Most of the time, I wore a sunbonnet or a scarf over my thick, flaming hair to keep back rebellious curls that were always drifting forward on my forehead. I had two calico dresses and one pansy-blue wool that had

9

been my mother's. I had found the gown in a trunk after her death and had treasured it until I finally grew old enough to alter the dress to fit. My father's eyes got misty when he saw me in it, and I wondered if it could have been my mother's wedding dress. My father's talk of dressing me up in finery seemed to ease the guilt he felt for seeing his daughter dressed poorly. All I owned were two flannel petticoats, three aprons made of bleached sacks, and one pair of shoes. In any case, I had little time to think about clothes. Managing the daily chores and looking after Davie demanded all my time and energy.

"Water," I said to Davie, making a sign, and pointing to a couple of empty buckets sitting on the wash bench.

He nodded and quickly grabbed one while I took the other. I loved my little brother. He was a sweet boy with an alertness in his manner that defied his silent world. Between us we had developed a sign language all our own that was primarily based on pantomime. I always mouthed the words at the same time I did the action. As understanding became faster, the signs became shorter, and Davie read my lips so that we could even laugh and joke with each other. His understanding of what was being said to him without hearing the words showed how smart he was. And he was a great little mime. I had to hold my sides sometimes, he had me laughing so hard when he imitated some good old boy shooting tobacco at a tin can or a fat woman bending over a washboard scrubbing clothes with a wiggling of her fanny.

Davie loved to hike all over the craggy hills, picking up pretty rocks and giving them to me as if they were precious treasures. He made games out of throwing sticks across the gully, or pointed excitedly at the high flight of an eagle or hawk overhead.

I found myself laughing with him and looking at him with maternal pride. As we walked to the creek, I noticed that touseled curls framed his face and hung low on his neck. I needed to get out the old scissors and give him another haircut. A splatter of freckles marched across his face and his lean cheeks. He seemed perfectly content with his place in life. He was unaware that his mended pants were above his high-top shoes and his bony wrists stuck out the sleeves of his faded shirt, making him look like an orphan ragamuffin. His basic, good-natured disposition was a mockery to my fits of anger and stubborn pride. I raged at a cruel fate that had cheated him of so much of life's joy.

But the day was not one for remorse. An azure sky was flecked with small clouds that looked like feathery puffs moving lazily across the heavens. The breeze that danced along the high walls of the canyon was warm, and I was glad that it was late May, even though I dreaded the hot, dusty summer ahead.

Swinging the buckets, we made our way down to a creek that twisted along the bottom of a rocky gulch. Refuse was piled everywhere along the path: old sardine boxes, broken picks and shovels, empty food tins, and rubbish of all kinds. Tents and crude buildings littered the slopes in tiers, and the hillside was pocketed with holes and tailings which showed where some prospector was digging for the earth's storehouse of gold.

Davie grabbed my arm and pointed. His large brown eyes were wide with excitement. A tiny puppy that was hardly more than a ball of fur came tumbling down a pile of refuse, obviously looking for something to eat. At our approach, the puppy raised his head, peered through a mass of tangled hair, and went bouncing over to Davie. He gave a friendly "woof" which my brother couldn't hear, but the wagging tail and slurping tongue spoke clearly enough. Davie leaned down and petted the puppy and then raised pleading eyes to me.

I shook my head firmly. We scarcely had enough food to keep body and soul together without trying to feed a growing puppy. My father hired out for meager day-pay work, helping other prospectors work their claims so he could keep us from starving while he sank every extra penny into his own diggings. I worried that Davie wasn't getting enough to eat most meals and halved most of my rations to try and keep him filled. I wasn't going to have my brother give his share to a dog.

The light went out of Davie's face, and I felt new pain at his disappointment. Anger quickly followed. I hated the horrible camp life, the dirt, the filth, the dreams that were nothing more than broken pottage bought by the sweat and sacrifice of men who were the worst kind of gamblers. They staked their lives and those of their families to find a capricious vein of gold that would make them rich. My father's stubborn determination to seek his fortune in the Sierra Nevadas was a sickness that prevailed in every dirty camp.

I strode ahead with my bucket, wondering what our lives would have been like if my mother had not died. She had been teaching school in a small Kansas town when my father met her, and she had conscientiously seen to my own upbringing until her health deteriorated after Davie's birth. My grandparents had died of influenza the winter before, and the family plot had three fresh graves within a year. If she had lived, I knew that Davie and I would never have heard of Rocky Gulch, Nevada. She would have accepted a deaf-mute son without the emo-

12

tional upheaval that had sent my father in a wild escape to the gold fields. If only . . . I impatiently shoved the thought aside. No use thinking about what might have been.

Davie kept looking back at the puppy as we made our way down to the stream.

"Morning." I nodded to women hunched on their knees over the water, washing gray clothes.

Some grunted in reply, others ignored my greeting. The May sun had not reached the depths of the gulch, and the water ran cold. I could see that the women's hands were chapped and red and I marveled at the tenacity with which they tried to perform their household chores under such miserable circumstances. It was here, listening to their conversations, that I had learned about the appetites of men and the fancy women who served them. I was appalled at some of the stories I heard and had to hide my blushing face as the women shared tales of the marriage bed or offered insights into the harlot's trade. Human nature was revealed in all its ugly forms, as crude and repugnant as the surrounding countryside. My father would have been horrified at the extent of my knowledge about the seamy side of life.

A wiry little woman smiled at me. "I'm always glad for a nice warm sun," she said as if sharing a special pleasure with me. "Thaws out the old bones, makes the blood run a little faster. 'Course, you young folks don't worry none about that."

"I'm ready for summer," I agreed, filling my bucket fuller than Davie's.

"God help us if we're here that long," snapped one of the women. "They've about dug up the whole mountain already."

"Wouldn't be surprised if Rocky Gulch is a ghost town in a couple more months," agreed another woman wearily, slapping a pair of overalls against a rock.

"Yep. Another rumor about a strike someplace else and every man and mule will be hightailing it out of here."

My stomach muscles twisted. Where next? On every move we left with fewer and fewer possessions. Even now, we had little more than the clothes on our backs.

Davie pointed to the stream. He loved to splash in the water, bobbing up and down in the slow-moving current and acting like a polliwog. He would be a good swimmer, given half a chance, I thought as I shook my head and signed, "Too cold."

On the way back to our lean-to shack, we dodged wagons drawn by mule teams and burros loaded down with prospectors' gear. The wagon road was scarcely more than two muddy ruts weaving around dilapidated buildings, horse troughs, and stacked kegs and boxes. As we walked, water splashed over the rim of our buckets. The puppy showed up again, and I sent a threatening look at Davie. He had a worried look on his face as the puppy scooted along in the road, narrowly missing flying hooves and creaking wheels. A couple of times he slipped in the mud and plopped down on his round little bottom. When he scrambled up, his fur was plastered down with mud. I sighed as the tiny mud ball barreled after us in a wobbly run.

My efforts to shoo him away were to no avail. I knew the dog was following us home and I would have to deal with the matter firmly. No, I would not give in. I had to think about our own survival. There was no place in our bare existence for a pet. I was trying to find a way to explain the situation to Davie when all thoughts of the

14

dog were driven from my mind.

Trapper McCloud, a middle-aged friend of my father's, came running toward us, and I knew from the expression on his ruddy face that something bad had happened.

A chill went through me. "What's the matter?"

"It's your pa," he said. "Rock slide. Came down on Ben without a warning."

I dropped my bucket and signed to Davie, "Go home." Then I picked up my skirts and ran.

"It happened all of a sudden," said Trapper, puffing along beside me as we hurried up the gulch toward the place where I knew my father had been working for Jeb Walters on his claim. "Somebody up above blew some dynamite. There was a rumble, and then the whole mountainside seemed to come tumbling down. I pressed up against the side of the hill and escaped, but your pa . . ."

I could see a gathering of men around an inert form. They had lifted the rocks off him, but my father's broken body lay motionless, his eyes glazed with pain and his mouth hanging slack.

"Papa. Papa." I flung myself down beside him.

He tried to move his head and couldn't. I bent over him, biting back the tears as I stroked his dirty face. His lips moved, and I could barely hear what he was saying.

"Lake Tahoe."

"Lake Tahoe?" I echoed, sure that I had not heard him correctly.

"Your aunt Minna . . . she'll look after you. Minna . . . Minna . . ." He said the name twice, as if fearful that I wouldn't hear him. The movement in his chest was so slight I could barely see it rise and fall. And then it was still.

"Do something!" I shrieked at Trapper and the other

15

men hovering close by.

Trapper touched my shoulder. "There's nothing to be done, lass. Your pa is gone."

It wasn't true. I wouldn't believe it. I pressed my face against my father's chest, letting the tears flow as I hugged him. What about his dreams? What about his dogged determination? He couldn't die like this. My shoulders heaved with sobs.

"I'm sorry, honey." Trapper closed my father's eyes and then pulled me to my feet. He cradled my shoulders as he led me back to our shack. Two men followed, carrying my father. People stopped whatever they were doing and watched us walk by. Their expressions were fixed and weary, and reflected an awareness of their own mortality.

My father is dead. The words kept running through my mind, but they had no meaning. My father's dominating authority had been at the center of our lives. We had felt protected because of him, we had endured the trials of dirt and poverty because of him, our lives had meaning because of him—and now he was gone. We had been a family . . . and now we were nothing.

Davie was sitting on a warped board that served as a step, holding the puppy. He looked into my face and knew. There was no need for words. Death was not unfamiliar to him. He had nursed baby birds that had died, made pets out of rabbits that were then killed for stew. He had seen men, women, and children sicken and grow weak until one day they were carried in a pine box to the burial ground. When I made a simple sign with my hands that meant "gone," he knew that our father had died.

He nodded and buried his face in the puppy's matted

fur, and his soundless sobs tore at my heart. I sat down beside him, numb with shock.

That same afternoon, my father was quickly laid to rest, as was the custom when someone in the camp died. Trapper, only a few years younger than my father, took care of burial. The women who had been washing clothes came by with small offerings, an apple, a bowl of watery stew, and a heel of stale bread. They patted my shoulder and shook their heads. Fear was reflected in the depths of their eyes.

Trapper took care of the selling of my father's tools. He placed the few dollars in my hand. "That should see you and Davie to your aunt's," he said.

I tried to focus my thoughts. Aunt Minna. Tahoe Lake. I had heard about the large body of water that lay on the borderline of two states, Nevada and California, but my father had never said anything about my having an aunt living there.

"I thought his sister, Minna, was dead." I told Trapper. "He always talked about the past, about how close they had been when they were young. He never indicated that she was still alive. And living so close!"

"You can take a stage to Glenbrook and a schooner across the lake to Blackbriar Bay."

My eyes widened. "You know where she lives?"

He nodded. "Your pa took me there once that time we went to Placerville last fall, remember?"

I was utterly bewildered. "I wonder why he didn't tell me. Except for showing us her picture in his watch, he never talked about his sister."

Trapper shrugged. "He didn't tell me much, either. I figured it was family business . . . something he didn't want to talk about."

17

"Tell me, what is she like?"

"Don't know. I just saw the woman once, when she came down to the lake's edge to talk with your pa. I reckon they didn't get along too well. Leastways, she never invited us to her house. They exchanged a few sharp words and we left. Your pa wouldn't talk about it."

Apprehension spread through me. "Maybe she won't want Davie and me to come and live with her."

From Trapper's frown, I could tell that the same thought had crossed his mind. "I guess your pa thought it was the best place for you. He told me once that his sister was his only kin. Her husband died a few years back, left her with quite a bit of property around the lake." He winked at me. "Sounds like you and Davie may have landed on a soft blanket."

"Or the hard ground," I retorted. If Aunt Minna wasn't friendly with her brother, the chance that she would receive us with open arms was pure wishful thinking.

"I guess they had a falling out years ago," said Trapper.

I wondered what could have kept them apart all these years. Why would she accept her brother's orphans with any more charity than she had accepted her brother's overtures?

"I wonder why my father wanted us to go there."

Trapper cleared his throat. "I don't reckon he had much choice. You don't have anybody else who will take you in, do you?"

"No."

He looked worried. "What'll you do if she won't?"

"I don't know," I said honestly. What would we do? Where would we go? My heart shrank into a tight little

18

knot when I looked at Davie.

"I'm on the move myself, or I'd look after you for a spell," said Trapper.

"Thank you. You've been a big help. But I guess Davie and I will have to find our own way."

I forced myself to act confident around my little brother. I had lost my battle over the puppy. Stunned by my father's death, I didn't have the strength or inclination to deprive Davie of the joy the puppy gave him.

"You can keep him," I said.

We would all starve together, I thought wryly, as I bought passage on a stage to Glenbrook, Nevada, a settlement on the east side of Lake Tahoe.

Chapter Two

Trapper saw us off on the overland stage. "Sure hope everything works out for you and Davie." I could tell from his tone that he had his doubts.

"I'm sure they will," I said with more conviction than I felt. I was still numb with shock over the loss of my father, the mainstay in my life, my protector and shield. He had always been there, and with the naïveté of youth, I thought he always would be.

"Things are about played out here, and I'll be moving on." A gray weariness coated Trapper's ruddy face, and his shoulders were as slumped as my father's had been.

I hugged his burly frame. "Take care of yourself, Trapper."

"It's pretty country you'll be seeing," he said in an awkward pause.

I nodded.

The older man tipped Davie's chin in a playful gesture, and my brother grinned back at him. Davie's eyes were bright and shiny. Standing there with the puppy clutched in his arms, worn and faded clothes hanging on his thin frame, he radiated his usual placid contentment. Even though he didn't understand completely where we were going, he showed no apprehension. His eagerness was a contrast to my nervousness. The responsibility of caring for him weighed heavily on me, and I forced myself to pretend a confidence I didn't feel.

"Here you go," said Trapper, helping us into the crowded stagecoach.

We had always done our traveling by wagon, and riding in a stagecoach was a new experience for both of us. Davie and I sat upright, knee-to-knee, with other passengers. I suppressed a flicker of pure panic as a crack from the driver's whip sent the stage lumbering down the rocky road. Besides the driver, five other men sat on the roof of the coach and gave a drunken "Hurrah" as Rocky Gulch was left behind. Those of us sitting inside struggled to keep from bumping heads as we were jostled about like lumps in a churn.

A team of six thick-withered horses drew the stage over a rutted road that varied from bare rock, dry creek beds, and craggy inclines to long stretches of prairie. Two lengths of strong steer hide suspended under the coach allowed it to rock fore and aft as wooden wheels rose and fell on the rugged ground. The constant movement made me weary after only a few miles.

A tiny baby wailed in the arms of a young mother. The sharp remarks of her husband made it clear that he held her responsible for the irritating cries. The infant obviously wanted to nurse, I decided, but propriety demanded that such a feeding be put off until the first relief station.

Davie seemed oblivious to the glares at the raggedy puppy he clutched on his lap. Rags, the name I had bestowed upon the mongrel, seemed utterly content to sleep in Davie's arms and twitched his ears as if delighting in some kind of puppy dream.

Four men sat across from us. Two young cowboys who were dressed in buckskins smelled like a livery stable. Dirty hair straggled out from under their water-stained, wide-brimmed hats. I learned their names were Zeke and Clyde. They laughed loudly and exchanged bawdy remarks that sent heat up into my cheeks. Both of them wore guns in holsters slung low on their hips.

Two older men, who were cleaner, and dressed in dark serge suits, were merchants of some kind. All four men eyed me with open curiosity, and I endured their measuring glances without changing my outwardly stiff demeanor. Inside I was trembling like a quaking leaf in a harsh wind. My father had always been very protective of me, making certain that no male attention came my way. I knew nothing about fending off masculine advances. The tales I had heard from the women washing in the stream had made me aware of the raw appetites of men. A woman of any age was in peril traveling without a male escort in these uncivilized territories. I was thankful for a sunbonnet that shaded my face, and I kept my old coat buttoned high to the neck, even though the heat of eight pressed bodies brought droplets of perspiration to my forehead. I was glad I was next to the window and could keep my gaze fixed on the passing landscape.

I prayed the driver of the wildly pitching stage was in control of the racing team that swerved around switchback curves over roads precariously dug into the mountainside. Tales of overturned coaches were frequent. Steep descents, rough roads, and the speed at which the teams were driven were often responsible for a stagecoach full of people vaulting to their deaths over a mountain cliff. Trapper had told me that the journey to Glenbrook took about three days. I despaired that any part of me would be in one piece by then.

Relay stations were twelve to fifteen miles apart, I soon discovered. Made of logs and dirt, they offered a brief respite from the jostling coach while the team of horses was being changed. Larger home stations were fifty to sixty miles apart, and they offered meals and sleeping accommodations, even though most travelers were like Davie and me, intent on getting to their destination as soon as possible. Only a broken coach, blinding blizzards, or some other unexpected disaster caused passengers to linger any longer than necessary.

"One hour," announced the driver at Soap Springs Station. A fresh team waited to be led into the traces as the flux of humanity poured off the coach and into the crude one-story building. Davie took the puppy for a walk while I visited one of the sagging privies at the back of the station before joining the other passengers inside.

The young mother riding with us disappeared behind a blanketed section in the long room and the wailing infant at last became quiet. The station was run by a buxom woman and her husband. Both of them bellowed at a passel of children who scurried about, doing everything from tending the horses to helping set out food for the travelers. A long table of rough pine boards flanked by benches was set with tin plates, iron knives, forks, and spoons, and heavy mugs. Meals were fifty cents, and I reckoned that Davie and I would have to limit our eating to once a day. Trapper had warned me that I would have to buy passage on a schooner to take us across the lake to Aunt Minna's place.

One of the cowboys, Zeke, took a place beside me on the bench. He leaned close and took away my appetite with one whiff of his sour breath. "Where's a pretty lady like yourself headed?"

"Not far," I said briskly, and turned to Davie on my other side.

His companion chuckled. "She ain't going to be friendly, Zeke. I've seen less prickles on a cactus."

"Oh, she's just a little timid, ain't ya, honey? Here, have some bread. Whatcha you say your name was?"

"I didn't." I took the platter of leathery "self-rising" bread. Each slice was heavy and gray. I saw that the men were slapping mustard on it.

A meat pie followed which had undefined pieces of meat floating in heavy grease. The crust was half-baked and leather hard. Strong lard pellets mixed with the flour gave the dish a soggy texture.

Davie looked at me and I answered with a quick hand motion: "Eat."

He watched me swallow down the badly cooked meal and obediently followed my lead. I didn't object when he gave his half-finished plate to Rags. I wondered if I would be able to keep down the meal once we returned to the bouncing coach.

Zeke grinned at me. "The food ain't to your liking?"

"Maybe she wants roast pheasant," smirked his friend, Clyde.

I ignored their laughter and went outside to wait for the stage to leave. The hope that the next home station would be better soon died; each meal seemed even more unpalatable than the last.

At every stop Zeke attached himself to me. He was in his early twenties, raw-boned, and he carried himself with a confident swagger. Unshaven, he wore his lanky brown hair caught in a leather strip at his neck. The man's sour-smelling breath and yellowed tobacco teeth nearly turned my already queasy stomach. No matter how I tried to avoid him, he always managed to be nearby, giving the impression that we were traveling together.

"Always wondered why redheads had fiery tempers to match." He smirked. "How about it, honey?"

I turned on him. "You don't want to find out!" I snapped. "Now leave me alone."

He gave a mock expression of surprise. "I was just trying to protect you from all these no-account fellows. You ought to be grateful to me. Show a little appreciation."

I jerked away from the hand he put on my arm. My heart was racing madly. What would I do if he managed to get me away from the others? He must have seen the fright in my eyes, for he laughed softly. "A wild filly, ain't you? Well, leave it to good old Zeke to gentle you in the ways of the world."

"If you don't leave me alone, I'll complain to the driver."

He grinned. "You do that, honey. Give us all a good laugh. Everybody minds their own business in this neck of the woods—unless they want to get shot between the eyes for interfering." He gave the gun in his holster a meaningful pat. "See what I mean, honey?"

I saw.

When we were in the crowded stage, the horrid man deliberately pressed his legs against mine as he sat facing me, looking at me in a lewd way that brought heated fury into my glare.

His companion chuckled. "Don't think the lady has

taken a liking to you, Zeke."

"Course, she has. She's just bashful, that's all. Ain't you, honey? By the time we get to Tahoe she'll be gentle as a kitten."

I despaired to think that he was going all the way to the lake. I had no experience in handling crude men like him. If my father had been here, he would have stomped Zeke into the ground. My lips quivered. There was no one to protect me from Zeke's advances. I would have to endure what I must, and avoid what I could.

When we reached Carson City, the young couple and their baby and the two merchants were replaced by a logger, his wife, and two little ones. Mrs. Greenberry, a rosy-cheeked, good-natured soul, held one baby on each knee and was quite gregarious, chatting away as if we were all on a holiday. Her husband was a silent hulk of a man who slept almost all the time with his mouth open, issuing loud nasal snores. His wife just laughed and ignored him. He had a job with the Delany Lumber Company in Glenbrook, she told me, and I was relieved that she would be with me the rest of the journey to the lake.

Zeke and his friend, Clyde, probably would have continued their obnoxious behavior in the stage, making me uncomfortable as before, but Mr. Greenberry was big enough to wipe them out with one hand. They slumped in their seats, and I kept my eyes away from Zeke's ugly face.

At every stop I used Mrs. Greenberry's presence as a buffer against the foul-smelling cowboy who continually eyed me with a lusty gleam in his eye. I wished he had gotten off at Carson City, but he and Clyde were hoping to get jobs in Glenbrook. Apparently the Delany Lumber

Company was a big operation.

Mrs. Greenberry had raised a questioning eyebrow at me when Davie didn't respond to her greeting, and I explained that he was deaf. "You poor darling," she said, patting Davie's arm. Davie felt her touch, looked up, and gave the woman a bright smile that mocked her pitying expression. His deep brown eyes were clear and alert. He had a way of communicating that often made words seem superfluous.

The arduous journey had not dampened my brother's good-natured acceptance of the situation. His continuing confidence that all was well rested heavily upon me. Even though we had missed meals on the journey and I had not spent a cent that wasn't a necessity, we were nearly out of money. I dared not think what would befall us if Aunt Minna refused to take us in. Would her anger against my father destroy any Christian charity she might offer to his orphaned children?

The passage from Carson City to Spooner's Pass was dramatic. On every side, tall evergreens blanketed the slopes, and I saw my first lumber flume carrying logs from the mountaintops down to points of distribution. I marveled at the engineering feat. These flumes followed the natural contours of the mountains and rested upon high wooden trestles.

"Some of them are twenty-five miles long," Mrs. Greenberry told me. "The sides are greased, so that logs coming hurtling down the chutes at terrific speed and will go for miles without having to be pushed along by teams of mules. The Delany Lumber Company is one of the largest," she bragged. "And pays the highest wages. Even provides housing for its workers. I haven't seen ours, but my husband says it's a nice little cabin just outside Glenbrook."

I was envious as she talked about her new home, and my apprehension increased. Surely, my aunt would offer her home to us when she knew we had no place else to go. By the time we arrived in Glenbrook late one afternoon, my fatigue had mounted with a growing uncertainty whether or not Davie and I would have a roof over our heads at the end of our journey.

My glimpses of Lake Tahoe out of the bouncing stagecoach window had not prepared me for a huge lake that was rimmed by forest-green mountains in every direction. A sudden view of the ocean wouldn't have been more startling than this first view of the deep indigo-blue water stretching in every direction.

"One of the world's biggest alpine lakes," said Mrs. Greenberry, seeing my astonished expression. "It was undiscovered for years. I guess if gold hadn't been discovered at Placerville, the Indians still might have this country all to themselves. Tucked away in the valley, the lake isn't visible even from some of the highest spots in the surrounding mountains."

"It's beautiful," I breathed. "How big is it?"

"About twenty-three miles long and thirteen miles wide. Half of it is in Nevada and the other half in California."

My heart sank. Somewhere along the banks of this mammoth lake my aunt lived in a house called Blackbriar House. The isolation of the lake and its separation from the rest of the world created a feeling that anyone could disappear in this virgin country and never be seen again.

The coach rattled into a small settlement that seemed composed of log buildings and wide, muddy streets, all ending at the lake's edge.

"Well, here we be," said Mrs. Greenberry, reaching across and giving her husband a shake on his arm. Her two little ones were asleep and she roused them, clucking as she straightened the little girl's bonnet and smoothed the infant boy's hair. "We're home," she said with a cheerfulness that created a emptiness deep in my own heart.

We alighted from the stage, and I just stood there looking across the vast body of water. Davie's eyes grew wide. He made the sign "water," and I laughed, nodding my head in agreement.

I picked up the canvas satchel holding our meager possessions and we walked toward the lake, the puppy bouncing around at our heels. Rags had endured the journey well, sleeping and playing with Davie as he teased him with a wad of string or handkerchief. The two of them were happy and contented. I was envious of their optimism as a sense of dread deepened within me.

We stood on the wharf and looked across the lake. I couldn't see the beginning nor end of the water. Where was Blackbriar Bay? Somewhere along the lake's irregular shoreline, shut off from the world except by boat, Trapper had said. In the darkening shadows of late afternoon, something ominous seemed to hover on the surface of the water, warning me. I had always been one to trust my feelings. If I'd had any other place to go, and the means to get there, Davie and I would have climbed back on the stage and departed with it.

There was no sign of a steamer to take us across the lake. The crude dock was empty, and I realized that the daily boat had already gone. I walked over to a sign.

In bold dark letters the placard advised us that the *Tahoe Queen* departed from Glenbrook at eight o'clock each morning, Monday through Saturday.

I realized we would have to stay the night in Glenbrook and buy passage on the next day's run. My heart sank. I didn't have money for a night's lodging. If I spent our passage money on shelter, we'd be stuck in Glenbrook without any resources.

Davie was watching my face. "Tomorrow," I signed and pointed to the lake.

He nodded his head, smiling at me as if I'd offered him a piece of sugar candy. His eyes were wide and excited, a sharp contrast to my growing apprehension and leaden spirits.

We left the dock and walked slowly back to the main street. The crude frontier town was filled with rugged, loud-talking men who undoubtedly worked for the Delany Logging Company. Above the saloon was a row of heavily curtained windows, and I guessed why Zeke and his friend had slapped each other on the back as they entered the Rawhide Saloon. We'd had a place like that in Rocky Gulch, and the saloon girls had provided the gossiping women with plenty of fuel for their wagging tongues. Some of the tales had been sad enough—young girls forced into a life of shame as a means of survival. These stories came back to me with double meaning now that I was facing an uncertain future with no assets, not even enough to buy a cheap room for the night.

I couldn't see any public place where we might sit out the night. Davie looked at me questioningly as we made our way along the narrow boardwalk. Rags darted ahead of us, tumbling, leaping, and wagging his tail as his black eyes peered at us through a mop of hair. I smiled reassuringly at Davie, hiding my growing anxiety.

My mind raced to solve the problem of shelter for the

night. Cold wind off the lake penetrated our shabby clothing, and I knew that trying to sleep on the ground would most likely settle a sickness on Davie. He fought battles with chest coughs every winter, and I feared that he would succumb to influenza as our mother had.

And I was frightened that Zeke might stagger out of the saloon at any moment and take advantage of the fact that we had nowhere to go. He would have been at me before this, if it hadn't been for the Greenberrys.

Through windows in the mercantile store, I saw them buying supplies. I remembered how Mrs. Greenberry had talked so enthusiastically about the cabin that was to be her new home. Smothering my pride, I waited outside the store until they came out.

"Oh, hello again," she said with a broad smile as I stepped forward. "It's great to get out of that stage and stretch our legs, isn't it? Guess you'll be going on to your aunt's . . . ?"

"Not until the morning," I said quickly. "The steamer won't be here until eight. I'm afraid we don't have anyplace to spend the night." I tried to keep my tone neutral, but there was still a pleading edge to it.

"Oh dear, that is a problem." She looked at her husband and he scowled.

"We don't have money for lodgings," I said quickly, "And it's too cold for Davie to sleep out."

"Of course, it is. You must stay with us! We'd be happy to have you, wouldn't we, Ed?" She glared at him as if he'd better say "yes" or be prepared to deal with her later.

"We've only got two rooms," her husband said shortly. "I told you it wasn't very big."

"That's all right," she assured him. "After the

confinement of a stage ride, we'll think we're in a mansion, for sure. We can't let these two spend the night without even a roof over their heads."

He growled something, but she just smiled at me and said, "Come along. As soon as we get the stove fired up, we'll have ourselves a homemade supper. My stomach will not take another meal like the ones those horrible stations force upon us."

"Thank you . . . for your hospitality." I wanted to hug her, and I had to blink rapidly to keep a sudden fullness out of my eyes.

"Think nothing of it. You and your brother are welcome."

We walked a short distance along the lake before we turned into a thick drift of trees. I looked back across the dark sheen of the lake. Deep. Dark. Waiting. Tomorrow I would meet the smiling young girl whose photo was in my father's watch. I had taken the watch out several times and studied the photograph, reassuring myself that once we reached Blackbriar Bay, we would no longer be alone and adrift in the world. Tomorrow . . . I took a deep breath to settle a foreboding that brought a trickle of fear slithering up my back.

Chapter Three

That night Davie and I slept on the floor of the Greenberrys' cabin. After our cramped journey, stretching our limbs in front of a glowing fireplace was pure delight. Shadows danced on the rafters, pine logs burning in the fireplace popped and crackled, and the sound of wind rustling trees outside was as soft as a lullaby. The rustic log cabin had luxurious accommodations compared to the shack we had left behind at Rocky Gulch.

Upon our arrival, I looked with envy at the long front room with a kitchen at one end and sitting room at the other. A small bedroom and porch opened off the main room. Mrs. Greenberry bustled around, cluckling like a hen as she inspected her new home. The furniture was made of sweet-smelling pine, clean and fresh, and I knew that she would soon have the family possessions scattered about, making it homey and comfortable. I wondered if Aunt Minna's home would offer us the same kind of family warmth. I wouldn't care how large or fancy it was, as long as we finally belonged somewhere.

At supper, Mrs. Greenberry filled our stomachs with

sausage, biscuits, and dried apples. She boiled coffee and poured us healthy mugs which warmed us to the soles of our worn shoes. After we had finished our meal and I had helped with the clean-up, the Greenberrys and their two little ones retired to the bedroom, and Davie and I bedded down in the main room on a quilt in front of the fire.

My brother fell right to sleep with Rags in the curve of his arm. My heart tightened as I watched the flickering firelight play upon his face. Thick auburn lashes lay upon his pale cheeks. His gentle mouth curved in a soft smile. Dear precious Davie. Whatever happened, I must protect him. But how? After I bought our passage on the lake schooner, my pockets would be empty. Except for my father's watch, I had nothing that could be sold, and I doubted that the old watch would bring more than a couple of dollars. There was a sentimental value that made the timepiece worth much more than that to me. I thought again of the picture that my father had carried for so many years. Tomorrow I would meet Aunt Minna, the woman who had once been a smiling young girl with her arm looped through my father's.

I had been startled to learn from Trapper that my father had paid her a visit not long ago. He had never mentioned it. Several times he had been away, working temporary jobs, or getting supplies. He must have visited her on one of these trips. If what Trapper had said was true, the reunion between them had not been a friendly one. If ill feelings remained between them, why would my father send us to her with his dying breath?

I closed my eyes with a prayer that all would be well once we reached our destination and met my aunt face to face.

Rags woke up that morning before we did and amused himself with my sunbonnet. He was dragging it about, tossing it in the air with gleeful joy, when I awoke and recognized his plaything. To my horror, I saw that he had chewed a hole in the top of it.

"No matter," said Mrs. Greenberry briskly. "I have more bonnets than I'll be wearing . . . and glad to be rid of one of them. Here, this will do nicely." She ignored my protests and handed me a natural straw bonnet with a loop of blue ribbon around the high crown. "That matches your dress nicely," she said in satisfaction.

I had put on my only good dress, the pansy-blue wool. The long sleeves were bell shaped at the wrist, with undersleeves of ecru lace that matched a rounded lace collar. The skirt was long enough to cover my scuffed shoes and warm enough to be worn without my old coat. I wanted to look my best when I met my aunt for the first time. The straw bonnet sat on top of my thick red curls, and I tied the ribbon streamers into a soft bow under my chin. Davie grinned in approval and relief. I knew that he had been worried that Rags was in deep trouble over his mischief.

"Thank you very much," I told Mrs. Greenberry, swallowing my pride and accepting the gift as graciously as I could. "You're very kind."

"Nonsense. That bonnet looks better on you than it ever did on me." Her bosom quivered with her hearty laughter. She gave both Davie and me a hug. "You take care of yourselves, now. I'm sure everything will be fine once you reach your aunt's house. Maybe she'll be living in a grand place and the two of you will be as happy as lambs rolling in clover."

37

"Maybe," I nodded, feeling confident in my new bonnet.

We bade the Greenberrys goodbye and made our way back to the center of Glenbrook. The steamer was already at the dock when we reached the main street.

"Hurry, Davie. Pick up the dog."

He nodded, swept Rags up from the ground, and tucked the pup under his arm. I grabbed Davie's free hand and pulled him along at a quickened pace.

My heart sank as I viewed the gleaming white hull and a mahogany deck cabin that looked large enough for a hundred people. I had expected something more like a scow than this sleek steamer. What would two tickets cost, I wondered as we walked along the wooden sidewalk.

The whole area was crowded with wagons and people. Some wandered about the busy wharf, gawking at the steamer, or hurried along as if they were going aboard. The air was filled with loud voices, creaking wheels, snorting horses, and the loud warning whistle from the steamer. We were forced to weave a path through the melee of people on the sidewalks, and horses, mules, and wagons in the street. Brawny workmen hurried to load cargo and stack cords of wood near the engine room. Dark smoke curled out of the center smokestack, and I could see two men wearing seamen caps moving about in the wheelhouse.

As we passed the men lounging up against the side of wooden buildings along the way, I was forced to endure their snickers and lewd remarks. With my eyes fixed straight ahead, I swept by them with as much dignity as I could manage.

"You going somewhere?" smirked a familiar voice. A

man's hand grabbed my arm and stopped me.

My nose told me who it was before I swung around. "Take your hands off me!"

Zeke's mouth spread in a yellow grin. Tobacco juice coated his teeth. "Still playing hard to get, honey? Poorer than a churchmouse and putting your nose in the air like you was somebody." Zeke laughed. "I'm your friend. And you'd better be nice to your friends."

I jerked away. "I'll . . . I'll have the law on you."

Gawking men standing around, taking in the whole thing, laughed along with Zeke.

"Honey, where you do think you are?" he snickered. "The only law around here is in a man's fists or his gun. Women do as they're told . . . and I'm telling you you'd better be nice to me. How about a little goodbye kiss?"

As he leaned his vile face toward me, I socked him in the nose as hard as I could. Surprised by the sudden attack and the pain, he stumbled backward, fell over a keg, and sprawled on the ground while the men around him roared with laughter.

I didn't wait to see what he would do next. I grabbed Davie's hand and we ran, reaching the *Tahoe Queen* out of breath. I flung a look backward and didn't see Zeke coming after us. I hoped his bloody nose was spouting like a geyser.

Quickly, we lost ourselves in a line of other people moving toward the steamer. A wizened little man at the bottom of the gangplank was selling tickets, and I nervously got my money ready to give to him. I prayed there was enough left for the tickets. The man squinted one eye against the swirling smoke coming from a corncob pipe clamped in one side of his mouth.

"How much . . . two tickets," I asked as we reached him. "To Blackbriar."

He peered one eye at me. "Whatcha say?"

"Blackbriar Bay. Will this steamer take us there?"

"I reckon it could . . . if a body was of a mind to go there." He shifted his pipe to the other side of his mouth.

Something in the way he was looking at me made my mouth dry. "Is there some reason why we shouldn't?"

He shrugged his bony shoulders. "That's ain't for me to say. But a young woman like yourself and . . ." he looked at Davie pressing against my side, and shrugged again. "Blackbriar, is it?"

"How much? Two tickets."

"Almost the whole distance around the lake. Two round trips will cost you . . ."

"No. Not round trips. One way."

He took out his pipe and knocked it against a piling. "You ever been there before?"

I shook my head.

"Then you'd better buy a round trip. Nobody stays at Blackbriar."

I swallowed back a sudden lump of fear. I said in an even voice that denied the tempest inside my chest. "Two tickets, please. One way."

He shrugged and named a price that was twice what I had in my pocket.

"That's one way?"

"Yep."

My mind raced. I only had enough money for one ticket. "Is there some way I could work out a passage? I could mop and clean and . . ."

"Nope. We got plenty of crew to do all that. Cash only.

If you don't have the price, you'll have to stay in Glenbrook until you get enough money for the fare."

Stay at Glenbrook? With Zeke at my heels?

"I can't stay here . . ."

He waved a scrawny hand in a gesture of dismissal. "Then move back. You're blocking the way."

A masculine voice floated over my shoulder. "What's the trouble, Hank?"

"This here young woman wants to go across to Blackbriar—but she ain't got the fare."

"Blackbriar?" The stranger's tone was also one of surprise.

My eyes traveled up a masculine torso to a tanned, strong face. In a fleeting appraisal, I decided his bold features just missed being handsome. Under the brim of a Western hat, his hair was sunbleached to the color of corn shucks. He wore leather trousers and a fringed doeskin jacket. He could have been one of the logging men, I thought, except his fine cambric shirt and soft black tie bespoke money and not labor.

"Blackbriar?" he echoed with a lift of his dark brown eyebrows. Blue eyes searched my face. "Nobody lives there except Minna McKenzie-Brown. Why would you be going to see her?"

My first impulse was to wither him with my drop-dead glare. "She's my aunt. Not that it's any of your business, sir," I replied haughtily.

The stranger gave me a smile that deepened the cleft in his chin. "Perhaps you'll allow me to make it my business. Permit me to advance you the fare?" He took a money clip from his pocket.

My pride bristled. I didn't want to be beholden to this

41

stranger, but at that moment my eyes swept beyond him and I saw Zeke coming toward the boat. He was mopping his bloody nose, and anger was in every stride of his body. Fear rushed through me. I couldn't stay in Glenbrook . . . not with that horrid man seeking revenge for his wounded pride.

Seeing my hesitation, the man said, "I'm certain that Mrs. Brown will see to it that it's repaid in full."

I reined in my pride. "A loan, then. To be repaid."

"A loan," he echoed in a lazy way that brought color up into my cheek.

"Come, Davie." I grabbed my brother's hand and swept up the gangplank while the stranger paid our fare. He needn't think his good deed has bought him any familiarities, I thought.

Glancing over the side of the boat, I saw Zeke shaking a fist at me and yelling something that must have been a curse. Thank God, he wasn't coming aboard.

Davie tugged at my skirt. Alarm was written on his face. In his silent world, he was adrift without comprehension.

"It's all right," I mouthed, smiling at him, and giving Rags' head a reassuring pat. The mongrel's pink tongue slurped a kiss on my hand.

We wove our way through passengers milling about the deck. I was surprised at the number of people aboard. Listening to exchanges of conversation among the passengers, I learned that the *Tahoe Queen* was the only means of travel around the lake. Only short sections of road had been built in scattered areas, and few of them were connected. The northern community of Truckee could be reached by a railroad running from Sacramento,

42

but most people living around the lake remained isolated. Apparently, there were few private boats, and daily mail, as well as ordered goods, freight, and passengers, went by steamer.

With Davie and the pup in tow, I led the way to the main cabin, a long room which ran nearly the whole length of the steamer. Wooden benches had been placed under the windows on both sides of the boat. In the middle section, tables and chairs offered additional seating for conversation and refreshments. I thought the boat was the grandest thing I'd ever seen. I know I must have stared like a bumpkin at walls of cedar paneling, lovely teak carvings, and pictures of seascapes that lent a homey feeling to the public cabin.

There were only a few women and children on the boat, and all of them were in the company of a male. Men passengers whom I judged to be prospectors, loggers, and other workmen mingled together, laughing and drinking at the tables and exchanging stories or news.

Davie and I sat down on one of the side benches. With his usual eagerness, my little brother peered out the window. Beside him, the puppy happily chewed on a piece of leather Mrs. Greenberry had given Davie. "That'll be saving your shoes and bonnets," she had said with a laugh.

I folded my hands in my lap and tried to look composed and confident, even though my heart was racing wildly in my chest. The swaying of the boat under my feet was a foreign sensation. I had never been on a boat in my life. A nervous sweat broke out on the palms of my hands, and I gripped them so tightly that my nails dug into the flesh. It seemed my whole life was adrift. My father had always been a firm anchor, even when our lives were in an upheaval. His authoritative figure had stood between me and the world. I had grieved for him, mourned his passing, and now a bewildering anger rose in me as if he had betrayed me by dying.

My eyes swept around the room, and I was relieved that I didn't see the stranger who had bought our tickets. I wondered who he was. How would I be able to return the money if I didn't even know his name? Did he know Aunt Minna? He must, I reasoned—otherwise, how would he know that she would be good for the loan?

A shrill whistle was followed by a rumbling and scraping of the *Tahoe Queen* as she eased away from her moorings. Davie's eyes were rounded, and he pointed at the wharf, which was getting smaller and smaller as the steamer moved out into the lake.

The steamer chugged southward, around the circumference of the lake cupped by forested green mountains and granite peaks. White swaths of clouds trailed across the sky and were reflected in the rippling blue-green water. After a few moments, the pristine brightness of sun and water and the rhythmic chug of the steamer eased away the tension in my shoulders. My spirits rose, and I put away all my worries about what awaited us and gave myself up to the dramatic panorama of the beautiful alpine lake.

Davie soon wearied of the view and stretched out on the bench. Rags curled up in his arms and laid a contented head on Davie's chest. I smiled as I looked at them.

"Some hot tea, miss?"

A smiling young man wearing a sailor's hat and blue

44

jacket and trousers offered me a steaming mug. A placard on his tray listed various drinks, and I saw that a mug of tea was five cents. The money in my coat pocket reminded me that the stranger had paid for two tickets.

"Yes, thank you." I gave him the coin.

"Nice day," he said.

"Lovely." I guessed him to be in his early twenties. Shocks of sandy hair stuck out under the white sailor's hat, which was tipped at a jaunty angle on his head. His gaze was blatantly curious as he surveyed me, Davie, and the sleeping puppy. "I hear you're going to Blackbriar."

"News travels fast, I see."

He laughed. "Sure does. The comings and going of people are about the only thing that keeps this job interesting." His smile was honest and disarmed me with its friendliness. "My name's Randy Bowles."

I smiled back. "Anna McKenzie." Nodding toward Davie and the sleeping puppy, I said, "My little brother, Davie, and Rags. Glad to make your acquaintance, Mr. Bowles."

"Randy," he corrected. "Folks would laugh if they heard you calling me Mister."

His grin was infectious. Without knowing why, I felt at ease with him. "I imagine you meet a lot of different people in your job," I said, selfishly wanting to prolong the conversation.

He shook his head. "Not all that many. Loggers, mostly. Not pretty young women like you, Miss McKenzie." he blushed as he said it, and I knew that he wasn't practiced in the art of flirting.

"Anna," I corrected, grinning back at him, suddenly feeling very feminine and foolish in my new bonnet.

"Would you like a biscuit . . . on me?" he said grandly, and handed me one before I could protest.

For a moment we just smiled at each other, and then my smile faded as my glance went beyond him to the doorway of the cabin. I stiffened. The man entering was the stranger who had paid for our tickets. "Do you know who that is?" I asked Randy in a quiet tone.

He turned his head, looked, turned back. "The man standing in the doorway?"

I nodded.

"That's Lyle Delany. You know . . . Delany Lumber Company. Biggest operation in these parts. Delany's got a hundred men working for him, I reckon." Randy frowned and I saw a tightening at the corner of his lips.

"What's the matter? Don't you like him?"

Randy shrugged. "What's to like? He's got a corner on the lumber business in these parts, and now he's buying up land around the lake as fast as he can. Pretty soon he'll own all the best locations. He's got the reputation for being as oily as they come. He'll cheat you of your eyeteeth and make you smile while he's doing it."

"Really?" The assessment of the man who had put me in his debt was hardly reassuring.

"Looks like he's heading this way. You take care." Randy's protective manner made me smile.

"Don't worry. I'll keep Mr. Delany in his place."

Randy moved on, acting as if he would enjoy the chance to throw the lumberman overboard.

The stranger's eyes met mine and held them in a commanding gaze as he moved purposefully toward the bench where I sat nervously holding my mug of tea and the crumbling biscuit.

46

I had never felt so uncomfortable in my life. What should I say to this prosperous man? What had I done, accepting money from someone so unscrupulous? I had little time to compose my thoughts before he stood in front of me.

Giving me a polite smile, he swept off his Western hat. "Enjoying the trip so far?" he asked pleasantly. His face was bronzed from the sun, sideburns curled at the side of his face, and a shock of hair the color of ripe wheat hung on his forehead. There was nothing in his manner to indicate any ill-mannered familiarity, and yet something flickering deep in those blue eyes made me uncomfortable.

My gaze was guarded as I replied, "Yes, thank you."

"Perhaps I'd better introduce myself," he said smoothly.

"I already know who you are," I said crisply.

"Indeed?" I thought there was amusement flickering at the corner of his lips. "My reputation must have preceded me, and from your tone, I gather not a very flattering one at that. May I sit down, Miss . . . ?"

"McKenzie," I said, wishing that he would go away but not knowing how to manage it.

Instead of sitting on the bench beside me, he pulled a chair from one of the tables and placed it so we were almost facing one another. He studied my stiff expression with infuriating boldness. "Miss McKenzie, you mustn't hold idle gossip against me."

"I assure you, Mr. Delany, your reputation is no affair of mine." It was difficult to avoid his steady gaze, but I managed to keep my eyes focused somewhere beyond his head. His solid frame filled the chair in front of me, and with Davie and the puppy asleep at my side, I was trapped on the bench, making a pretense of drinking my tea with perfect composure.

I thought he was laughing at me, and the suspicion made me even more disconcerted. He must be as muscular as any of his loggers, I thought, on some detached level. I didn't know what to say to this man. He frightened me. I was beholden to him for our journey, and I feared that being in his debt might prove to be a horrible mistake.

"So you are going to Blackbriar House," he said in a conversational tone. "Beautiful spot on the lake. Have you ever been there?"

I shook my head, determined not to show my confusion by nervous chatter.

"It has its own bay."

My eyes must have betrayed my interest in the place I hoped would be our new home because he continued in a conversational tone. "Years ago a glacier must have dumped rocks and earth to one side as it moved and left a large piece of water surrounded by land except for a narrow opening into the lake. There's even a small island in the middle. An excellent example of a glacial moraine . . . truly a lovely spot."

And you would like to buy it. The thought was like the cutting edge of a knife. I wondered what kind of payment Mr. Delany would expect in return for his generosity.

"Lucky woman, your aunt," he continued. "Her husband left her quite a bit of property, didn't he?"

"I don't know."

"Really. You didn't know that she's quite well off . . . as far as property goes? Her rambling old house looks out on a magnificent view—not that anyone is welcome to enjoy it. A real hermit, your aunt. Does she know you're coming?"

The casual question was an arrow striking at the heart of my fears. "No."

"Have you ever met her?"

In spite of my determination to remain aloof, I looked him directly in the face. "No, I haven't. Do you know my aunt?"

"Never had the pleasure. I've tried a couple of times, but that caretaker of hers ran me off with a gun."

I swallowed hard. "Caretaker? A gun?"

"The old boy wasn't fooling. Nobody gets near Mrs. McKenzie-Brown unless Jem Erskine says so."

I must have paled, for he said quickly, "Strangers, of course. Not kin."

But I wondered if the distinction meant anything to a woman who had held such rancor for my father all these years.

"Is something the matter, Miss McKenzie? You look quite ill."

I managed a smile. "Must be the motion of the boat," I lied. "Maybe I'm not much of a sailor."

He nodded at Davie. "He seems to be content."

"Tired out from our journey. We were on the stage for three days."

He raised a questioning eyebrow. I could have ignored the unspoken question, but I didn't. "We came from Rocky Gulch, where my father had been prospecting for gold. He was killed in a rock slide . . ."

"Oh, I am sorry." Before I knew what he was doing, he had taken my hand. His fingers closed warmly around mine in a gentle squeeze. "And your mother?"

"She died several years ago. So it's just Davie and me."
I drew away my hand and firmed my chin. "We're going
to make our home with Aunt Minna, my father's sister. I
know we'll be happy there."

He didn't say anything, but a narrowing of his eyes did
little to reassure me that my brave words had any basis in
reality.

"Is there something I should know?" I asked him
bluntly.

"Know? About what?"

"About the situation . . . at Blackbriar House?"

He seemed ready to speak and then changed his mind.
"I'm sure your aunt will be delighted to have company,"
he said with a measured smile—and I knew he lied.

Chapter Four

Davie woke up, jostling the puppy when he moved. Rags bounced all over his lap and stretched up on his short legs to land some sloppy kisses on Davie's face.

Delany laughed. "That's quite a pup," he said to Davie. "What's his name?"

My brother wasn't looking at the stranger and wasn't aware that the man was speaking to him.

"His name is Rags," I said quickly. "And my brother, Davie, is a deaf-mute." I waited for the usual expression of embarrassment and pity that followed this information. Instead, much to my surprise, Delany reached over and started petting the puppy. When Davie looked up, the man smiled and Davie smiled back. Instead of being pleased, I was furious that this stranger was capable of using Davie to ingratiate himself with me.

"How old is your brother?"

"Eight."

"Has he been deaf since birth?"

"Yes . . . but his mind is sharp. He catches on very quickly," I bragged. "We can communicate with each other, and he's learning to write his name."

"What method of sign language do you use?"

"Method?" I laughed. "The McKenzie, I guess. Between us we've developed kind of a shorthand system. Even the flicker of a little finger can communicate a rather complicated message. We've learned to tell jokes and gossip . . ."

"All by yourselves?"

"Of course." I looked puzzled.

"You haven't made use of the sign language developed by Abbé de l-Epée, the Frenchman who is credited with inventing a system of communicating with the deaf?"

I shook my head. "I didn't know there was one."

"Yes. He is a Catholic priest who formulated the first system of hand signs, but I suppose not many people know about it, at least in this part of the country."

I couldn't keep the excitement from my voice. "I've never heard of any books that would teach me how to talk to him."

"I'm sure there are some. Strides are being made to establish schools for the deaf in the East. An educator named Thomas Gallaudet became acquainted with a deaf little girl and went to Paris to learn how to become a teacher for the deaf. He established a school in Hartford, Connecticut, where people can study to be teachers and deaf students can learn how to sign."

I was saddened to think that Davie had no one but me to teach him. Most of our signs were pantomine and dealt with concrete concepts. It was only because of Davie's

52

intelligence that he had been able to interpret subtle communications. If he had a real teacher, there was no telling what he could do. I voiced my regrets to Delany.

"I'm sure you're doing a fine job."

"It's all trial and error, I'm afraid."

"How would it be if I tried to get you some material on teaching the deaf?"

I forgot all about my hesitation to be indebted to this man. His interest in Davie lulled my suspicions. I would swallow my pride in the matter if it would help Davie to communicate better. Helping him break free of the limitations of his deafness was worth any sacrifice on my part. "I would be most appreciative if you could get me some books . . ."

"Of course. It would be my pleasure, Miss McKenzie." He grinned. "Do you think you might tell me your first name."

"Anna," I said readily.

He nodded, as if he thought the name suited me. "Mine is Lyle. And it's my pleasure to meet you, Anna."

I know a blush was mounting in my face. It was too soon for me to be on a first-name basis with this man. After all, I had little in common with such a person, and I felt he was secretly amused at my gauche behavior.

I was glad when Davie touched my arm and pointed out the window. The steamer was heading into the bank near a dramatic formation of rock that rose tall and bare from the water's edge. A dark depression like a tunnel or cave ran through the center of it.

"Cave Rock," said Delany.

Both Davie and I craned our necks, peering out the window at the rising mass of rock.

"The Indians have a legend about it," said Delany, as if he enjoyed the role of storyteller. "In seasons of high rain, the lake overflowed its banks and flooded out villages, so the story goes. The Indians prayed to the Great Spirit for help, and He made a hole in this rock so that high waters could run out of the lake instead of overflowing."

Davie was watching Delany's lips, and I took time to repeat the legend as best as I could. Davie seemed to understand, and pantomimed a high lake and then the sweep of water through the hole.

"I'm impressed," said Delany, laughing. "He told the story better than I did."

The *Tahoe Queen* stayed long enough for us to walk out on deck and let Davie take the puppy for a run along the bank. Cargo and mail was left at a cluster of cabins, and then we were on our way again.

I expected Delany to take his leave when the steamer was back on the lake again, but he stood beside me, casually putting one boot on the lowest railing and resting his hands on the top one. Standing next to him, I was aware that my head came only to his shoulder. His muscular frame dwarfed my small figure, and I had to tip my head back to look up at his vigorous features and fair hair.

"Cave Rock is one of the few landmarks on the lake that will give a traveler his bearings," he explained in a conversational tone, as if he were eager for me to become acclimated to the Lake Tahoe area. "It's very easy to become disoriented on the lake. Miles and miles of shoreline look just the same from a boat in the middle of the lake. People get lost and end up miles from where they thought they were. It's dangerous to take a boat out very far unless you know what you're doing."

As my eyes roved over the miles of blue lake and tiny edge of distant hills, I was caught in a kaleidoscope of sky and water. "Spectacular," I breathed.

His blue eyes reflected the brightness of the scene around us. "And to think this wondrous body of water lay hidden for hundreds of years before the white man found it!"

"And now that he has," I said rather pointedly, "it won't be long until people and boats spoil it."

"Not spoil—enjoy," he corrected. "Lake Tahoe is too beautiful to have its loveliness remain unseen."

"And of course, you intend to remedy that situation by buying and selling property." My tone reflected Randy's disdain when he had told me how this lumberman was trying to buy up lakefront property.

"Better than stripping the hills of all their trees, don't you think? At the moment, logging is the main industry in the area. And it's very profitable, but I'm trying to look ahead. I've acquired some nice property—but I'm not a robber baron."

I thought there was an amused glint in his eyes, as if my tone had accused him of being one. "I suppose there are some who might question that," I answered frigidly, remembering what Randy had said about Delany's oily dealings.

He chuckled. "You don't look like the kind who puts much store in rumors. I imagine you like to make up your own mind, Anna."

Was that a challenge? Suddenly I felt very inept at sparring with this shrewd businessman. From the first he had handled the situation to his satisfaction, smoothly and purposefully. He gave every indication that he was a man of pragmatic concerns . . . and I wondered why he was giving me his attention. I knew that other passengers were wondering the same thing. There was a deferential attitude toward Lyle Delany that marked him as a man of importance. Several men made a point of speaking to him, their speculative glances passing over me as they walked by.

"Do you have a family?" I asked Delany, telling myself the question was purely a superficial polite inquiry. When he shook his head, I ignored a peculiar sense of satisfaction that he wasn't married.

"I am building a lodge at the southern tip of the lake. It's almost finished, so I'll be spending most of the year up here. And what about you? Where are you from?"

Only a deep sense of loneliness made me willing to tell him about myself. "Originally from Kansas. My parents had a farm, and my father worked the land until my mother's death. Since then, we've been on the move, stopping long enough for my father to find work but never staying in one place very long. My father had a dream of finding a rich vein of gold, and he stubbornly prospected as hard as he could to find it." I firmed my chin. "Before he died he told me that he wanted Davie and me to go to his sister—so here we are. Alone and . . ."

"Not alone," he corrected with a firmness that startled me. His commanding strength reached me through the warm smile that bathed my face. For a moment our gaze held. "Please allow me the pleasure of being your friend, Anna."

I could feel my face grow hot. Even though hard life in the camps had aged me beyond my seventeen years, I lacked experience handling someone like this. His smooth, confident manner both frightened and attracted me.

"Why would you want to be my friend, Mr. Delany?" I asked him with my usual candor. "If you think that I can't take care of myself, you're wrong."

He laughed. "I knew from the first moment you flashed those amber eyes at me that you resisted help of any kind. Believe me, I have no doubt whatever that you can manage quite nicely on your own, but surely you don't intend to live shut off from the world like your aunt."

"I don't know," I said honestly. "At the moment, I have no choice but to throw myself upon her bounty and abide by her wishes."

"And what if she makes you a hermit like herself? Without friends . . . without visitors . . ."

"If that's what she wants, I'll have no choice but to obey." Silently I vowed that for Davie's sake, I would turn my back on the world and suffer the torments of a hermit if I must.

"Well, I hope you will extend me a welcome if I come to Blackbriar. And perhaps introduce me to your aunt. She owns a large acreage that borders mine at the southern tip of the lake."

His smile was still warm, but it brought a chill to my heart. I knew then why he was interested in my friendship—he was going to use me to make contact with Aunt Minna. I was not quite the fool that he thought. It was apparent that his attentions to me had been calculated: he wanted to buy her property. How smoothly he had orchestrated an invitation to her home.

"I'll mail you the fare money," I answered crisply. "The Delany Lumber Company in Glenbrook, is that correct?"

"There's no hurry."

I regretted the necessity of having to borrow from him and silently vowed I would send him the money as quickly as possible. I didn't want to be indebted to Lyle Delany for anything. It was obvious he intended to use me and Davie for his own purposes. "I like to pay my debts promptly."

Once more I thought he was amused. "If you insist. I hope you will be warmly received at Blackbriar," he said "And if I can be of any further assistance . . ."

"Thank you, but we'll be fine . . . once we reach my aunt's home."

He straightened up and squinted across the water. "We're almost to my stop." He smiled at me. "It's been a pleasure to have shared your company."

My smile was stiff and my goodbye very firm and final as he prepared to leave the steamer. As the *Tahoe Queen* pulled to shore, I glimpsed unfinished buildings through the trees. A lodge, cabins, and an impressive boat dock were in various stages of completion.

"All kinds of delays," he said with a frown. Then his expression softened, "But it's a beautiful spot, isn't it?"

Thick drifts of tall trees spread down wooded slopes to the lake's edge. A narrow beach of white sand curved in a half-moon and was edged with rippling water in shades of aquamarine and violet. Even the mess of construction had not marred the natural splendor of the scene, and I murmured, "Beautiful." If Aunt Minna owned property like this, she could command a nice price if she decided to sell it. No wonder Lyle Delany was cultivating my friendship.

"Till we meet again," he said with such obvious intent that I found myself laughing. He raised an eyebrow as though perplexed by my mirth.

He stood on the dock waving as the steamer pulled away. My feelings were at odds with a sense of satisfaction that I had seen through his little ploy. Impatient with a foolish sense of loss, I took Davie back into the cabin and we sat down to wait for the steamer to travel up the California side of the lake. The bright, sunny morning had given way to afternoon rainclouds, and as the bright colors of the lake faded, my mood grew more sober.

Randy, the friendly steward, came by, and I bought two sandwiches for lunch. I asked him how long it would be before we reached Blackbriar.

"About thirty minutes. Most of the time the *Tahoe Queen* doesn't stop there. Seldom any mail to deliver . . . and no visitors."

"Not ever?" I asked with a lump in my throat.

"Not usually. The caretaker has a small skiff, and he runs most of the errands. A little while ago he took a new housekeeper back with him—but I guess she didn't last long. None of 'em do." He eyed me sadly. "Are you going for a visit?"

"No. To live there, I hope," I said with more certainty than I felt.

"You won't like it," he added, before I had time to

59

explain. "Widow Brown ain't left the place in ages. Her husband died about ten years back. That's when Erskine, her caretaker, began to look after things for her. Her husband left her property all around the lake. Doesn't spend a dime unless she has to. Never keeps help. You'd do better to live some place else."

"Mrs. Brown is my aunt."

"Oh, I didn't know . . ." Randy looked embarrassed. "So that's why Mr. Delany was paying you all that attention."

"What do you mean?" I asked, even though I knew exactly what the steward meant. The smooth Mr. Delany had already shown his interest and his enthusiasm for opening up the lake to the tourist trade.

"Mr. Delany's property extends nearly as far up the western side of the lake as Blackbriar Bay," the young man explained. "He's been wanting to make it a part of his new fancy resort. But your aunt won't even talk with him. That caretaker of hers drives him off every time . . . at the end of a shotgun, we hear." He chuckled. "We've all had a good laugh over it."

"Yes, I bet you have," I said dryly. And now the laugh's on me, I thought, remembering how warm Delany's smile had made me feel.

"You really going there to live?" His eyes widened, and I felt new apprehension sluicing through me at his appalled expression. The young man shook his head. "I bet Jim Erskine won't like it. He doesn't have the welcome mat out for anybody."

"I'm kin—he'll have to accept Davie and me," I said with more confidence than I felt. Everything I heard about my aunt refuted any assurance that she would take in her estranged brother's children.

"I guess you could always leave—if you don't like it."

"Of course," I said, as if I had dozens of options for taking care of myself and my little brother.

He sighed. "I know how hard it is, trying to find a place to call home. I left mine a couple of years ago, thinking I'd make it rich along with some of the lucky ones finding gold and silver all over the place. Never got anything for two years of misery. Never had a dime to send back home, let alone enough for decent food and a roof over my head."

I nodded. "I have heard the story often enough."

"Anyway, I decided to get myself a job. This one doesn't pay much, but I've been able to save a few dollars, almost enough to go back home without feeling like a complete failure."

"I think you did the wise thing. For every millionaire, there are thousands who never see a cent for all their sacrifice." I didn't tell him I knew from experience.

Shadows stretched long over land and water. The lake's surface reflected the sullen sky, and a dull pewter color had replaced the earlier sheen of blue-green. A chill went through me, and I clutched my shawl tighter at the neck. A sense of brooding disaster ran coldly through my veins. For a brief, unrealistic moment, I almost sent a message to the pilot that we had changed our minds. He could put us off at some other stop on the lake—anyplace but Blackbriar Bay. Common sense overrode the impulse. My father had sent us here. I drew on the memory of his soft gaze when he looked at the photograph in his watch. Surely, whatever had happened between him and his sister would not warrant a hardness of heart that would cause Aunt Minna to turn us away from her door.

The steamer chugged through a narrow outlet that opened into a small bay. Sloping, wooded hillsides stopped abruptly at the edge of the water, and I could see why my aunt's house was accessible only by boat. A road into the area would have to be built over huge boulders and rocky shelves. A small rocky island rose in the middle of the circled bay.

Davie pointed to it and nodded. It looked like a storybook island, the kind that would appeal to the adventurous activities of a small boy. I could see Davie scampering over the rocks to the highest pinnacle and surveying the scene like king of the hill.

As we chugged toward the shore, I glimpsed a stark wooden building almost secluded from view. The main section appeared to be two stories tall, with a narrow addition at one end that rose three stories to a pointed cupola. Chimneys jutted up into the air like appendages from a huge insect cowering in the trees. The style was like that of a mining shafthouse—narrow windows, plain walls, and no exterior adornment.

"That's Blackbriar," said Randy Bowles, appearing at my elbow. "Funny-looking place, isn't it?" Then, seeing my expression, he added quickly, "Old man Brown kept adding to it. Never did look much like a house, but I bet it's better on the inside."

I mentally crossed my fingers with the hope that he spoke the truth.

The competent pilot brought the steamer close enough for us to climb down a ladder to a small, weathered dock that looked old enough to crumble under our weight.

Randy waved goodbye as the *Tahoe Queen* headed back across the small bay and slipped through the narrow opening into the lake beyond. We stood there for a moment like castaways as the steamer faded to a black dot on the lake. I felt Davie's small hand in mine and gave it a reassuring squeeze.

"Let's go meet Aunt Minna," I said, more to myself than to him. My heart was knocking loudly in my chest as we turned and started up a rock path toward the ugly house.

Chapter Five

We're here, I thought with nervous excitement. Our journey had been long and tiring; now it was ending. I put aside the apprehension that had been growing ever since we'd left Rocky Gulch. I reasoned that most of the things Randy and Delany had told me about Aunt Minna had been hearsay. They knew nothing firsthand. After living in several camps, I knew how rumors and stories could get twisted. Someone could have misinterpreted the situation at Blackbriar, jumping to all kinds of conclusions, and spreading ugly tales about my aunt and her caretaker. I had a basic trust in people, and I drew on that trust now as Davie and I walked hand-in-hand down the long pier with Rags bouncing along at our heels.

A sprinkling of rain hurried our steps, and a quickening wind sent rough swells of water against green pilings, an old boathouse, and two slips for boats. Gray logs, frayed ropes, and an old rowboat turned upside down on the sand provided a desolate welcome.

The path from the lake to the house was rough and narrow, hemmed in by tall pines and masses of low-growing cedar. Deadfall of dry needles and bleached twigs and branches had collected into thick undergrowth, making a stroll under the trees almost impossible. We had just reached a narrow clearing in front of the house when I heard someone cry out in pain.

I quickened my steps, pulling Davie along with me. "Oh, my heavens!" I gasped as I saw a gray-haired woman crumpled in a heap at the foot of the uneven steps that led into the house.

"Aunt Minna!" I rushed forward.

"My ankle!" She writhed in pain. "I think it's broken." Her foot was twisted under her in a grotesque fashion. She was a woman of average height, but flesh hung loosely on her frame, giving her a delicate look.

I put my arms around her shoulders and helped her into a sitting position. She cried out as she straightened the injured leg.

The years had not been kind to my Aunt Minna. The laughing girl in the photograph was now a gaunt woman with furrowed lines in her cheeks. Her McKenzie-red hair had faded to an ugly gray. Her sparse figure was all sharp angles and flat planes; nothing remained of the full-faced girl with her arm looped through my father's. An ugly brown dress hung from bony shoulders, and a worn lace collar circled a sagging neck.

She managed to get up on her one good leg by leaning heavily upon me. Limping and groaning, she hobbled with my help back into the house and collapsed in a worn chair near a blackened fireplace. I motioned for Davie to stay outside with the puppy while I tended to my aunt.

"Get me that footstool," she ordered in a querulous tone. "My ankle's burning like a hot poker." She groaned and stroked her leg as if the movement would help the pain go away.

I brought a leather-covered stool and helped place her injured foot on it. "Is that better?"

She made a grimace that answered my question.

"We'd better take off your shoe," I said, seeing how quickly the flesh was swelling around the top of her worn button shoes.

She nodded. As I loosened the fastenings, explosive cries protested the job of slipping it off her foot. Already a puffy swelling was making the ankle twice its size.

"You should soak it," I said, having treated my father for a similar injury a few months back. "Warm water and salt."

Her biting brown eyes snapped at me. "Well, get some—and be quick about it." She gave a jerk of her head toward the hall.

I credited the pain in her ankle for her rude behavior and hurried to do as she bade. She was in too much agony to be gracious about my sudden appearance at her house. I was glad that I had arrived at a moment of need. By the time the crisis was over, all stiffness between us would be gone.

A narrow corridor running from the front of the house to the back was as shadowy as a tunnel. Dark walls, a smoky high ceiling, and worn floorboards lent the passage a stifling oppressiveness. The inside of the house lived up to its dreary exterior, I thought, as a musty, sour smell filled my nostrils. The house was like a rabbit's warren, with short flights of stairs going up and down along the passage. Rooms opening off it were dark and drab.

I kept going down the serpentine hall until I reached a cold and colorless kitchen at the back of the house. Pine trees pressed against dirty windows, shutting out light and scraping the sides of the house with nerve-wracking scratching noises. A blackened stove held only cold, gray ashes, and a crude table was littered with dirty dishes that smelled like spoiled fish. My nostrils quivered, and I wondered how anyone could live in such squalor. No wonder a housekeeper refused to stay for very long.

A water jug on the washbench was nearly empty, so I pumped it full and then filled a blackened teakettle sitting on the back of a cold stove. I wondered how long it had been since a meal had been cooked there, or a pan of biscuits or sourdough bread put in the oven.

I rolled back the sleeves of my dress, and as quickly as I could, I shoveled ashes out of the stove into an almost overflowing bucket. I laid a couple of chunks of kindling from the nearly empty woodbox and struck several matches before I coaxed the wood into flames. While the water heated, I looked around for a large pan. The only one I found was being used to store fishing gear. I emptied out the hooks, lines, and tackle in a pile on the table and searched a messy cupboard for some salt until I found an open jar that was half-filled.

While the water in the teakettle slowly heated to a tepid warmth, I washed out the dirty pan, drying it with a cloth that was scarcely more than a rag.

"Took you long enough," snapped my aunt when I hurried back to her with the pan of warmed water. Her thin mouth was held in a grimace as I gently lowered her foot into the water. She sat forward in the chair, her head bent so that a stringy mass of gray hair drifted over her face.

I stood there, wondering what I should say or do. At least I had gained entrance into the house, I thought wryly. I was certain that my aunt had been on her way out when the schooner dropped us off. If she hadn't fallen, we might not have been allowed to leave the boat. "Does that feel better?" I asked.

She shoved back a shock of hair and glared at me. "Who are you?"

"Anna McKenzie. My little brother, Davie, is outside. We're your brother's children."

"I don't have any brother," she said flatly, and I knew that she had long ago decided to deny my father's existence.

"He talked about you a lot," I countered. "And kept your picture. See." I took out the pocket watch and flipped open the lid.

She stared at the photograph. I saw her hands tighten in her lap.

"Do you remember when it was taken?"

Her tumbled hair hid her expression from me.

When she didn't answer, I added quietly, "My father said that the two of you had gone to a fair and a man with a camera was there taking pictures. It must have been a happy time for you. Both of you are laughing."

She shoved back her hair with an impatient gesture. Her eyes were as cold as before. "Why'd you come here?" she demanded.

I firmed my chin. "My father was killed . . . in a rock slide . . . prospecting for gold. Before he died, he told me to bring my little brother and come here." I swallowed against a dry mouth. "So here we are." I tried to keep all traces of anxiety from my tone. I wasn't going to snivel nor throw myself upon her mercy. I had too much pride to beg with tears and pleas. "He said you'd take us in, Aunt Minna."

Before she could answer, Davie darted into the room, clutching the puppy in a stranglehold. He scooted behind my skirts. His eyes were rounded and his face bleached of color.

I followed his frightened gaze to a man who stood in the doorway, leveling a rifle at me. He was huge and heavy-chested, with thorny black eyebrows that matted over the bridge of his crooked nose. In a swarthy face, his eyes were as hard as chips of shale. A mouth that once might have been curved and sensual was pulled into a sneering, hard line, and a smell of liquor and tobacco suddenly dominated the room. He looked as if he would delight in blowing my brains out and laugh while he was doing it.

Erskine, the caretaker, I thought instantly. He was much younger than I had pictured when Randy Bowles had talked about him, no more than thirty-five or forty, and I felt his smoldering, discordant energy as one feels the destructive forces of a threatening volcano.

"What in the hell is going on?" he bellowed. His black eyes scorched my aunt. "I leave for a couple of hours and come back to find ye entertaining company."

"They're not company." My aunt gave a short laugh as if somehow the joke was on him. "This is my niece . . . and nephew. Come to live with me, they have." Her chest suddenly heaved with mirth, a crazy, hysterical kind of laughter that made my skin prickle.

"What ye talking about?" he snarled.

She muffled her laughter with her hand. I thought her eyes danced with some kind of maniacal joy. She looked at me and gave a wave of her hand. "This here is Jem Erskine, my handyman and caretaker. Isn't that right, Jem?" She seemed to be baiting him.

For a moment, I thought he was going to reach out with one of his broad hands and slap her face. Instead, his piercing stony eyes swept to me. "How'd ye get here?"

I was surprised to find my voice quite strong despite the fright that threatened to buckle my knees. "On the schooner. Just a few minutes ago." Only a few minutes, I thought. Already it seemed like an eternity.

The man swore again and leaned over my aunt. "Why'd ye let them get off? Haven't I warned ye . . ." He said in a threatening tone.

Aunt Minna sobered. "I couldn't help it, Jem. Honest, I couldn't. I saw the *Tahoe Queen* pulling in and was hurrying to see who was coming—when I fell on that blasted step. I told you it needed fixin'. My ankle's throbbing with the beat of a sledgehammer," she said in a petulant tone. "I can't stand to put my weight on it. Maybe it will be a good thing to have some help—"

"They're leaving," he said flatly. "I'll row 'em to Tahoe City. Ye shouldn't have let them get off the boat."

"I told you that I fell. Look at that foot. Bigger than a bloated pig's stomach." She lifted her foot out of the water, wincing as she laid it on the footstool. "I'm not going to be doing much walking for a spell." She squinted at him. "Might not be a bad idea to have the girl around for awhile. After all, they *are* my kin."

"Are ye out of your mind?" He sent her a wordless message that was vile enough to shrink her back into her chair.

"It won't hurt nothing," she pleaded. A wordless exchange flashed between them.

My heart was suddenly knocking in my chest. I knew at that moment the ugly man was in charge here, utterly and completely. My Aunt's eyes were the first to lower.

"Well, whatever you think, Jem."

"I've heard talk about that brother. Hated Ben McKenzie's guts, ye did." He glared at her. "Ye don't owe him nothing, and his kids less than that. Parasites, that's what they be."

"But I need some help with this place," she countered in a wheedling tone. "And the girl could give it."

"Yer as lazy and shiftless as they come." His contemptuous tone was appalling.

"How dare you speak to my aunt like that?" I flared.

"Yes, how indeed?" echoed Aunt Minna. My impulsive support seemed to strength her resolve in the manner. "I'm thinking they can stay awhile. At least till I get on my feet."

"It's a mistake. The longer they stay, the harder it will be to get rid of them."

I wished that Davie and I could walk out the door and slam it in their faces, but I had to swallow my pride for my little brother's sake. I put my hand on his shoulder and pulled him close. I knew that he was bewildered by the hostile expressions and talk which he could not hear. His frightened eyes darted from the scowling caretaker to Aunt Minna. I signed as best I could that the woman was one of our family. He had no concept of "aunt," so I tried to draw a comparison between the woman and our father—"Just like you and me. Family."

He nodded, but I coud tell that his comprehension of the relationships was vague. The woman wasn't acting like family. Our father had been firm but gentle, and Davie wasn't used to having someone glare at him with such malice.

I sensed a good deal of maneuvering going on between them. My aunt seemed to be under the man's control, rather than the other way around. If he was the hired help, why was he exerting so much authority? Why was my aunt frightened of him? Was that fear in her eyes, or something else? She might be the owner of Blackbriar House, but I suspected that the decision whether we went or stayed rested with Erskine.

My measuring glance traveled over the man's wide shoulders, rugged features, and dagger-sharp eyes, which were as black as his thick eyebrows. I felt the domination of his aggressive animal-like maleness. He was at least ten years younger than Aunt Minna, but I wondered if she was taken with him in a romantic way. For some reason, my aunt had been willing to remain isolated from the world since her husband's death. Could they be lovers? Maybe Erskine was afraid I would find out that he was manipulating my aunt's affections to gain control of her land.

After a moment, a silent understanding between them seemed to put them in agreement. Erskine's black glare centered on me. "Where'd ye come from?"

I sensed that the decision to allow us to stay had been reached, but a sense of relief was drowned by a rising tide of apprehension. How could we live in this house? What would life be like even for a short time?

"I asked ye a question!" he bellowed at me, leaning his rifle against the fireplace.

I suspected that he was the kind of bully to feed on fright. I couldn't let him know how scared I was. "Rocky Gulch, Nevada," I responded. "East of Carson City."

"I know where it is. I suppose yer pa was one of them crazy-eyed gold hunters?"

"He was a farmer, laborer, and prospector," I said with a lift of my chin.

He snorted. "And a loser at all of them, I'll wager."

"My father was an honest, hard-working man."

"A no-account drifter," growled Erskine. "And jealous of yer aunt's well-being, I'll wager. She gave him short shrift when he came snooping around a while back. He wasn't welcome here then—and neither are his brats."

"Why don't you let my aunt speak for herself?" I snapped, angry at the way he'd put himself in charge of the situation.

Aunt Minna shot a look at Erskine and then turned to me. "What about your ma?"

"She died several years ago. My father decided to sell our farm in Kansas, and we moved first to Idaho and then to Nevada. Last week my father was killed in a rock slide."

I looked for some sign of grief in my aunt's face. None. She tightened her lips. I wondered why she hated my father so much that she couldn't even mourn his passing.

"So ye decided to put the touch on your aunt, eh?" the caretaker said in a ugly tone that made me feel like dirt.

"With his last breath, my father told me to come here." I firmed my voice. "He was sure his sister would offer us a home."

"So yer poor as church mice, are ye? Looking for a handout." He spat on the floor. "Beggars. Well, ye'll damn well earn yer keep, or out the two of ye go." He moved closer to me, leering down from his great height. "And ye'd best learn how to please me. Ye get my meaning?"

"Jem!" said my aunt. "Leave the girl be. Can't you see she's the kind that would run a blade between your ribs if you put a hand on her? We don't need that kind of trouble!"

He gave a deep laugh. "Trouble is the spice of life, my dear. I always did like fiery red hair, but you know that, Auntie." He laughed again. "Auntie Minna. What a joke!" His eyes fell to Davie and the puppy that was wiggling in protest. His scowl was instantly ugly. "The mutt goes! The lake's deep enough to get rid of him in short order."

"No." I took a step forward, surprised at the fury that sped through me. "The dog belongs to my brother. Don't you dare do him harm."

"And who be ye, telling me what to do? I could wring that slender neck of yers with one twist of my hand." He put a thick finger against my cheek as if in warning.

I knocked it away. My glare bit into his smoldering gray eyes. "You'll keep your hands off me, my brother, and the pup."

"Oh, I will, will I? Well, now, look who's telling me what I can do and what I can't!" He seemed more amused than angry. "Might have some sport teaching ye to pull in your claws. How old ye be?"

"Seventeen."

He nodded in satisfaction, as if he found my answer to his liking. I wanted to turn from his lusty gaze and run away as fast as I could. But where?

Before I could stop him, he reached and jerked Davie away from my side. My brother let out a gasp of air. Rags leaped out of his arms, and Erskine gave the dog a kick with his huge boot, lifting in into the air. It yelped and scurried away.

"As for you," he bellowed at Davie. "Git yourself out to the shed and bring in some wood. It's fixing for a windblow."

Davie jerked and writhed, trying to get free of the man's iron grasp on his arm. "You need some persuasion, too?" he demanded.

Garbled, senseless sounds came from Davie's mouth. Erskine stared at him. "Good Lord! He's an idiot. The boy's looney."

"No, he's not. He's deaf. He doesn't hear what you're saying. Let him go or I'll—"

In one movement Erskine dropped Davie's arm and forced me back against the wall, leering into my face, turning my stomach with the onslaught of his foul breath. "Don't ye be threatening me or I'll bash yer head in like a ripe pumpkin, ye hear me? I'll skin ye alive and drop yer bleeding corpse in the lake. Nobody threatens Jem Erskine—nobody!"

Only Davie's strangled whimpers kept me from fainting dead away. My eyes froze on Erskine's face. For a moment I thought he was going to bludgeon me to death.

Instead he stepped back. Deep within his black eyes, an unreadable emotion flickered. "Ye have much to learn, Anna McKenzie," he said in a deadly tone. "Keep that brother of yers and that mutt out of my sight. Hear?"

I managed a stiff nod.

"And ye'd better be able to cook better than your Auntie." He gave a smirking laugh. "Maybe we'll have something better than burned potatoes and raw fish for a change."

My heart lurched about in my chest, and I took a deep breath to counter my weak knees. "Get the dog," I signed to Davie. He dived under a chair and pulled out the cowering puppy. Rags whimpered in Davie's arms as he came back and pressed up against my side. I kept a protective hand on his shoulder, waiting for the man's wrath to settle upon us again. I could feel Davie tremble. No one had ever touched him like that. How terrified he must be in his soundless world! I held him close to my side, hoping he wouldn't feel the tremors within my own body.

Erskine grabbed up a half-empty bottle from the floor beside my aunt's chair. He plopped down on an elkhide couch whose cushions bore the indentations of a heavy body. He tipped his black head backward and drank deeply from the whiskey bottle. His rugged profile was like chiseled granite, lined and pock-marked, fierce and ominous.

My aunt laid her head back against her chair and closed her eyes. Davie and I just stood there. No one spoke, and for a moment the only sounds were wind and rain. Outside an eerie wailing crept under the eaves and echoed in the blackened chimney. Strange cries like tormented souls rose and fell, as if we had somehow descended into a pagan hell. Evil was a miasma that seeped through the house. For the first time, I was grateful that Davie could not hear the horrible rattling that shook the unfinished walls and rough floors.

The white whiskey gurgled in Erskine's throat as he drank deeply. When the bottle was empty, he threw it into a pile of refuse near the fireplace. I felt his searing eyes upon me. A mocking smile curved his moist lips, and like a grappling hook his expression sank into me. Dear God, how could we stay here, under the same roof with this man?

"Git!" Erskine snarled. "I'm hungry."

"Yes," said my aunt, lifting her head and turning to look at me with eyes as cold as the wet panes of glass. "Fix us supper."

"What is there to cook?" I demanded, moving toward the door, remembering the horrid state of the kitchen.

"Find something," ordered Aunt Minna.

"And be quick about it," growled Erskine. "Or ye and the dummy'll find yerselves out in the rain for the night."

I wanted to protest. I had not seen any foodstuffs in the filthy kitchen, and the remembered sour smells warned me that whatever I found would probably be spoiled or rancid.

"Well, don't just stand there," he bellowed.

Taking Davie's hand, we made our way back to the kitchen while outside the wind rose and battered the house, reaching my ears as mocking laughter.

Chapter Six

I discarded my bonnet, pinned my heavy hair into a coil on the nape of my neck, and put on one of my aprons. I would have preferred to change into one of my worn day dresses, but I didn't dare take the time. The rebellious wisps of red hair that fringed my forehead were moist from nervous sweat that beaded there.

I found a couple of tallow candles and placed one on the littered table and carried the other about, peering into cupboards and a long pantry that was filled with everything but foodstuffs. My eyes smarted from smoke circling up into my eyes as I pawed through empty, smelly stone crocks, boxes, kegs, and tins. A half-filled sack of flour was alive with weevils, and rodents had left tracks upon every surface. A scurried rustling as I moved things about informed me that nesting rats and mice were not pleased with my intrusion. A few withered potatoes and one sprouted onion was all I found for my efforts.

I was appalled by the filth I saw everywhere I looked. I couldn't believe that any woman would allow her kitchen to sink into such a deplorable state. Even though our home in Rocky Gulch had been barely more than a shack, I had proudly kept the small cook stove clean, the walls scrubbed, and homemade shelves and meager foodstuff in order. My father never came home to a cold meal or a slovenly house. We had lived in near poverty but never in dirty squalor. Our home had been a place of warmth and caring. Tears welled up in my eyes as painful longing and loneliness swept over me. I clenched my hands at my side. My insides revolted against the stench and filth.

I was about to give in to tears when I felt Davie tugging at my skirt. Quickly I blinked back the fullness in my eyes.

"What's wrong?" he signed.

His concerned, worried look gave me the strength I needed. I didn't know how, but I vowed that I would do what I must to keep a roof over his head. "I have to find something to cook. Food," I said quickly with my hands.

He nodded and rubbed his stomach in boyish fashion.

Together we finished a tour of the kitchen and found nothing. The strong fish odor was undoubtedly left by the last meal. What did they eat besides fish? In desperation I opened a door which I thought opened to the outside, but holding out my flickering candle, I saw steps leading downward. A cellar of sorts, I thought, even though it looked more like a hole dug in the earth.

Every part of my being wanted to slam the door shut and ignore the possibility that food might be stored in the cold dugout beneath the house. I didn't like small, closed-in places even when there was plenty of air. The worst torture I could think of was to descend into a dark mine tunnel. That feeling of abhorrence overwhelmed me as I stood in the doorway and the pit of darkness beckoned.

In the yellow candlelight, I could see that the walls

were dirt and rock, as if the cavern had been dug out of the mountainside. Cool air bathed my face and I shivered.

Davie waited, looking at me questioningly. I feared that Erskine might lurch into the kitchen at any moment, demanding his food. He would be ugly, his belly full of the home-brewed whiskey. Apprehension of his anger overrode my fear of going down the rickety steps into the dark abyss.

"Stay here," I ordered Davie.

His eyes rounded with fear. He looked down into the black hole and blanched.

"It's all right." I smiled reassuringly.

Void of a sense of hearing, Davie depended upon tactile and visual stimuli to keep in touch with the world—and he hated the dark.

"You stay here." I guided him to a stool by the fire. "Be back in a minute."

He clung to my hand. I bent and kissed his forehead. Then I signed, "Don't worry. Nothing's going to hurt me."

The puppy followed me over to the doorway and then stopped. His little nose quivered as if feeling the air. He gave a short woof and then backed up.

His behavior was less than reassuring, I thought, as I steeled myself to descend into the gloomy abyss. Holding the candle out in front of me, I started slowly down the crude stairway. After three steps, I discovered that I couldn't stand up straight. The cellar was nothing more than an earthen pit . . . a hole scooped out of the ground. The roof wasn't even timbered. Rock and dirt had fallen down in tumbled piles, making the hole smaller and smaller with time. A sensation of being buried alive was triggered by dust floating up my nostrils and a smothering of stale air that had never seen the light of day or felt the warmth of the sun.

I took a few hunched steps, turned in a circle, and then screamed!

A corpse hung by the neck, dangling in the still air right in front of me. The smell of blood and flesh was strong enough to turn my stomach.

Mesmerized by fright, I couldn't move forward nor back. My hand trembled, threatening to drop the candle. My eyes adjusted to the darkness, and in the wavering radius of flickering candlelight, I saw the hanging body more clearly. I stared. Then I gave a weak laugh. At that moment I recognized it for what it was—a deer carcass.

A sudden weakness followed a flood of relief. It wasn't a human body that hung there. I chided myself for thinking such a thing. What a deplorable state my nerves were in. I'd better get them under control and quick. I took a deep breath, allowing relief to ease away my tension. I had found meat for supper!

The animal had been cleaned and skinned, and a carving knife was handily stuck into it. I was not squeamish about butchering. Chickens, wild turkeys, pigs, and deer had to be killed, cleaned, and preserved in order for us to have food to eat. Very quickly, I sliced off several thick portions of the meat and made my way back upstairs.

I held out the booty with a smile, and Davie gave me his soundless grin. With warm water remaining in the teakettle, I cleaned a blackened skillet and cooked some suet from the meat until I had enough grease to fry the meat, potatoes, and onion. Soon the lingering smell of fish was lost and an aroma of venison and vegetables filled the kitchen.

I gave meat scraps to the puppy and a tin plate of food to Davie. He sat on his stool by the stove and gobbled his supper with the appetite of a hungry eight-year-old.

I had just finished washing three more plates when I heard loud footsteps coming down the hall into the kitchen. Stiffening, I swung around.

"Where's my supper?" Erskine bellowed, stomping in with a full bottle of whiskey in his hand. His eyes landed on Davie. "What the hell—?"

My brother froze with a piece of meat halfway to his mouth. "It's all right," I signed and put my hand on his shoulder.

"Feeding yourself and the little beggar, are ye, while I go hungry."

I turned to the stove, gingerly picked up the hot skillet, and thrust it at him. "Here's your supper! Eat it!"

He looked at the steaming food, and then at me. I could tell that the appetizing aroma had dulled his anger. "Well, don't just stand there. Fill me a plate." He jerked a chair from the wall, knocked off a pile of papers that had been set on the seat, and dropped heavily into it.

I put a clean plate, knife, and fork in front of him and served him the food before I put the skillet back on the stove. In the process I knocked on the floor some fishing gear which I had emptied on the table earlier.

"What's my fishing stuff doing here?" he bellowed.

"I needed the pan for Aunt Minna's ankle."

"So yer throwing my things around, are ye?" He jabbed a finger at me. "Let's get something straight. Ye keep yer meddling hands off my things! If ye don't, ye'll be taking on a hell of a lot more than ye can handle."

"I don't intend to live in a pigpen!" I flared back.

"Fishing gear doesn't belong in a kitchen washbasin."

"Oh, doesn't it now? It belongs wherever I say it belongs. And anything else in this house. Ye'd better learn that right now."

If I had any doubts about who was in charge, they were settled by the challenging fury in his eyes. Still, some stubborn bent in my nature would not let the matter rest. "If you expect me to cook the meals, I'll be in charge of the kitchen."

For a moment I thought he might lurch from his chair in anger. Instead he gestured with his knife. "Sit down."

"No. I have to see to Aunt Minna's dinner."

"Ye'll bloody well sit down before I knock you down." I sat.

He chomped on a piece of venison, glaring at me with every bite. "Now listen. Your auntie is—" He made a telling gesture to his head. "Got it?"

"What are you saying? She's—ill?"

He gave an ugly guffaw. "I'm telling ye that sometimes she don't make sense. Don't believe nothing she says. She's sick in the head, all right. I've been seeing to her for nigh on ten years." He leaned forward, his voice harsh and deep. "I'm telling ye that I'm master of Blackbriar House. Ye'll do as *I* tell ye. If ye don't, I'll toss ye and that dummy brother of yern in the middle of the lake— and that will be end of that."

I sat there in silence as he ate. I kept my hands folded in my lap. My fingernails dug into my flesh, so tight was my grip. I knew that Davie was watching my every move. He'd learn to read my expressions as deftly as if he heard the words that passed my lips.

"I am not here to challenge you or your position," I said evenly, hoping that I hid the fear and anger raging

84

inside. "This place is obviously in need of a housekeeper. As long as you permit my brother and me to live here, I'll gladly work for our keep. As for my aunt, I'm happy to care for her in any way I can."

He snorted. "And ye'll get the back of her hand for yer efforts, I'll wager." He tipped the bottle and drank heavily from it. I must have betrayed my disgust, for he slammed it down and shouted, "And don't be looking at me like I was scum beneath your feet. I ain't some no-account bastard. I got dreams—and the guts to make them come true. Ye hear me?" he shouted in a drunken slur. "You won't find me on my belly digging in the earth like yer pa. I'll get mine. And I'll peel the skin from anyone who tries to stop me." His voice had lowered to a near whisper. "What's mine is mine."

I sat very still, not daring to flick an eyelid. Any response could trigger his fury. His thorny eyebrows and coarse features were the devil's own countenance. He must have read the repulsion in my eyes, for suddenly he stood up and tipped the table over, sending it crashing to the floor, scattering everything on it.

I leapt out of the way, expecting his fury to be turned on me. He bellowed a loud curse, shaking his fist at me, and then he threw open the back door and went out into the rain and whipping wind. I saw lightning forking across the sky, touching his huge form with an eerie light. Booming thunder drowned out his roaring curses as he disappeared into the night.

I hurriedly closed the door against the rain and leaned up against it, trying to get my breath. Erskine was a drunken lunatic. An unpredictable, savage devil. How had my aunt lived with him for ten years? Had she always been his prisoner? Had she been kept here by his maniac

85

fury? No wonder she was mentally sick and confused.

Davie was clutching the puppy and cowering against the wall. I went to him and tried to assure him as best I could. What could I say—that we had put oursevles in the hands of the devil himself?

As quickly as I could, I righted the table and filled two plates from the skillet I had luckily left on the stove. Otherwise, the food would have been scattered all over the dirty floor.

I motioned to Davie to come with me. I would eat my supper with Aunt Minna. With Erskine out of the house, we would have time to get acquainted.

Davie went ahead of me, holding out a smoky candle to light our steps as we made our way back through the dark laybrinth of halls to the front of the house. I wondered if Minna's husband had planned the house or just added additions as the fancy took him. From what I had seen, he had never put the finishing touches on anything.

The front sitting room seemed to be the only one finished with wallpaper, and I wondered if it could have been the original room of the house. Aunt Minna still sat in the chair where we had left her. Her head lolled to one side, her mouth open in a deep snore. An open bottle of strong-smelling whiskey leaned against her side. There was little food in the house but plenty of whiskey, I thought with disgust. I knew then that the satanic caretaker had made a drunkard out of Minna McKenzie-Brown. No wonder the house was in such a deplorable state. For the first time I realized that my arrival might save my aunt from a tragic end. It had always been a weakness of mine to think I could change the course of fate if given the chance.

"Aunt Minna. Aunt Minna." I jostled her bony

shoulder. "I've brought your supper. Wake up."

She groaned, opened one eye, and then jerked awake as if prepared to defend herself against me. A befuddled expression chased across her face and alarm shone in her glassy eyes.

I patted her shoulder reassuringly. "It's me, Anna. Remember? Your niece."

She gave me a drunken stare, and then her moist lips curved. "My niece?"

"Yes. Your brother Benjamin's children. Don't you remember?"

The smile was almost a sneer. "Oh, yes . . . come to live with me, have you?"

"Yes."

"Leeches!"

"No! We'll earn our keep. I'll do the cooking and cleaning. You don't have to treat me or Davie as kin, Aunt Minna. We'll work for you for board and room. That's all we ask."

She looked at me as I placed the plate in her lap. "Here's your supper. Now, eat some meat and vegetables. . . ."

She grabbed my arm. "Jem?" A worried frown creased her face.

"He's already eaten. He . . . he went out."

She nodded. "The boathouse. He likes to spend time in the boathouse. Got a cot there . . . and small stove. He likes to be alone. All alone." She took the fork and began to peck at the food.

Even though I had little appetite because of the upheaval of emotions that had overtaken me, I knew that I must eat. I took my plate and sat down on the battered couch. Davie curled up beside me with the puppy snuggled against him.

I began talking about our trip around the lake. How beautiful Lake Tahoe was. I told my aunt about Mrs. Greenberry and her family. I searched for any subject that would keep the conversation on some kind of a normal tone, even though my aunt seemed indifferent to my presence. She never answered nor made any comments of her own. I wondered what she was thinking as she kept her blurry eyes focused on the food that she lifted listlessly to her lips.

Davie and the puppy were soon fast asleep on the couch. In the flickering candlelight, my brother's childish countenance was angelic. A tight cap of auburn curls framed his pale face, and dark brown lashes curled on his cheeks. In sleep his mouth was soft and innocent, like that of a newborn baby. A surge of love and tenderness brought moisture to my eyes just gazing upon him. A maternal fierceness fired my determination to protect him at all costs. He had no one in the world but me. Any hopes I had that my aunt would offer a safe haven for us had been dispelled with the knowledge that Blackbriar House was under the domination of her caretaker. Jem Erskine had warned me that he was master of the house, and I had no cause to disbelieve him.

My aunt groaned as she moved her foot. The swelling had doubled the size of her ankle.

"If I had some wrappings I could bind it," I said, getting to my feet. "Some rags . . ."

She grimaced and reached for the whiskey bottle. Like Erskine, she tipped her head back and took a deep swig. She made a sweep of her hand that knocked her plate on the floor and then leaned her head back as if she were going to pass out again in a drunken stupor.

"You need to go to bed," I said briskly, bending over her. "Come on. I'll help you." I reached out to her.

Her hand came up fast and hard. The vicious blow knocked my head to one side, and my cheek burned from the impact. I staggered back.

She looked like a cornered wild animal. Her gray hair was a tangled mass around her face. Her glazed eyes were tiny black points, a smoldering hatred in their depths.

Was my aunt mad? Erskine had warned me that she was irrational at times, but I had not believed him. I touched my burning cheek, appalled as she stared at me like a wild animal ready to spring.

I had never been struck in my life. The shock of it breathed terror into me. For a brief instant anger surged before dissipating into helplessness. I had never thought myself a coward—but my mettle had never been tested. My father had been stern in our upbringing, but he had never been given to harsh physical discipline. Anyone who had dared lay a hand on his children would have had to answer to him. From my childhood, I had been taught to treat adults with respect, and from the moment I had learned that we must make our home with Aunt Minna, I had been prepared to give her the same kind of loyal family obedience that I had given my father. She was, after all, my flesh and blood. But that didn't give her the right to abuse me. I would do her bidding, but I would not suffer physical abuse at her hands.

"Why did you do that?" I asked as calmly as my racing emotions would allow. "I wasn't going to hurt you, Aunt Minna."

"Then keep your hands to yourself!"

Was Erskine responsible for the violent reaction that my touch had engendered? Did Aunt Minna have to defend herself against him? I resisted the temptation to touch her placid hand resting on the arm of the chair as I looked straight into her face. "I'm here to help you. Don't you understand? If Erskine is mean to you—"

She surprised me by laughing. "Little Miss Fix-It. Knows how to make everything all sweetness and light. Going to rescue her poor, inebriated Auntie from the big bad man . . . and everybody will live happily ever after." Her shoulders shook with drunken mirth.

"Aunt Minna. You are the mistress here. I don't think Erskine should be in charge," I said firmly. "This is your home . . . and he is just hired help."

"You don't know nothing!" Her mouth twisted in an angry line. "And none of it's your business. Jem was right. He should have taken you to Tahoe City and dumped you there. If I had two good legs under me, you'd find yourself out in the rain right now."

She's going to turn us out. I looked at Davie sleeping on the couch. Whatever the emotional storms raging in the house, at least we had a roof over our heads. My determination to put Erskine in his place was only going to rob us of a chance to stay here long enough to solve our homeless situation. No good would come out of trying to talk to Aunt Minna now. She was too far gone in drink. "All right, Aunt Minna. I'll hold my tongue. Now tell me what you want me to do."

"Leave me alone."

"Can I help you to bed?" I asked, wondering if there was a first-floor bedroom somewhere in the rabbit warren of rooms.

"Leave me be," she said in a tired voice, and rested her head back against the chair. I knew that in another minute she'd be lost in a stupor.

"Where do you want Davie and me to sleep?"

She gave a wave of a hand which could have meant anything.

"Upstairs?"

She grunted, which I took to mean we'd have to find our own beds.

I woke Davie up, and we let the puppy out the front door for a short run before we went upstairs. The rain had stopped, and the air was heavy with moisture. The sound of water dripping through needled branches and off the house's eaves blended with sucking and slapping water at the lake's edge. Whorls of mist floated over the dark lake like ghostly galleons.

I could see the boathouse and a watery glow of light through a high window. I shivered, picturing Erskine drinking and shouting drunkenly into the night. What diabolical plans fermented in that devilish brain? What evil possessed him?

Feeble moonlight did nothing to dispel black shadows in nearby dark woods, rocky crags, and dense undergrowth. A cry of pain, or a shout for joy, I thought with a prickling on the nape of my neck, would be all the same—lost in the vastness of hard rock and cold water.

I hurried Davie and the puppy inside, and shut the door. But I knew that impending danger was not outside—but in!

Chapter Seven

"We have to find a bed," I told Davie. "Bed," I repeated, laying my hand against my cheek.

He nodded. The puppy was wide awake after his romp in the cool air outside. He squirmed in Davie's arm and gave joyful "woofs" as if it were time to play. That's all I needed, a rowdy puppy to bring more wrath down upon our heads.

Aunt Minna was still snoring noisily in the living room when we passed. Her head lay to one side, facing the hall doorway, and she looked much older than my father had at his death, although I knew there was only a year's difference in their ages. Life had not been kind to her. Every line in her sagging face was evidence of deep unhappiness. What had my father done to her to bring such revulsion to her face when she looked at me? Any brotherly love she had once felt for him had died, and I feared that anything I did would fail to lessen her cold hatred. The sight of her passed out drunk in her chair sickened me. And yet I felt pity for her, and guilt for not insisting that she go to bed, but my smarting cheek reminded me that I would only get battered for my help.

I took a candle, picked up our worn satchel, and led the way up a narrow staircase rising into darkness above. Somewhere in this ugly, rambling structure there must be a corner that we could claim as ours.

Our footsteps sounded loudly on the creaking boards, and in some places the steps sagged in a dangerous fashion. When I reached out a hand to the wall to steady myself, my fingers touched rough, dusty, unfinished boards. I had seen mining structures that were sanded and finished in better fashion than Blackbriar, I thought. Nothing about the place was like a home. I shivered as a bank of cold air came down the staircase to greet me.

When we reached the first landing, I held out the candle. A hall ran a short distance from the stairs in each direction before it turned and disappeared in the darkness. Dave hugged my skirts as we walked down the left hall and peered into the first open doorway.

This cold chamber must belong to my aunt, I decided quickly. Women' clothes were strewn everywhere, and an unmade bed was piled high with rumpled pillows and covers. Even by candlelight, I saw that the room was crowded with heavy, dark furniture. Musty, close air reeked with unwashed clothes and soiled carpets, and soot and ashes overflowed from a blackened fireplace.

Across the hall was a larger chamber, sparsely furnished, not littered, but reeking of tobacco and sour whiskey. Erskine's room! No doubt about it. The man seemed to rise up out of the shadows, his remembered hot breath and fiery eyes sending an uncontrollable shiver through me.

We quickly retraced our steps and started down the

hall in the opposite direction. I wanted to get as far from Erskine as I could. When we passed a large bathroom, I entered and saw a claw-footed tub and boxed water closet gray with dust. Only one ragged towel lay in a heap on a marble washstand. Because we were used to outdoor facilities, the inside plumbing seemed like a touch of luxury.

The puppy sat on the floor, cocking his head while Davie and I refreshed ourselves. Then he wagged his tail and followed at our heels as we made our way up another set of stairs in the part of the house which I judged to be the addition that boasted the cupola on the roof.

The staircase twisted crazily, finally coming out on a landing which had to be the third floor, I thought. Our passage was halted by closed door. I turned the blackened copper knob, and the door swung open at my touch.

Holding out my candle, I expected to find another crude room with dirty furnishings. In my weariness, I thought for a moment that my eyes must be deceiving me. The small room stretching under the eaves was pleasantly furnished, with a bed, chair, oval braided rug, and tall wardrobe. Unlike the other rooms, a fresh smell of cedar came from the paneled walls. A quick survey revealed one window, overlooking the lake, and a slanted ceiling, but no source of heat. We could see our breath in the chilled air, but somehow I felt a sense of belonging and, even though I knew it to be foolish, a feeling of safety.

I set the candle down on a small table near the window. "We'll stay here," I signed to Davie, nodding at the bed. "But we'll have to find some blankets," I said, thinking aloud, seeing that the bed had been stripped except for a thin mattress of dubious color.

"Blankets," I repeated, looking in the empty wardrobe.

Davie pointed. His quick eyes had discerned a long, narrow chest under the bed. I drew it out and found two comforters carefully folded there. The tiny stitches in an elaborate quilting pattern verified painstaking efforts that could have been my aunt's handiwork. Several lengths of material were also in the chest and some unfinished embroidered pillowcases. All of the items had a musty smell, as if the chest had not been opened for a long time.

I decided that Aunt Minna might have enjoyed this room when her husband was alive, before Erskine worked his satanic power over her. Somehow it was reassuring to know that the drunken woman downstairs had surely once cared about things like lovely comforters, embroidered pillowcases, and fresh-smelling cedar walls.

Davie was exhausted, and I feared that tomorrow's demands might be greater than any we had endured so far. We quickly dressed in our night clothes, lay down on the narrow bed, and wrapped ourselves in the thick comforters. The three of us snuggled together like cupped spoons, Davie curled against me and the puppy against him.

Slowly my frayed nerves gave way to feelings of renewed hope. The worst was surely over. We had found sanctuary, at least temporarily. I would work for our keep, suffer what I must, and try to improve things as I could. My mind refused to go beyond this point. Enveloped by an overpowering fatigue, I let go of tension and apprehension and slept.

I must have been asleep a couple of hours when the sound of lumbering footsteps jerked me to an instant stiffening. Even before my mind registered the reason, I was filled with fright. Then I remembered where I was. Erskine! Was he coming up the stairs to the attic room?

I waited, not daring to breathe. My heart knocked wildly in my chest as I listened. What would I do? Why hadn't I pushed the wardrobe against the door? In my need for sleep I had been lulled into carelessness. Now it was too late. I couldn't tell if he was walking on the floor below or coming up the attic steps. My body was hot with sweat. I remembered the way the man had overturned the table and shouted at me in his hoarse, drunken fury. No telling how much drinking he had done in the boathouse or what condition he was in.

I listened to his heavy walk on the boards below. Then I heard my aunt's simpering, slurred voice. "My foot . . . my foot . . . don't hurt my foot."

"I'm putting you to bed, woman. Shut up, or I'll let you stagger around by yourself. Where's the girl?"

"How should I know? Maybe she lit out, for all I know. I don't think she likes her Auntie much. . . ." Her voice trailed off, and I couldn't hear any more.

A few minutes later, I realized with something akin to horror—the attic room spanned Erskine's on the floor below! I could hear him banging around. A hollow echoing of his footsteps, a slamming of drawers, and then muffled swearing. The noises floated up through the floorboards. Finally all human sounds faded.

In the hushed stillness, the house seemed to come alive with the creaking and groaning of weathered boards and shifting walls. Outside needled branches scraped against the house and gusts of wind tortured loosened shingles and sagging windows. I lay wide awake as slowly my breathing and heartbeat regained their normal pace. I tightened my arms around Davie and closed my eyes, certain that I would not sleep another wink. The day's events flashed through my mind, twisting and turning, overlapping patterns of people and places—the long journey, the Greenberrys, Zeke's bloody nose and his raised fist. On the steamer, Randy's friendliness that had made him seem like an old friend. I hoped things worked out for him so he could go home with money in his pocket. Not many men did that once they left everything to follow the goldfields.

And more poignant than everything else was the time I had spent in Lyle Delany's company. Even in memory his intense blue eyes and smiling lips brought a peculiar warmth to my chilled body. I had never had a man stir my feelings to a point of foolish blushing. I must have seemed terribly gauche to him. Before I knew what the situation was with my aunt, I had haughtily scorned his offer of friendship. Now I knew I needed it desperately, even if he only offered his attentions because he wanted to buy Aunt Minna's land. Would he come to Black-briar? Randy had said he'd been trying to make contact with my aunt. I no longer resented him using me as a way to get to her. Surely he would be able to offer me some help and advice if I was honest with him about the situation here. I couldn't afford to indulge in any stiff-necked pride. Not when he might be able to do something to get Erskine out of his position of authority. I was certain that once the evil man was gone and his influence on Aunt Minna removed, she would recover and be the woman she used to be.

Yes, Lyle Delany would come. My heart quickened at the thought. I had told him that I would send him the amount owed, but now I realized that getting money from Aunt Minna to repay him for the steamer tickets was but a foolish hope. From what I had seen, she lived in abject poverty. Had her husband left her in such straits when he died? I thought not. Erskine had said that he had been her caretaker for ten yers. During that time he could have stripped her of all her money, leaving nothing but her land. Apparently she had refused to sell it. Perhaps she wasn't so enamored of Erskine as not to realize that once everything was gone, she'd have no hold on him. A fierce protectiveness rose in me. My father would have wanted me to do what I could to get her out from under Erskine's influence. Aunt Minna needed support and strength as much as Davie and I needed a home. She was alone in the world, just as we were, beaten down and turning to drink to escape a deplorable situation. I didn't know how I was going to do it, but somehow I would try to break the hold the vile man had over her. With such naive optimism surging through my veins, my body muscles relaxed and I finally fell asleep again.

It was the puppy, bouncing on top of me, that awoke me to early morning sunshine. He licked my face with enthusiasm, and I laughed as I sat up to escape his attack. "Down . . . down."

Undaunted, Rags jumped on Davie, giving him the same good morning awakening. The puppy bounded on top of us, tumbling over legs and arms, issuing happy, high barks, and shaking his raggedy tail so hard, it threatened to fall off. He tugged at the covers with a baby growl, and I made a grab for the disappearing blanket. I was laughing when the door suddenly flew open!

As if ice water had been poured on us, we froze.

"So this is where ye be!" Erskine stood there, his black hair falling wildly down on his forehead, his unruly eyebrows sticking out like thorns. He wore baggy pants with dangling suspenders pulled over gray underwear. Too late I remembered that his room was below ours. Our play with the puppy had awakened him.

His scathing eyes passed over my copper-red hair tumbling loosely around my shoulders and down my back. Even though I was covered to my neck by my nightgown, his gaze made me feel undressed. I touched the top button, uncertain from his lusty stare whether it was still fastened. Davie trembled and I firmed my chin. "No one told us where we were to sleep."

He smirked. "Well, now, ye'll have to forgive the oversight," he answered in a mockng tone, "but seeing as how ye've made yerselves to home, the attic's as good a place as any for beggars." He leaned up against the door frame; his black eyes held points of smoldering lust as they traveled over me. "Yep, close enough for me to watch out for ye."

"I don't need watching after."

He gave me a lusty leer. "Ye be looking like a red witch for sure with all that fiery hair hanging down yer back." Then he sobered. "What's happened to yer face?"

"My face?" I touched my cheek and then I remembered. It must be bruised. "I must have bumped it."

Erskine's eyes gleamed. He knew my answer for the lie that it was. He grinned, his lips pulling back from ugly,

100

yellowed teeth. "Knocked ye about, did she? I'd be staying clear of Auntie, if I was ye."

"You'd like that, wouldn't you?" I flared. "Well, I'm going to care for Aunt Minna. Fix her some good meals and clean her house. It's time someone looked after her." I flung the words at him like a gauntlet.

His hoarse laugh surprised me. "Then ye be a bigger fool that I gave ye credit for." He straightened and pointed his finger at me. "Ye'd best keep yer pretty nose out of things that don't concern ye. Hear?"

"My aunt's welfare concerns me very much," I lashed out, fool that I was.

"She'll put ye in yer place fast enough," He predicted. "Now git yerself down to the kitchen and fix me some breakfast. I'm rowing to Tahoe City. Be back this afternoon with company."

"Company?" My heart lurched. Maybe Blackbriar wasn't as isolated as I had been led to believe.

"Ye heard me. And be quick about me breakfast." He turned and stomped downstairs to his bedroom.

A few minutes later, Davie and I descended into the kitchen. By daylight, the kitchen looked to be in worse shambles than the day before. The fire in the monstrous cookstove had gone out, and it took me several minutes to take out the ashes and lay another fire. Luckily the woodbox had been filled recently. Erskine must have brought in some wood. In a few minutes a crimson fire was heating four black lids and setting the blackened teakettle to humming.

I found a sack of coffee beans and a small grinder. The aroma of boiled coffee soon overpowered the kitchen's unpleasant odors. While Davie played with the puppy

101

outside the back door, I tried in vain to find something to cook for breakfast. No meal, no flour, no gruel. I dreaded going back down into the cellar to cut more venison, but I was about to do it when the sound of a rooster crowing brought my heard around with a jerk.

I bounded out the back door. "Chickens?" I asked Davie with my hands.

He nodded and pointed. Sure enough, a dilapidated chickenhouse stood a short distance from the house. I could see a rooster and several dirty white hens plucking around inside the wire shelter.

With Rags bounding at my heels, I unlatched a sagging gate. "Keep him out," I motioned to Davie. I didn't want the puppy to send the chickens into a panic.

The rooster flew at me and the scrawny hens flapped and scattered with hysterical clucking. The odor in the henhouse was so offensive that I wondered how I would ever be able to gather any eggs. By a force of will I managed to keep from gagging while I searched six nests and found four eggs.

Triumphantly, I returned to the kitchen with my booty. A couple of withered potatoes remained in the gunny sack after last night's meal. I diced the blackened culls, fried them, and added them to the scrambled eggs. I had just finished when Erskine lumbered into the room, and dropped down into a chair.

"Coffee," he barked.

I handed him a steaming mug. Nervously I dished up a plate of eggs and potatoes and set it in front of him.

He glared at the food and then roughly shoved the plate away. "Where's me meat?" he bellowed. "I'll be rowing ten miles to Tahoe City. This ain't enough food

102

for a peahen." His thorny eyebrows matted over the bridge of his nose. "Cook me some decent food. Red meat. And be quick about it." Dark and smoldering eyes held mine.

My hands gripped the edge of the table. A roaring thundered through my head. I wanted to shout at him to get his own breakfast, but I knew that the test had come. What happened now would determine my future, my brother's, and my aunt's. The battle had begun. Would I be able to contain my fury and pride no matter what happened? Subjugate myself to being treated like an animal? Suffer his crude and cruel behavior? Would I end up like my aunt, crushed and broken by his ruthless domination? There was no hope for her unless I stayed. I felt my father's presence strengthening me as I gave Erskine a measured smile that denied the quivering inside me. I turned and went down into the cold earthen pit and slashed away another hunk of venison.

I served it to him half-raw with warmed blood oozing from it. I stilled a rising nausea in my stomach as he chewed the meat like a wild animal. When he had finished, he shoved back his chair and grabbed a weathered hat off a wall rack made of deer antlers.

"Set out supper in the dining room tonight," he ordered. "For our special company."

My heart sank. The dining room? Company? "And what am I supposed to fix?" I flared. "Venison again? There's nothing but the deer carcass for food."

"Then ye'd better catch some fish. There's a pole outside the boathouse. Put that dummy brother of yours to catching us a mess. He's got enough sense for that, ain't he?"

103

I ignored the thrust which he knew would rile me. "And what else am I to prepare for company? Weevil bread and mice-riddled gruel? Or will you and my aunt be drinking your supper?"

"Don't be smartin' off at me," he growled. "Ye keep that saucy mouth to yerself. I've a half mind to dump ye and that idiot kid in the middle of the lake and be done with ye."

Suddenly he was towering over me. His rancid breath was a hot blast on my face. He reached out and jerked my hair free of its pins. His rough hands spread it out over my shoulders. "That's the way ye ought to wear it, Witch." His eyes gleamed and his mouth was moist. "Ye don't fool me none. Yer ripe for the taking."

I backed up, but he deftly pinned me against the wash bench. His walrus frame and his hard, broad chest pressed against me, driving the air from my lungs. Thick sinews bulged in his arms, legs, and torso. I pounded my fists on his chest with blows as effective as feathers brushing against an iron shield.

"Yer a fiery wench," he smirked as he pressed his vile body harder against me.

"Get away from me." My terror was razor sharp. I could feel hardened lust swelling within him.

He laughed and caught both my hands in one of his. I was so helpless as a fly in the hands of a bully who laughingly pulled off the insect's wings.

"Let me go!"

Smirking, he bent his moist mouth to kiss me, but before his lips met mine, he jerked back, swearing and wincing from pain as he favored one of his legs.

I saw then that Davie stood behind him clutching a

thick piece of firewood. He must have clubbed one of Erskine's legs.

"You blasted—!" Like a crazed animal, he lunged toward Davie, but I was quicker. With a frantic thrust, I pushed my brother aside and put the table between us and Erskine. Davie backed up into a corner, watching with rounded eyes.

For a moment I thought Erskine was going to turn the table over as he had done the night before. I stood there, my flaming hair flowing around my face and a knife from the table clutched in my hand.

A flow of expressions crossed his face as he stared at me. Then, slowly, his lips lost their angry tight line and a spine-chilling twist appeared at the corners of his mouth. "A couple of redheaded wildcats, ye be. Well, now, it's a bit of a sport we'll be having." His eyes glinted with excitement. "Aye, a lesson the two of ye will be learning. And when I'm finished, ye'll be glad to do my bidding." His eyes hardened as they bit into me. "Yea, ye'll be grateful to lick my boots before I'm through."

"Never!" I spat, foolishly allowing my fears to come out as arrogance.

His eyes slid to Davie and then back again. "We'll see."

My blood ran cold. He had found my Achilles' heel. He knew I would do what I must to protect my brother.

His smile echoed my thoughts. "We'll see," he repeated.

I stood my ground, keeping my eyes on his face, and my body poised for any attack.

He gave a deep laugh and then made his way to the door. "I'll be back late this afternoon. And ye'd better have supper ready!" The next moment the door slammed behind him, leaving me shaken and near tears.

For a moment I couldn't move. Then I felt Davie's hand slipping into mine. My lips trembled as I smiled down at him. With the ugly bruise on my face and my hair tumbling over my shoulders in wild array, my appearance was surely less than reassuring. A bewildered questioning deepened the anxious lines in his young face.

At that moment I heard my aunt screaming my name from upstairs. I quickly coiled my hair, smoothed my apron, and told myself that everything would settle down now that the vile caretaker had gone. Aunt Minna had told Erskine to leave me alone. Surely, she wouldn't stand by and let him rape me!

Chapter Eight

The scene with Erskine had left my heart pumping furiously and my face flushed. For an irrational moment, I wanted to grab Davie's hand and flee from the house. Erskine's lustful behavior had destroyed my belief that I could handle any situation if I was determined enough. Now I knew with sickening certainty I was no match for the evil man. The memory of his lusting body pressed against mine filled me with terror and shattered any hope that I would be able to keep my distance from him.

I hastily fixed a plate of eggs and potatoes. Leaving Davie and the pup in the kitchen, I made my way upstairs to my aunt's room. What if Aunt Minna turned her eyes away from what was happening? How could she, when common decency demanded that she accept some responsibility toward us? I feared that little protection would be coming from the woman who had already been overpowered by the saturnine Erskine. We couldn't stay here. We had to get away. Aunt Minna would have to make some arrangement for our safety. Her hatred of my father could not be strong enough to allow her to see her niece ravished and her nephew abused. Even in her befuddled state, she couldn't possibly close her eyes to what could happen if we stayed here.

"Good morning," I said with false brightness as I entered her room. I was surprised to find her hobbling about, already dressed, muttering and tossing things about, apparently looking for something.

"Where'd you hide it?" she screeched at me. Wild-eyed, the woman had trembling hands, and her mouth sagged in a pitiful fashion.

"Hide what?"

"You stole it." She picked up a hairbrush and threw it at me.

I managed to duck, almost spilling the plate of food that I had in my hands. "I don't know what you're talking about. I haven't stolen anything, Aunt Minna."

"Where'd you hide my bottle?" she screeched. She was a pathetic figure, her gray hair falling in a matted braid that hadn't seen a comb for days, her complexion a lifeless gray, and her gaunt figure trembling like a withered tree before a wind.

"Aunt Minna—" I said again softly.

"Don't call me that!" Tears welled up in her eyes, her mouth drooped, and she dropped down on the edge of the messy bed. "I need a drink," she whimpered, putting her hands over her face. Her thin shoulders shook.

"You need food. You'll feel better when your stomach's full. I've brought you a nice breakfast," I said, looking about for a place to set down the plate.

Every surface was piled high. The floor was littered with everything imaginable, clothes, papers, shoes, dishes, towels, and broken mirrors. Dust and grime lay heavy on floors and windowsills. There was little space between the dark furniture, which was all crowded together. This place was a contrast to the orderly attic room with its sparse furnishings. A small table loaded down with a stack of newspapers was the closest thing within reach.

"Here you are." I scooted the papers on the floor and moved the small table in front of her. "You can sit on the bed and eat your breakfast."

She lowered her hands from her face and for a long, long moment stared at me as if trying to remember who I was. "What are you doing here?" she croaked. "Go away." Her expression was that of a petulant child who had wearied of a playmate. "I don't want you here. Go home."

I swallowed to get some moisture in my dry mouth. "I can't go home, Aunt Minna. Don't you remember? My father's dead . . . your brother, Benjamin. He sent us to live with you."

"I don't want you here."

"You need me, Aunt Minna." All my determination to abandon her as quickly as possible faded as I saw her pathetic weakness. She would soon die if I left her. Between us we would have to save ourselves from the evil man who would destroy us all.

"I don't need you. I don't need anybody. I just need a drink."

"You need food . . . and someone to help you get back your strength. I'm going to clean the house, cook your meals, and look after you. We'll be a family." My voice trailed off as a sudden rise of emotion threatened to bring tears to my eyes. I wanted to embrace her and find strength for both of us. We were kin, after all. And I knew my father had loved her despite the differences that had separated them. I wanted to show her that I was ready to love her, too, but her flat stare stopped me from showing any display of affection.

"I don't have a brother," she said with that glint of hatred in her eyes.

"Can't you let the past go? He never denied his love for you. I saw him looking at your picture with tender eyes. He wanted to make his peace with you. Can't you be forgiving?" I pleaded. "I don't know what happened between you and my father, but I'm your niece, and Davie's your nephew. You're not alone. We want to stay with you, Aunt Minna."

"You're a fool," she said with a pitying smirk. "Erskine will break you as easily as he snaps a willow twig."

"You mustn't let him!" I countered angrily. "This morning he put his hands on me. I'm afraid, Aunt Minna . . ." My voice broke.

Her expression was unreadable. "Jem is a healthy, lustful man. His blood runs hot when a wench parades herself in front of him."

My mouth dropped open, but no sound came from it for a moment, then anger exploded. "How can you suggest that I invited his abominable behavior! You can't be that blind! Surely you don't condone his assault on me. How dare you uphold that horrid man against your own flesh and blood?"

"And how dare you come here uninvited? Nobody asked you." She shook a wobbly finger at me. "You don't know anything about me or my life. With your nose in the air, you come in here and act like you're aiming to take charge. Well, you got it all wrong. Auntie isn't handing over anything! If you think you're going to get your hands on Blackbriar House, Erskine will stop you fast enough."

"I don't want anything from you—just a chance to help you out of this deplorable situation. You can't let a horrible man like Erskine run you or this house, Aunt Minna," I said with a rush. "After all, he's just hired help. A servant, really."

Aunt Minna's laughter was a pitiful, high-pitched sound without mirth. "A servant—Jem Erskine?"

"Isn't he? What is his position, Aunt Minna? Caretaker? Can't you discharge him?" My tone pleaded with her to take some action against the vile man. "He's not good for you. You can see that. This house is a shambles. He must have been stealing you blind for a long time. And you don't have to put up with it." I looked her straight in the eye, trying to instill some strength into her sagging body. "We can manage nicely, just the two of us. Get rid of him, Aunt Minna."

"Get rid of him?" she echoed. Her rheumy eyes held an unreadable glint that might have been amusement. "And how would I do that?" She gave a raspy laugh. "You're crazy if you think Jem would say a nice fare-thee-well and be on his way. He's a stubborn man," she said with a hint of pride in her voice. "Doesn't let anybody push him around."

"We could send word by the *Tahoe Queen* that we need someone in authority to come and evict him. There's a nice man on the boat, Randy Bowles. He'd help us, I know. All you have to do is make the decision to get rid of him. I'll help in any way I can."

"I bet you would. A thieving busybody, that's what you are. Well, Jem ain't a man to brook any interference from an outsider, and neither am I. Now bring me a bottle."

A wash of disappointment made my voice strident.

111

"We'll talk about this later. Why don't you eat your breakfast—"

The rest of the sentence was cut off as she picked up the plate and heaved it against the wall. Eggs and potatoes made a greasy splatter all over the wall and floor. I jerked back just in time to miss the clenched fist she swung at me.

"You and I had better come to some understanding," she snarled. "Your Auntie ain't taking orders from the likes of you. If you want to keep your mouth shut and do my bidding, you can stay. If not, I'll turn you over to Jem and let him deal with you. Now, help me downstairs. I'll find my own bottle."

Her behavior was so irrational that I couldn't think of any way to appeal to her.

Leaning heavily on me, she limped down the stairs and back to the chair in the front room where she had sat the night before. A half-empty bottle sat on the floor beside the chair, and she grabbed it the minute she eased down in the chair and put her foot up on the stool.

She took a healthy swig and then glared at me. "Git out of my sight. The only way you stay is to earn your keep . . . one way or another." Her implication was clear. I knew then she'd never raise her hand if Erskine went after me. She nodded as if my thoughts had matched hers. "Now, you'd better get this place cleaned up before Jem gets back." Her rheumy eyes narrowed. "Bringing a gentleman with him, he is."

"A gentleman? Who?"

"You'll find out." She took another swig on the bottle. "We'll want to put our best foot forward, won't we?" She gave a drunken giggle. "It isn't often we have company."

My heart was suddenly racing. Anyone with a decent

bone in his body surely would be receptive to Davie's and my plight. I wished I knew who Erskine was bringing back from Tahoe City, but it wouldn't do any good to try and pump Aunt Minna for more information. As I went back to my kitchen chores, the prospect of making contact with someone from the outside world lifted my spirits.

I tackled the kitchen mess with a fury that released smoldering emotions and simmering apprehension. Davie carted out armfuls of litter and refuse while I turned my hands red and raw, scrubbing everything in sight with harsh lye soap and hot water. I realized by mid-afternoon that the job of getting the kitchen into a respectable condition was going to take days.

"That's enough," I signed to Davie, throwing aside my soiled apron. I had put a venison roast in the oven, but failed to see anything else to add to the meal. I had depleted my supply of eggs, and the scrawny chickens didn't look as if they were very productive. I had no idea what else I could prepare for company dinner. "Let's walk down to the lake," I signed to him.

Davie's spirits had risen during the day, and he was his usual happy, contented self. He bounded out the back door with exuberance. I had taught my brother to clap his hands when he wanted someone's attention, and apparently the puppy had already caught on, for Rags came bounding out from under a pine tree at the signal.

A furry ball of tumbling energy, he came toward us in a lopsided run. Dry needles had caught in his tangled fur, and his nose was dirty from rooting in the dirt. I laughed at his clumsy, enthusiastic greeting, thanking God for puppies and kittens and other delightful young things that could innocently lighten the human spirit.

113

We made our way through a drift of trees hugging the hillside and took a narrow path that led in a downward direction, away from the house. Azure water in the oval-shaped bay was embraced by wooded hillsides like two arms extending on both sides and not quite closed to allow passage from the lake into the bay. Thick swatches of forest-green conifers rose high above pink-and-cream-colored boulders which had tumbled from rock shelves down to the water's edge. An afternoon sun glazed the water, creating a blinding glare on the surface like that of a polished emerald.

We walked along a narrow beach and I was breathing heavily before we had gone very far. The six-thousand-foot altitude was having its effect, I thought, as I sat down on a boulder. Fatigue that had nothing to do with work I'd done settled upon me, a kind of lassitude that brought a peculiar kind of peace. Physically weary and emotionally drained, I was content to sit there and watch Davie happily throwing rocks into the water, splashing himself and Rags with childish glee.

Yesterday the water had been a gray mirror reflecting the sullen sky, drawing into its depths the black shadows of rain clouds. Today the lake was like an inverted bowl, blending shades of aquamarine water, white clouds, and heavenly blue skies. As I looked beyond the small rocky island out into the lake, a dark object caught my eye. The steamer! The *Tahoe Queen* chugged across the water, trailing white streamers behind it. Was it going to enter the bay or continue northward?

As if some eagle eye aboard would see me standing there, a dot upon the pale rocks, I waved foolishly. If only there were mail that would bring the *Tahoe Queen* into the bay, I thought with a prayerful breath. How wonderful it would be to see Randy's broad smile again and exchange a few words with him. Little more than twenty-four hours had passed since we'd landed at Blackbriar Bay, but fear, anxiety, anger, and apprehension had made it seem like an eternity.

Please, stop. Please, stop. I desperately needed to maintain some contact that would offset the threatening brutality of Erskine and the deplorable drunken behavior of my aunt. If only . . . My powerful prayers died when the *Tahoe Queen* became a fading dot on the horizon, continuing its northern tour of the lake without entering the bay. Randy had said that the steamer rarely stopped at Blackbriar Bay, and I had been foolish to think that my contact with him was going to be renewed. A new sense of desolation settled upon me. What was I going to do? How could I live shut off from the world, surrounded by ugliness and fear? My stubborn optimism failed me. I wanted to run away, leave my aunt in the clutches of Erskine, and face whatever dangers might lie among strangers. If my aunt refused my help, what could I do to change the evil power Erskine had over her?

Wearily I motioned to Davie and we started back to the house. We had just reached the boathouse when a swiftly moving skiff entered the bay.

Erskine was back.

Davie looked frightened. I hesitated, debating whether to remain on the pier, forcing a meeting with him and his "gentleman" guest, or to retreat to the house. Remembering the morning's scene made me decide on the latter. Just like Davie, I wasn't ready to face the ugly man any sooner than we must. I didn't know who the man might be in the skiff with him, but I would make certain I had a chance to talk to him alone.

Davie looked relieved when I motioned toward the house. He scurried ahead with Rags threading his legs, nearly causing him to trip. Back in the kitchen, I checked on my roast. It was a nice savory brown, with juices just waiting for the flour I didn't have. Erskine would be furious with the meager offering, but there was absolutely nothing else to prepare.

Davie and I fled upstairs to get ready for dinner. As I changed into my blue wool dress, my fingers trembled. I smoothed the lace collar and pinned my hair into a prim coil on my neck. I wanted to look presentable when I made my plea for help. I was certain that Erskine wouldn't push himself on me in the presence of a guest.

Davie looked disgusted when I made him change his pants and shirt, and comb rebellious hair that hugged his head with curls. Satisfied that my brother and I looked presentable, we went back downstairs to the kitchen.

My mouth dropped open when I saw the kitchen table. It was loaded with supplies: flour, dried yeast, beans, a brace of bacon, dried apples, and sacks of onions, potatoes, and corn. I had never seen such bounty all at one time. At least a month's supply! My father scarcely had enough money to buy more than we needed for a few days, and I couldn't help but be excited by the chance to cook a generous meal for the visitor.

I set vegetables to boiling, put biscuits in the oven, and boiled apples for applesauce. Almost too late, I remembered what Erskine had said about eating in the dining room, a dark, dusty room which had folding doors that could be opened into the sitting room.

A kind of butler's pantry opened into the room at one end, and searching some built-in cupboards, I found several table cloths edged with yellowed crocheted lace and others that were embroidered elaborately like the pillowcases I had discovered in the attic room.

Hurriedly I chose a cloth and spread it over a wide table that would have seated ten people comfortably. When had that many visitors ever come to Blackbriar House? A walnut sideboard with elaborate carvings of grapes and vines was six feet tall and dominated one wall. A dusty large mirror with a wide gilded frame dimly reflected the two lamps, which I quickly lit. I despaired that there wasn't time to put the room to rights.

A dusty set of dishes and fancy tableware had been stored in the bottom drawer of the sideboard. I quickly carried them to the kitchen, and a delicate pattern of wood violets gleamed in the oyster-white porcelain after I had given them a good washing.

For a moment I stared at the lovely plate in my hand, a symbol of gracious living and perhaps a clue to the woman my aunt had once been. A new resolve blossomed within me. These lovely dishes, the intricate handiwork, and the attic room spoke of a mistress who had cared for her home and its belongings. Somehow I must fan the ember of that former pride until she could regain herself.

As I set the table, I heard her drunken laughter through the closed doors. Repeatedly, throughout the day, I had tried to get her to eat, but she had scarcely touched enough food to fill the stomach of a songbird. When I had refused to hunt up another bottle of whiskey, she had hobbled about until she found a full bottle in one of the darkened rooms. Apparently there was enough money to keep her and Erskine in whiskey, I thought angrily. Her hair remained uncombed, her dress soiled, and her appearance unkempt. I was ashamed to have anyone see her in such a condition.

Erskine's booming voice and Aunt Minna's laughter were all I could hear. As I worked in the dining room, my ears strained to hear the conversation they were having with their guest. He must be soft spoken, I thought, failing to hear a third voice. The clinking of glass told me they must be drinking.

I don't know what I expected but when the dining room door suddenly opened, I was startled to see a dried-up, doddering old man come in with Erskine. I know I must have registered my surprise—and disappointment. Erskine's eyes met mine with derisive amusement, as if he enjoyed my disconcerted reaction.

"My dear," he said in an oily tone that turned my stomach, "I want you to meet Herman Hackerman." His smile was taunting. "Judge Hackerman."

The judge's veined eyelids raised, showing pale gray eyes so light in color that he seemed sightless. Fumbling with a pair of rimless glasses, he peered through them at me.

"This lady is Anna McKenzie," said Erskine, continuing the introduction with a politeness that was sickening.

"Pleased to meet you, Miss McKenzie," whined the Judge, holding out a gnarled hand ribbed with purple veins. His facial skin was like dried parchment threatening to crack with every movement of his mouth and eyes.

Erskine helped the feeble old man to a chair. Obviously he was exhausted, and I wondered if he would stay awake long enough to eat. With the same kind of false solicitous manner, Erskine helped Aunt Minna to the table. The day-long communion with a bottle had left her in a near stupor. She sat at the foot of the table, nodding and hiccuping in an obscene fashion. I was mortified at her appearance, but Erskine looked at her with an expression akin to pure satisfaction. I don't think I ever hated him as much as I did at that moment.

Davie helped me carry in the food, and I was surprised when Erskine indicated that he expected us to join them. Quickly setting two more plates, Davie and I sat down opposite the frail judge. I offered food to Aunt Minna, which she proceeded to spill and drop on both herself and the table.

When I offered her a buttered biscuit, she screeched at me and knocked it from my hand. The judge's colorless eyes widened, and I thought Erskine chuckled in satisfaction. He seemed bent on disgracing my aunt in every way possible. In her inebriated state she was incapable of following a topic of conversation. When she did make a slurred remark, it was completely irrelevant.

I did my best to cover for her, asking the judge about himself and pressing food upon him. For such a feeble-looking man his appetite was quite healthy, and I was pleased that I had managed to offer him an acceptable meal.

Erskine complimented me on almost every dish, and I saw a malicious humor in his eyes as I was forced to offer a polite "Thank you." The situation was so bizarre that I wondered if some form of insanity had overtaken me.

I asked Judge Hackerman if he'd ever been to Blackbriar before, and he shook his head and said he'd never had the pleasure. However, he had heard a great deal about Minna McKenzie-Brown, he told me. His old eyes settled on my aunt, and I wondered what he had heard—and from whom.

Davie sat very quietly in his silent world. When the

Judge addressed a remark to him, I explained that my brother was a deaf-mute. A flicker of interest crossed his wizened face. "He seems alert."

"He's very smart. And a happy child."

"And lucky to have someone like Anna looking after him," interposed Erskine. His smile would have been the same if he were reaching out a hand to push me over a cliff.

My eyes fled to the old man, and my heart sank in disappointment. The help I needed wasn't going to come from this frail visitor, who chewed his food with difficulty and had trouble following the conversation. It was obvious that Erskine's physical strength and commanding manner impressed the judge. It made me sick to see the way Erskine deftly handled him.

My aunt's head lolled forward, and I feared she was going to fall over onto the table. She gave a drunken fling of her hand, knocking her plate off the table and breaking the lovely china into a hundred pieces.

Shoving back my chair, I stood up and glared at Erskine. "Please, carry Aunt Minna upstairs and I'll see her to bed." I had had enough.

His mouth spread in a victorious grin. "She's a bit under the weather."

I wanted to scream at him . . . *she's drunk* . . . *because of you!*

Erskine walked around the table and lifted her up in his bearlike arms. "I'll see to her. You stay here, Anna, and visit with our guest."

I started to protest, but the judge said, "Yes, Miss McKenzie, please do. I would like to hear about you and your brother. Your father was Benjamin McKenzie, wasn't he?"

120

I sat back down, startled that this old gentleman was showing interest in me and knew my father's name. I nodded.

"And he recently died?" I nodded again and then repeated the story of his accident. I told him about the photograph in my father's pocket watch and he asked to see it.

"Of course." I told Davie with a quick sign to run up to our room and get it. When he brought back the gold pocket watch, I handed it to the judge. The old man squinted at the picture, studying the two smiling young people. Then he sighed, snapped the lid shut, and handed it back to me.

I held it protectively in my hands. "My father always spoke affectionately about his sister, even though there had been some trouble between them. I want to help her," I lowered my voice, "but the situation here is dire—"

"The years make strange changes in people," he said, cutting off my whispered words. "Would you believe that once I was the best rower on the Delaware River? Set the best time for a five-mile course, I did." His smile was misty. "Long time ago."

"Judge, I need your help. Davie and I can't stay here."

He raised one of his white eyebrows. "And where will you go?"

"I don't know, but we have to get away."

He shook his head. "Life is hard for single women. Better you remain with your aunt. The West is still uncivilized. Not like the East. I came west right after I got my law degree. Never went back. Spent most of my life in Sacramento."

I tried again to tell him about the way Erskine

dominated my aunt. "He's looked after her a long time," he chided. "Lived here for ten years or more."

"But he—"

"A beautiful spot. One of the prettiest places on the lake. God's country on earth. Well, now, we'd best get down to business," he said, reaching into the inside of his pocket.

"Business?" I must have misunderstood him. What business did he have with me?

"I have some papers here that will give you power of attorney over your aunt's business affairs."

"Me? I—I don't understand."

"You are Mrs. McKenzie-Brown's nearest relative, and I have satisfied myself that you will be looking after her interests. Mr. Erskine brought me here to see for myself what state your aunt is in. Deplorable. Certainly not of sound mind. Obviously not capable of handling her financial affairs. She has extensive holdings around the lake . . . increasing in value all the time. Someone needs to look after them."

Erskine came in the room during this last remark and stood behind my chair. "I couldn't agree more. Hard as it is on Anna, her aunt cuffing her about and all—the bruise on her cheek—" he added knowingly.

"Yes, deplorable," nodded the Judge. He spread papers in front of me. "I need your signature to make everything legal, Miss McKenzie."

I couldn't move. I didn't understand what was happening, but I feared that danger lay ahead in signing those papers.

"There's nothing to be frightened of," the old man assured me. "You have a sensible head on your shoulders. And Mr. Erskine will remain here to advise you."

It came to me in a flash: somehow, Erskine was going to get his hands on my aunt's property through me. I didn't know why he had chosen this circuitous route. Did he think he could manipulate me more easily than he could my aunt? Had she stood up to him when it came to selling her property? So many questions—and no answers.

"Go ahead, Anna." Erskine urged.

He was shrewd, wily, and unscrupulous. I was no match for his villainous cunning. "I don't want to sign anything," I said firmly.

"Of course, ye do, Anna," he countered. "It'll be best for ye—and the boy."

I saw then that he had moved behind Davie's chair and his thick hands were settled on my brother's slender shoulders. "So many things can happen unexpectedly . . . a fall . . . a broken neck."

My mouth went dry. The threat in his smoldering eyes was a promise, one that he would carry out without hesitation.

I signed the paper.

Chapter Nine

Hours later I sat on the floor in front of the attic window and stared out into the night. My mind raced with questions—ominous, frightening, and bewildering. Davie lay asleep in the bed, and the puppy had climbed onto my lap, accepting my absent-minded strokes. Outside, a night owl hooted in the crown of a ponderosa pine, a night wind made soft noises like whispers as it rustled needled branches, and the lake moved in a pattern of dark shadows and swatches of moonlight. I leaned my forehead against the cool pane of glass, closed my eyes, and searched for any reason that Erskine had for arranging to put the control of my aunt's property into my hands. Why? He already dominated Aunt Minna. I couldn't believe that she would hold out against him if he put pressure on her to sell everything she owned. In her pathetic drunken state, it seemed likely that she would do his bidding no matter what he asked. I had seen the way he'd manipulated her into presenting herself as a pitiful drunk in front of Judge Hackerman. Surely all he had to do was put a paper in front of her and for another bottle of whiskey she would sign it. The condition of the house suggested that everything of value and any money had long disappeared, probably into Erskine's pockets. Why did he need me?

The puppy nudged my hand with his cold nose. His black eyes were like jet buttons catching the moonlight. "What am I going to do, Rags?" I felt that I was caught in a diabolical net and the more I struggled, the tighter it would fold around me. The memory of Erskine's hairy hands on Davie's slender neck brought a chill racing up my back. I didn't doubt for a moment that he would brutally use the child to control me. And once I was of no further use to him, what then?

The judge was spending the night at Blackbriar House and had arranged for the steamer to pick him up on the next day's run. The *Tahoe Queen* would be stopping at Blackbriar Bay. I still had a little money, probably enough to buy passage for Davie and me to Tahoe City. Erskine wouldn't dare to forcibly retain us in front of everyone after the boat arrived. Randy would be there to see us aboard and we would be safe enough in the company of the judge and the steamer's crew. I didn't know what we would do once we got to Tahoe City. At the moment, any dangers we faced there would be better than the ones threatening us here. What about Aunt Minna? I felt a twinge of guilt about leaving her, but Davie was my first responsibility. The present situation was fraught with danger for him. With Erskine threatening to harm him, I had no choice. Whatever help I could provide Aunt Minna would have to be given to her away from Blackbriar House.

It was nearly dawn before I had a plan. I put the clothes in the worn satchel, and slipped down the attic steps. I didn't dare light a candle to show my way.

On the second floor, I stopped and listened. Hardly daring to breathe, I kept the movement of my chest shallow. I knew that Erskine roved about at night, staying in the boathouse until all hours. I thought he might have come to bed, but I couldn't be sure. He could walk softly when he wanted to, like a demon devil afoot in the night.

My heart thumped loudly as I stealthily descended the darkened stairs one by one, feeling my way in the darkness. The thought of Erskine's drunken laughter and grappling hands was enough to paralyze me at every step. The shadows were alive. Settling boards in the house mocked every movement. Only my desperation kept me moving downward. The soft patter of my shoes and the whispering of my skirts along the floor sounded loudly in my ears. Every second I expected to hear Erskine's loud, gleeful roar and feel his pawing hands upon me.

At the bottom of the stairs, I froze against the rough newel post, all moisture drained from my mouth. The main floor was enveloped in a hushed, waiting silence. As I looked toward the front of the house, the sitting room was dark. No light from any of the maze of rooms filtered into the long hall extending to the front door.

I lifted my skirts with one hand and kept the satchel motionless at my side with the other. As I made my way down the back hall, every one of my senses strained for a clue that would betray Erskine's waiting presence at every turn. By the time I reached the kitchen, my heart was pounding and my chest rising and falling like the frantic breathing of a trapped bird.

Watery moonlight filtered through the dirty windows. I stepped around the familiar furniture, careful not to bump against any of the kitchen chairs or table. Rusty hinges scraped loudly as I gingerly opened the back door. A night breeze hit my face as I slipped outside. Pressing up against the side of the house, I waited a long moment, listening, half-expecting to hear thundering footsteps after me. Then came no sound from the kitchen, but as I trembled there, I was prepared to see Erskine's huge frame rise up from the shadows to grab me with his mauling hands.

I heard nothing above the whisper of needled branches dancing in the night wind. Reassured that my exit from the house had not been noticed, I hurried around the side of the house, keeping in the shadows. When I reached the front path, I tried to stay close to trees hugging the sides of the narrow passage. The path was so uneven and rough that despite my caution, my footsteps caused rocks to crack and shift under my weight. About half-way down the path, I froze. A flickering light wavered through the window of the small boathouse.

Erskine! When I had looked out from the attic window a few minutes earlier, the boathouse had been dark, influencing my decision to slip out and hide the satchel close enough to the dock to grab it up at the last moment before we boarded the steamer.

Now I was certain that Erskine was in the boathouse. What should I do? I didn't dare gamble that he wouldn't hear me if I came any closer. Moonlight fell upon the water and upon dark clumps of trees and shrubs—and upon me standing in the middle of the path. The realization made me dart to one side, into a mass of prickly cedar trees bordering the path. I had no sooner gained concealment than I heard the sound of the boathouse door creaking.

Had he seen me?

Heavy footsteps sounded hollow as he walked down the weathered boards of the pier extending out into the water. Then he started up the dirt path. Rocks crackled under his feet. He was coming. Slowly. Deliberately. Closer and closer.

Hunched in the cluster of trees, only a breath away from the path, I resisted the impulse to flee further into the stand of pine and cedar. *Don't move!* The order came from some rational part of my mind, detached from the swelling hysteria that threatened to send me into panic. Even the slight shifting of my weight would crackle dry needles under my feet, and the slightest sound would betray my presence. Cowering there, only a few feet off the path, I froze like a hunted animal, stiff and waiting. I closed my eyes, listening to the heavy rhythm of his steps coming nearer and nearer.

Then the footsteps stopped . . . *at the spot where I'd fled the path!* I waited for his roaring laughter and the lunge of his thick body toward me through the trees. If he had been looking out the window, he could have seen me dart for cover.

The moment stretched into an eternity of torture before my senses registered that he was moving on up the path. *He hadn't seen me.* Relief like a sickness made my body weak. Nausea rose in my stomach, and I fought down the flow of bitter bile into my mouth.

I heard him enter the front of the house, making no effort to close the door quietly. In my mind's eye, I saw him climbing the stairs and making the sounds I had heard so often in the room below us.

What if he came to the attic and found me gone? A quiver of new fright sped through me before common sense conquered it. With the judge in the house, Erskine wasn't likely to create any kind of scene. I mustn't let my fear torment me with unfounded "what ifs."

In case he was looking out a window, I decided to leave the satchel where I was crouching in the trees instead of taking it closer to the dock as I had planned. After waiting for a few minutes which seemed like an hour, I left my hiding place, retraced my steps, and hurried back around the house to the kitchen.

Once I was inside the house, weakness sluiced through me. I sat down in a kitchen chair, my mind racing with the details that must be put in order for our escape.

Soon it would be dawn. I must carry out the cooking and cleaning jobs as if nothing was amiss. Getting through the day until mid-afternoon when the steamer arrived would be the hardest part. I sat in the darkness and went over the plan in my mind. It would work . . . I was sure of it. We would make our escape. At the moment, getting out from under the domination of a cruel, unscrupulous tyrant outweighed the apprehension about what we would do once away from Blackbriar Bay. Whatever awaited two penniless orphans out there would not be as dire as remaining under this roof. At dawn I fired up the stove, boiled some coffee, fried slabs of bacon, mixed up some sourdough biscuits, and had just taken them from the oven when I heard uneven footsteps coming down the hall. My nervousness made me burn a finger as I hastily put the pan into the warming oven of the stove. I quickly swung around.

Aunt Minna came into the room, walking quite steadily as she leaned on a homemade cane and hobbled over to a chair by the table. Her eyes were clear and cold, and her drawn expression lacked the sagging lines evident when she was drinking. A lopsided gray braid down her back was evidence of an attempt to brush her hair. Her wrapper was dirty but buttoned to the neck and tied at the waist.

"Good morning, Aunt Minna," I said. My heart leapt with relief to see her sober. "Would you like some breakfast? I baked—"

"Coffee," she snapped.

I nodded and poured her a cup. Her hands trembled as she used both of them to raise the hot liquid to her mouth. Her stony glare settled on me over the rim of the mug. Even though I was perspiring from the heat of the stove, I felt chilled in her presence. Cold sober, my aunt still exuded a hostility so strong it was almost palpable. For the hundredth time, I wondered what had passed between her and my father to bring such hatred into her eyes when she looked at me. I was certain that my father had felt a deep affection for her and had not been fearful of sending his orphaned children to her. He could not have known that she would receive us with such bitter rancor.

"That man?" she growled, "The one who was here last night? I can't remember—" She faltered and her forehead furrowed as if she were trying to sort out some drunken impressions.

"Judge Hackerman . . . from Tahoe City."

"Jem brought him here?"

I nodded, trying not to wilt beneath her accusing eyes.

"Jem never allows anyone to set foot at Blackbriar House," she snapped. "Unless—" She slammed down the mug, sloshing the steamy liquid over the side. "What are you two up to?"

"Nothing . . . I mean, I didn't know anything about

131

Judge Hackerman . . . or why he was here. You have to believe me, Aunt Minna. Jem forced me to sign some papers. He threatened to hurt Davie if I didn't. I—"

"Papers?" She frowned. "Papers? What papers?"

I swallowed, not knowing how to tell her that the judge had deemed her incompetent to handle her own affairs. "It was Jem's doing," I said quickly, grasping at this chance to show her caretaker in his true colors. "Erskine saw the chance to get control of your holdings. He arranged for you to be good and drunk last night. Since I'm kin, the judge was willing to put your financial affairs in my hands, but I don't want—"

"Liar!" Her voice was a screech. "The two of you— trying to cheat me! Had it all arranged, didn't you? Behind my back, Jem sent for you to come here, didn't he? Arranged for you to sneak into the house like a sly fox—"

"*No, that's not true!* You have to believe me, Aunt Minna. I came here because Davie and I needed a home. That's all! I had nothing to do with his scheme to get his hands on your property. He used me!" I leaned toward her. "But we can beat him, Aunt Minna. Between the two of us we can show the judge exactly what kind of man Erskine is and he'll help us get rid of him. Trust me, Aunt Minna. Please."

"Trust you?" Her voice was ugly. "You lying, cheating bitch!" I leapt back as she threw the steaming coffee at me, dousing the back of my right hand with the hot liquid. I cried out in pain. At that moment Judge Hackerman entered the kitchen with Erskine at his heels.

"Oh, my!" The old man's eyes took in the scene in one horrified glance.

Aunt Minna lurched to her feet. Her anger dissipated

instantly. "I didn't do anything, Jem." Terror flashed in her eyes.

Erskine's glare went from her to my red hand. "What are ye doing, woman?"

Aunt Minna seemed to shrivel before my eyes. "She was telling me all kinds of lies. I'm sorry, Jem. I'm sorry," she blubbered, holding out her hands in a beseeching manner. "Please, don't be angry."

"It's all right, Aunt Minna," I said quickly, hating to see her grovel so. Obviously Erskine had terrorized her to the point that she feared him. No wonder drink had become her only salvation, I thought. Like a dog whipped too long and too harshly, she seemed beyond rational thought. She put her hands over her face and wept.

"Don't cry, Aunt Minna," I pleaded. My heart ached for the young girl who had laughingly posed for a picture with my father and now was a defeated woman, cowering and begging like a tormented animal.

Erskine smiled at her, that cruel, moist smile of his. "You must behave yourself . . . in front of company," he told her.

"Leave her alone," I snapped. "Can't you see you're to blame for all this." I put my arm around her shoulders but she knocked it away. "Go away," she screamed at me.

Erskine laughed as if he enjoyed watching the ugly scene. Holding my burned hand, I turned and fled the room. My aunt's pitiful pleading and Erskine's booming responses followed me up the stairs. Tears burned in my eyes and I knew that we must leave that afternoon or suffer the same evil that had destroyed my aunt.

"What's wrong with your hand?" Davie's hands sliced the air, fright back in his eyes.

"I burned it . . . on the stove," I lied. Thank heavens

133

the coffee had not been hot enough to scald me. An ugly redness covered three fingers, but there were no blisters.

I was appalled by Aunt Minna's accusations that Erskine and I were in league on some foul plan to cheat her. How could she believe such a thing? Her mind was so twisted that she was incapable of rational thought. Yet she had every reason to be suspicious of Erskine's activities. He hadn't brought me to Blackbriar House as she had accused me, but he had been quick to exploit my presence. For some reason he wanted my aunt's financial reins in my hands instead of hers. More than ever, it was crucial that I escape from Erskine's domination. I couldn't help Aunt Minna by staying, but perhaps I could do something once Davie and I were safely away.

How was I going to get through the day? The steamer would not arrive until late afternoon. We waited in the attic room until I was sure that Erskine and the judge had eaten breakfast. Looking out the window, I saw them sailing out to the island in the skiff. They were probably going fishing. Thank God. I began to breathe easier with Erskine out of the house.

The morning hours went by with excruciating slowness. I spent time with Davie and Rags, and kept busy working in the kitchen. I set out some lunch in the dining room and ate with Davie. No one bothered us.

Aunt Minna spent the day in her usual chair in the front room, and I despaired to see another bottle of whiskey in her hands every time I looked in. Her head slumped forward, and all the spirit I had seen that morning had disappeared. My conscience pricked at me for leaving her in such a state, but for the moment I had to see to Davie's safety. There was nothing I could do to rescue her from Erskine by staying at Blackbriar Bay.

When my father's watch told me it was about time for the *Tahoe Queen*'s run, Davie and I went down the stairs from the attic room just as Erskine came into the hall.

"There you are!" he bellowed. "I was coming after you. The judge has some last-minute instructions for you. Wants to talk to you before he leaves." His dark eyes glinted at me as he gave a nod toward the sitting room.

My chest tightened. I had planned to be waiting out of sight near the pier when the *Tahoe Queen* pulled in. I was terrified that the steamer would come and go before Davie and I had a chance to board her. If I refused to do as Erskine ordered, he might get suspicious. Besides, I reassured myself, the steamer was coming to pick up Judge Hackerman, and it wouldn't leave without him.

I signed to Davie to collect Rags and wait for me at the back door. I went into the sitting room expecting to find the Judge waiting there. Aunt Minna was alone, her pathetically thin body slumped listlessly in her chair. Her glazed eyes squinted at me, and her head lolled heavily from side to side. Her eyelids seemed too heavy to hold open. They closed. Her head fell back and her mouth sagged open with a drunken snore.

Impulsively, I paused by her chair and then leaned over and kissed her pallid cheek. "Goodbye, Aunt Minna," I whispered.

The judge must be in the dining room, I thought, and opened one of the folding doors. I peered in. It was empty. The sound of a shrill whistle stabbed me like a knife. The *Tahoe Queen*! I had to get Davie and get down to the dock without delay. Lifting the skirts of my calico dress, I ran through the house and out the back door where I had told him to wait.

Davie? Where was he? The boy and his dog were nowhere in sight. The temptation was there to yell his name, but the act was fruitless as a means of catching his attention. Stamping on floorboards might catch my brother's attention if he were in the same room, but creating strong enough vibrations on the ground was almost impossible.

Panic and fury surged through me. Why hadn't Davie done as I had told him! He must have misunderstood my flying fingers when I told him to wait by the back door. Maybe he had gone down to the lake?

I was just about to race around the corner of the house when the shrill bark of the puppy somewhere on the sloping hill above the house stopped me.

"Rags!" I yelled. "Come here, Rags." Relieved, I knew that Davie would see Rags' head cocked in a listening slant and he would know that I had called him. I waited for both of them to appear. Another bark, but no sign of the puppy or Davie.

I swore. The steamer would be docking at any moment. I lifted up my skirts and hurriedly climbed the hill. The puppy, ears twitching, stood barking at a red squirrel perched on a branch of a pine tree.

No sign of Davie.

The first lurch of fear went through me. Where was he? I had told him to wait for me while I talked to the judge. The judge! Erskine had lied. The judge had not wanted to speak to me at all. It had been a ruse, a way to delay me in the house. Davie! What had Erskine done with Davie?

Rocks and dirt spilled in front of me as I raced down the hill and bounded around the house. I could see the steamer at the end of the pier. The judge was just being helped aboard. I recognized Randy's lanky frame. I waved frantically and ran as fast as I could down to the weathered pier.

"Anna!" Randy waved back, leaning his lanky frame on the railing of the steamer, his freckled face spread in a wide smile.

The steamer gave a warning whistle.

I waved frantically. "Wait . . . Wait!"

"What's the matter?" he shouted back.

"I—"

My next word was cut off as a hand like an iron pincer sent pain radiating through my arm. "Ye gonna cause trouble? Run off—and leave yer little brother?" I swung around to face Erskine. His smile was a satisfied leer.

"What have you done with him?" I gasped.

"Yer idiot brother's in safe keeping . . . unless ye do something stupid to change all that. Get me meaning?"

He had Davie; his satisfied grunt and cruel amusement left no doubt in my mind.

"Anna?" Randy called out my name again. Suddenly he was on his way down the ladder.

"Ye'd better watch your tongue," warned Erskine, "if ye know what I mean. Ye start any rumors and I'll see to it that yer little brother's broken up in little pieces." He dropped his arm, and then turned and purposefully walked up the path to the house as if he were not the least concerned about what I might do or say.

How cleverly he had checkmated me.

"Anna, is everything all right?" asked Randy in a rush when he reached my side. "I was glad when I heard we were going to stop here . . . I wanted to check on you, and all." His concerned eyes swept my face. "You okay?"

My lips seemed stiff as I tried to smile. "Fine."

"You sure? You look kinda peaked. Is your aunt working you too hard?"

I shook my head. My mind raced ahead. Erskine had outwitted me this time, but I had to make certain I got another chance. "Randy, could you write me a letter?"

"A letter?"

"So the steamer would have to make a mail stop here?"

The *Tahoe Queen* gave another warning whistle. The pilot was getting impatient.

"Sure . . . sure. Will do." He frowned. "You take care, hear?"

I nodded, blinking back a fullness in my eyes as I watched him hurry aboard. The steamer headed out of the bay, taking the judge and all my hopes with it.

I raced back to the house. Erskine was sprawled in a kitchen chair, his fishing gear spread all over the table. He gave me a triumphant sneer as I came in. "So ye decided not to go. I thought ye'd be changing yer mind," he smirked. "Thought ye was pretty clever . . . but I saw through yer plan last night when I saw ye on the path. Found the satchel this morning and figured out what ye was up to."

"Where's my brother? If you've hurt him, I'll kill you."

Erskine laughed mirthlessly as he jerked his head toward the meat cellar.

I flew down the steps and reached out in the darkness to a crumpled heap on the dank ground. Davie! He had been tied hand and foot and as I struggled with the knots, his body shivered from fright and cold. I half-carried him up the stairs and set him on the stool near the fire, rubbing his clammy hands and stroking his blue cheeks. His frightened gaze fled to Erskine and back again, new tremors rising in his body.

His rounded eyes pleaded with me, asking for reassurance and explanation. Trapped in silence, not understanding why he had been treated so callously, his fear was multiplied. I gathered him in my arms and held him close. Slowly his tremors faded away. I vowed that Erskine would not touch him again.

The fiery determination must have been in my eyes, for Erskine grinned at me as he picked up his fishing gear. "Quite the little mother lion, ain't ye?"

"And what kind of a beast are you to misuse a helpless little boy?" I taunted, fury overriding caution. "You must be proud of yourself. A big, brave man . . . terrifying two women and a child," I said in a mocking tone. "You've destroyed my aunt with drink and frightened a little boy to death, and you think you've got the best of me. But you haven't! You'd better keep one eye open as you sleep or you'll find a butcher knife buried in your throat," I warned recklessly.

He pointed a menacing finger at me. "Ye'll be doing as I say. If ye don't, I'll be the one handling a knife." A quick slice of his hand across his neck punctuated the sentence.

Davie saw the gesture and understood it well. He buried his face against my chest. His shoulders heaved with silent whimpers.

Erskine grunted in disgust. He stomped out of the house, leaving Davie in a state of terror.

I took the boy upstairs and put him to bed. He held

139

onto my hand as if he feared I would slip away from him.

"I wouldn't leave you, Davie. We'll get away from here together." I knew he couldn't understand all the words, but his feeble smile told he had understood enough. "Next time, we'll make it."

The trusting look in his eyes tore at my heart . . . and it fueled my anger. For the first time in my life, I realized I was capable of murder.

Chapter Ten

Time passed and the steamer did not stop at Blackbriar Bay. Then, unexpectedly, nearly two weeks after the judge's visit, I heard its whistle. The *Tahoe Queen* was going to make a mail stop! If Davie and I could get down to the pier—!

I flung down my dishtowel, grabbed Davie's hand, and scooped up the puppy at a near run. Before we reached the back door, I heard a coarse laugh from the hallway. "Going somewhere?"

Erskine stood in the kitchen doorway, daring me with a twisted grin to try and make a dash for it. Like a hunter watching his prey, he was poised, every muscle rippling, his apelike frame challenging me to try and outdistance him. Alone I might have gambled, but with Davie's safety at stake, I couldn't.

I turned away from the door, putting Davie behind me as I faced the vile man. "You can't keep us prisoners forever."

"I wouldn't be betting on it if I were ye. Not if ye want to keep yerself and that kid all in one piece. Now, why don't the two of ye sit down all nice and quiet-like . . . unless ye'd rather pay another visit to the pit?"

Davie began to tremble, correctly reading Erskine's gesture toward the cellar door. I took his hand and we sat down at the kitchen table. In a couple of minutes we heard the steamer's departing whistle and I knew that our chance had gone.

Erskine laughed at my expression. "Thought ye'd pull a fast one, didn't ye? Yer about as clever as a mouse trying to get out of a hole when the cat's only a tongue-licking away."

Despair was like a knot in my stomach. No telling when the steamer would return again. Would Randy send me another letter, or would he decide I was playing games with him?

"Guess I'd better wander down and see what's in the mail pouch. I don't suppose ye have any idea." His lips twisted in mocking grin. "I've been watching ye waiting for it. Every afternoon yer as anxious as a brooding mare." He laughed. "I'm betting that beanpole sailor sent ye a letter."

He swaggered out of the room, and I sat down in a chair and put my head in my hands. Davie tugged at my arm. I looked at him, and he made a sign that belonged in the privy.

I laughed and felt my spirits rebounding. "We'll get him yet," I said with foolish bravado. "Let's go fishing," I signed, and immediately the anxious frown left his face. How little it took to reassure him, I thought. Such is the innocence of childhood that a fishing pole can solve all problems.

We came back to the house a couple of hours later with five beautiful cutthroat trout. Davie was wet and smelled of fish, but he was happy and life seemed a little more normal than it had since our arrival.

I never saw the letter that Randy sent. In the days that followed I immersed myself in hard work. The house was a dark, rambling place, with shadowy halls connecting scattered rooms smelling of smoke, sour drink, and dirt. Every window had collected so much grime that it was nearly impossible to see through the panes. With warm water in a bucket, a hunk of lye soap, and elbow grease, I tackled the windows in the kitchen and dining room.

My aunt chided my labors. "They'll just get dirty again."

"Maybe, but for a while they'll be clean enough to let the sunshine in. It's a pretty day, Aunt Minna. Why don't you sit under the trees while I tackle the outside windows? The sun will do you good."

Much to my surprise, she let me help her down the rickety front steps to a bench that had been placed close to the front door where she could look across the bay to the small island and the lake. I wondered what her thoughts were as she sat there, a pitiful creature with sagging skin and flaccid muscles. Was she remembering her married life and what her days had been like when they were building the house and accumulating property around the lake?

I heard her sigh deeply and lift her pallid face to the sun. My heart leapt with hope. Any sign of sobriety was encouraging. She made curt replies to my attempts to involve her in any conversation, but I ignored her abruptness and was as cheerful and positive as I could be. For the first time I felt that I was making progress. She seemed to be content in my company.

My back threatened to break as I scrubbed the outside windows. With every swish of my cloth, my thoughts whirled with frantic plans to make an escape. I had never handled a boat, but watching Erskine come and go in the skiff centered my thoughts on stealing it as a way to get away. I even eyed the old rowboat turned upside down on the dock, waiting for caulking. Dry, shrunken boards warned that any attempt to float the old boat would only result in sinking it in the middle of the bay.

Just about the time I thought I was making progress with Aunt Minna, she started drinking again. I decided that her suspicions about a conspiracy between me and Erskine had been lulled to the point that she saw no need for staying sober. She began drinking early in the day and by evening was lost in a drunken stupor.

On one of our hikes, Davie and I discovered a source of the endless bottles of white whiskey—a mountain still. We found it quite by accident. In fact, Rags led us to it, bounding through the underbrush to a crude affair built under an outcropping of rock and hidden from above and below. I wondered if Erskine was selling some of the "white lightning" whiskey. I saw no other means of his putting money in his pocket. He had obviously robbed Aunt Minna of all of hers. I raged that homebrew whiskey was in ample supply but no garden had been planted to provide decent fresh food, no goat was kept for milk, and only a few poorly laying, vermin-ridden chickens scratched for food.

I reasoned that the situation must have been different when Aunt Minna's husband was alive. We came across a tumble down barn and leaning fences which hinted that Blackbriar House had once been a self-sufficient, well-ordered property. Things must have deteriorated after Erskine came on the scene. What had happened to the place—and to my aunt? And what was going to happen to us?

Escape was always at the front of my mind. While Davie fished along the lake's edge, my eyes searched the surrounding hillside. Thick virgin drifts of trees and rugged slopes of tumbled rocks made impossible any thought of trying to hike around the lake. The only way out of the area was by boat.

We hiked farther and farther away from the house in every direction, always with the same result—viewing miles of rugged territory and water in every direction.

On one of our explorations on the hillside behind the house, we came upon a crude rock sepulchre with a wooden cross mounted upon it. I suspected that Aunt Minna's husband was buried there.

Davie looked puzzled, and I tried to explain that some people were buried above ground instead of in graves. His eyes widened, and he stared at the pile of rocks as if the corpse were going to appear in front of us at any moment.

I wondered what Horace Brown had been like. Had he treated Aunt Minna well? Apparently there had been no children from the union. The isolation of Blackbriar must have been hard to bear when my aunt was a young woman, but after his death, she had continued to stay isolated from the world.

Davie tugged at my arm. He pointed to the sepulchre. "Who?"

"Aunt Minna's husband," I signed back.

He looked perplexed. Relationships were difficult to explain. I thought of the schools Delany had told me about. If only I knew how to teach Davie everything he needed to know. Would the lumberman remember his promise to send me a book on sign language? I doubted it. He had probably forgotten all about us by now. And the memory of the time we had spent with him on the steamer was fading. I decided that my belief that he had been interested in Aunt Minna's property had been wrong.

Then something happened to change my mind.

I was in the attic room with Davie one morning when I glanced out of the window and my heart jerked to a stop.

A sailboat! Tied up to the pier. Who could it be?

Two men stood by the boathouse. Erskine and. . . ? I squinted against the morning sun. Yes, it must be. There was no mistaking that flaxen hair nor the masculine stature of the man. Lyle Delany!

My first impulse was to raise the window and cry out to him, but as I saw him throw back his head and laugh, my hands froze on the window sash.

He touched Erskine's arm, and the two men walked over to a pile of crates and sat down. My joy withered and died as I watched them sit there smoking, chatting and laughing. The companionable scene sent a bone-deep chill through me. In my foolish daydreams, I had pictured the attractive Delany arriving at Blackbriar like a knight on a white stallion, rescuing me from the vile

146

situation in which I found myself. Now such fantasy was a mockery of the truth.

Erskine was shaking Delany's hand, nodding and smiling. They stood up and walked down to the end of the pier in a companionable stride. *Like conspirators.* The ugly things Randy had said about Lyle Delany came rushing back. What was he doing here? Why hadn't he made some effort to see me? Why was he hand-in-glove with Erskine?

I watched Delany shove his boat away from the dock, and in a few minutes he was gone. Erskine came back to the house with a satisfied twist to his lips.

Better to know the truth, I thought, moving back from the window. I sat down on the bed, fighting a deep sense of betrayal and loss. All my foolish dreams had best be laid to rest. Lyle Delany's interest in Blackbriar House obviously had nothing to do with me. It was foolish to think that his attentions on the boat had meant anything. After all, I had spent only a few hours in the man's company. I wondered if he had used me as an excuse to talk with Erskine. A kernel of bitterness grew as I remembered the scene between them.

I tried to get it out of my mind, but I couldn't. I realized then how much my fantasy of love and romance had settled upon the fair-haired Delany. He had been at the back of my mind all the time, when I was up to my elbows in dirty water, when my face was smeared with dirt and grime. The last thing at night when I fell exhausted into bed, there had been a warm memory of his deep blue eyes and bold mouth to lull me to sleep. Now that was gone. I had seen him laughing and smiling with Erskine—and something inside me had died.

147

I cooked and cleaned with a fury that released some of my pent-up emotions. Davie and I explored the rambling house. In one room we found stacked boxes covered with dust. Curious, we opened some of them and found old clothes, some pictures and letters. A tintype caught my attention because "Horace Brown, Captain," was written on the back. A thickish man in army uniform looked formidable as he shouldered an army rifle. Aunt Minna's husband. I wondered if he had shown the same kind of military hauteur to his wife.

My heart began to beat faster when I found a packet of four letters written to Aunt Minna—*from my father*. The sight of his familiar handwriting made my hands tremble as I held them. Davie looked at me in concern. He had been busy rescuing Rags from the middle of the things we had taken out of the box.

"Papa's," I signed.

Davie's touched the letters, tears forming in his eyes. I realized how much he missed the strong, loving man who had filled his life with tender care and strength. Like me, Davie had lost the anchor of his security. For a moment we stared at the handwriting and grieved for our father.

I knew I shouldn't read the letters. My father had taught me to respect other people's property, and I breathed a prayer of forgiveness as I slipped them out of the envelopes. When I had finished reading them, I dropped them in my lap, leaned my head back against the wall, and tried to absorb what I had learned.

The story was a simple one. From my father's pleas for forgiveness, I learned that he had interfered in a love match between his sister and a young man named Richard. My father, a protective older brother, had come upon them in each other's arms one evening in the garden, and in his anger my father had beaten Aunt Minna's sweetheart soundly. Fearful for his life, the young man had fled, never knowing that Minna was bearing his child. He was killed a few months later while wrangling some wild horses in Wyoming. Minna had his baby in disgrace and gave it away at birth. She married an older man, Horace Brown, who took her away from the wagging tongues and the brand of a fallen woman. Isolated from the rest of the world, she had spent her life at Blackbriar. From the tone of my father's letters, I knew she had never forgiven him. I was surprised that she had even kept his letters. My heart went out to her.

But if Aunt Minna was firmly under her caretaker's control, why did Erskine go to all the trouble to have her affairs put in my hands? If she would sign anything he put in front of her, why did he need me? The same question that had plagued me since the judge's visit rose to the front of my mind, demanding an answer. Was Erskine intent upon cutting my aunt out of her share?

I put the letter back and vowed I would try to be more understanding of her. A few days later Erskine strode into the kitchen and ordered me to get ready to board the steamer that afternoon.

"What—?" I dropped the tin plate I had been drying, and it made a harsh clatter on the floor.

"Are ye hard of hearing? I'm telling ye to get yer bonnet on! The steamer will be here in a few minutes. Yer going to Tahoe City."

I blinked. "You're sending me to Tahoe City?"

"Blast it all! Are ye as stupid as yer brother? I've sent word for the steamer to pick ye up. There's legal things that need doin'. Now git ready." He read the hope that lurched into my eyes. "And don't be getting any foolhardy ideas. Ye'll go and take care of business and . . ." he gave that malicious smirk, "and I'll take care of yer brother."

"No." My tone was hard and flat. "I'm not going anywhere without Davie." My thoughts raced. Davie was up in the attic room, playing with some pieces of wood that I had collected as building blocks. I wasn't going to let Erskine get his hands on him the way he had before.

"Go get yer bonnet," he snarled, starting toward me in a threatening manner.

"No." I turned and ran, bounding up the steps. I would try to block the attic door with something so he couldn't drag me from it. I reached the top of the stairs and glanced back over my shoulder, expecting that he would have darted up after me. But he hadn't. I raced into the small room—and cried out!

Davie wasn't there! Blocks of wood were all over the floor, and Rags was curled up on the bed asleep. The puppy raised his head and gave a welcoming woof.

"Davie! Where's Davie?" I gasped aloud as if the pup could tell me. Then I knew—Erskine had whisked my brother away from his play before coming to the kitchen.

I fled back down the stairs. The horrible man waited for me at the bottom, that sneering smile on his face.

"Where's Davie?" I screeched at him.

He grabbed my arm and gave it a vicious twist. "Now, listen fast. We ain't got much time. Yer brother's safe as long as ye do as yer told. Ye'll go to Tahoe City, sign

150

some papers at the judge's office, and come back tomorrow with the money. If ye open yer mouth to anyone . . . anyone . . . I'll give ye back yer brother in pieces. And I have ways of knowing if ye go shooting off yer mouth." He gave my arm another cruel twist, then gave me a vicious shove up the stairs. "Now, change yer dress, git yer bonnet, pack a few night things. Then meet me at the dock!"

I stumbled back up the stairs to the attic. My mind raced as I threw my blue wool dress over my head, fastened the mother-of-pearl buttons, and shoved some hairpins into my hair. My hand trembled as I tied the streamers of my bonnet. Did I have any choice? What would he do to Davie if I refused to go?

I heard the whistle just as I finished throwing some night things in the canvas satchel. Through the window I saw the *Tahoe Queen* making her way toward the bay. Racing downstairs, I went directly to the cellar, knowing it was stupid to think Erskine would hide Davie in the same place a second time.

The dark pit was empty.

There were dozens of places in the house and outside where Erskine could have hidden Davie. I couldn't possibly search all of them in time.

"There ye be!" bellowed Erskine, waiting for me as I came up the cellar steps. "I told ye to meet me at the dock." He grabbed my arm.

I jerked away from him. "I'm not going unless you tell me where Davie is!" Anger, fear, and desperation made my voice shrill and my manner reckless. "And you can't make me go."

"The devil, I can't!"

"You won't kill Davie, because he's the hold you have over me. If you hurt him, I don't care what you do to me. And if you kill me, you'll never get your hands on my aunt's property. You need me . . . alive."

He stood there, his breath coming from deep in his chest like the rumbling of a hurricane. I thought I saw a glint of admiration in his eyes as he growled, "That leaves yer aunt, don't it? She's no good to nobody."

The shrill of the steamer's whistle warned that the *Tahoe Queen* was approaching the dock.

Erskine's eyes glowed with a demon's gleam. "If ye don't get on that boat, I'll kill her in front of yer eyes . . . and pour her hot blood over yer head."

My stomach turned over. He had won, and he knew it.

"All right. I'll go, but I'd better find Aunt Minna and Davie unharmed when I get back, or—"

"Or what?" His jeering laugh followed me as I turned and fled out the back door.

Randy was waiting for me on deck and helped me up the ladder. "I was hoping it was you we were picking up. Didn't know who had sent in passage money." He looked at the expression on my face and frowned. "Is something the matter?"

Was something the matter? Hysteria swept over me. My brother and aunt were in the hands of a crazed madman, and their lives depended upon my ability to keep the horror a secret. *I have ways of knowing if ye go shooting off yer mouth.* I didn't dare say anything. I couldn't chance anything happening to Davie while I was gone. "I was rushed . . . getting ready," I said lamely.

"I sent you a letter, but you didn't come down to the dock to get it."

"I couldn't. But thanks, anyway." I didn't tell him Erskine must have destroyed the letter. I couldn't control a shiver.

"Come on in the cabin and have a spot of tea. It's a good hour to Tahoe City."

"Thanks, but I'd rather stay outside for a little while." I gave him a feeble smile. "I need to do some thinking."

"Good place to think, on the deck of a boat. The rhythm of the water soothes a troubled spirit. Let me know if you need anything." With a warm grin, he left me standing at the railing, staring down into the deep waters of Lake Tahoe.

The events of the last hour had shaken me like the onslaught of a raging fever. My hands were clammy, my head whirled, and a quivering in the pit of my stomach lent a weakness to my legs. I gripped the iron railing and tried to get control of myself. I mustn't let myself give way to a debilitating upheaval of emotions. More than ever, I needed to think rationally, somehow turn the situation to my advantage. The lives of Davie and Aunt Minna depended upon it.

A foamy wake spread out behind the boat, rippling in long, mesmerizing streamers across the surface of the lake. A low sun was already disappearing behind a rim of mountains, and elongated shadows were rapidly changing the lake's aquamarine color to a pewter gray. Looking down into the clear water, I saw huge dark rocks rise in a threatening fashion under the surface and I expected the steamer to crash upon them at any moment. Miraculously, it seemed, the steamer slipped over them, and the illusion that the rocks were close to the surface faded away.

I breathed deeply, straightened my back, and firmed my chin. The crisp, cool air and the rhythmic chug of the engine returned my pulse to normal and cleared my head. Erskine would not have allowed me to go by myself to Tahoe City if he'd had any other choice. I was supposed to sign some papers and return with money. If I didn't, I had no doubt that he would turn his fury upon the hostages I had left behind. How could I thwart him and still protect Davie and Aunt Minna?

Davie. A sob broke in my throat, and I stiffened against the knowledge that he was alone and terrified. If only—! I jerked my mind away from fruitless agonizing about what I should have done. I mustn't think about my brother, nor Aunt Minna, but keep my mind centered on finding a way to save us all from Erskine, a diabolical beast who would forfeit our lives without a pang of remorse.

"Well, now, there's some color in your cheeks," said Randy as he joined me at the railing. "I think you're feeling better. Want to talk about it? You'd be surprised how many people share their troubles with me."

Sharing my heavy burden would have eased my worry and pain. More than anything I wanted to pour out my fears and anxieties—but I didn't dare. He might do something that would endanger all our lives. Better that I keep my silence for the moment. "I appreciate the offer," I said sincerely. "Maybe later."

"How long you staying in Tahoe City?"

"Overnight. I'll be coming back tomorrow."

"Darn it. I have to work tonight, getting some things done on the steamer before tomorrow's run. Otherwise, I could show you around a bit. Where you going to be staying?"

I looked blank. Erskine had told me to go to Judge Hackerman's office to sign some papers . . . and nothing more. "Is there a hotel?"

"The Timberline. Not very fancy, but clean, and the cooking's good. A little expensive." He eyed my modest dress and bonnet and I knew he was wondering if I had the price of lodgings.

I didn't. In my haste I hadn't even brought the few dollars I had left over from our stage journey. I would have to find Judge Hackerman's office first thing, I thought as apprehension brought a tightening to my stomach. What kind of papers was I expected to sign? Erskine had said I would be bringing back money. What kind of a deal had he made? Was there any way I could protect my aunt's interests without endangering all our lives?

"Well, here we are . . . Tahoe City," said Guy, pointing across the water.

As we drew closer, I saw numerous small docks and a variety of boats along the water's edge. Beyond the wharf, log buildings lined streets that rose steeply on wooded hillsides. I was used to bustling mining camps, stark, dirty, and crowded, but Tahoe City was none of these. Small but attractive houses dotted the shoreline, and the steeple of a pretty white church was etched against the forest-green backdrop. A swarm of rugged men shouted at each other, swaggered about, and leaned up against nearby buildings, smoking and watching as the *Tahoe Queen* pulled in. Memories of Zeke's crude attentions brought a flicker of apprehension.

"Do you know where Judge Hackerman's office is?" I

asked Randy.

"Just beyond the jail . . . on the second floor of the post office. You can't miss it. You got business there?"

I nodded.

"Your aunt selling some property?"

Was she? I didn't know what was happening? I tried to murmur something that Randy could take either way. The *Tahoe Queen* bumped against the dock. I took a deep breath to quiet the tightening muscles in my stomach. "Thanks, Randy, for your friendship. You'll never know what it means to me."

His smile was warm. "Never had a pretty girl for a friend before."

For a second, I almost told him everything, but the insane impulse fled and I dropped my gaze from his. *If you tell anyone . . . anyone . . .* Erskine's threat echoed in my ears. "I'm glad you're my friend, Randy," I said simply.

"Well, got to go. See you tomorrow, Anna. Hope you have a good stay." He cocked his head. "You'll be all right, won't you?"

I nodded. "Fine . . . just fine."

He hurried away to fasten the lines and finish his duties.

I tightened the streamers on my bonnet and picked up my satchel. I was halfway down the gangplank when all breath left my chest. I put one hand on a rope bannister to steady myself.

At the bottom of the ramp, waiting for me, was Lyle Delany. He smiled, doffed his hat, and held his silver-blond head at a rakish angle.

"Welcome to Tahoe City, Miss McKenzie."

If I hadn't seen him talking and laughing with Erskine, I would have been fooled. I would have accepted the foolish pleasure that rose in me as he took my satchel and guided me off the boat.

"Good afternoon," I said coldly, knowing now what Erskine had meant when he said, *I have ways of knowing if ye go shooting off yer mouth.*

Chapter Eleven

I couldn't think of anything to say to Lyle Delany, who kept a possessive guiding hand on my elbow as we left the wharf. I was raging inside at how deftly I had been shuttled like a prisoner from one warden to the next. Erskine had put me on the steamer . . . and Delany had taken me off.

I glanced back at the boat and saw Randy staring at us from the steamer's deck. I think he would have come barreling off the boat after us if I had called his name. The impulse was there, but I controlled it. I had to guard every action. *Davie . . . Davie.* I smothered an urge to flee back to the boat. I was caught in a vicious net, and the mesh was being pulled tighter and tighter around me. I had to do as I was told. If I didn't, I might never see my little brother again.

There was a familiarity in the way Delany was smiling that made me terribly uneasy. At the same time, I was grateful for his escort when I passed by the gauntlet of men lounging near the wharf. Their lustful smirks and whispered exchanges reminded me of Zeke, and I prayed that I would never see that crude man again.

The man at my side caused everyone to give us a wide berth as we walked away from the lake. Lyly Delany was well known in this town, I decided, seeing the reaction of those around us. Open speculation glinted in the eyes of men who greeted Delany by name, and there was a guarded respect from rough-looking men that could have been in his employ. I intercepted admiring glances from women, young and old, as they passed us or came out of stores like Leed's Mercantile Mart, their arms loaded with packages.

One gaudily dressed woman with a brazen smile and dyed red hair looked me over as she swept by in a small black buggy. I was glad I had worn my best dress and Mrs. Greenberry's bonnet. Such a foolish feminine satisfaction gave me the courage to hold my head high. Delany ignored all the attention that centered on us as we strolled down the boardwalk.

"I understand you've been under the weather since your arrival," Delany said, as if this were an ordinary walk requiring social amenities.

I frowned. "Under the weather?"

"That's what Erskine told me when I dropped by the other day."

"He lied," I said flatly, ignoring a cautious voice that warned me to watch what I said to this man who was obviously a confidant of Erskine's.

"I see." His discerning gaze swept over my stiff expression. "Well, I'm sorry I didn't insist. How are things going? How is your aunt?"

"The same as always," I said flatly. How stupid did he think I was? Everything had been arranged between him and Erskine, my coming here to sign papers which would undoubtedly give Delany the land he wanted to buy. The power of attorney had probably been his idea, too. After having met me on the steamer, he and Erskine must have decided that they could put through the deal without Aunt Minna. They were using me, and I couldn't do anything about it. For some reason my aunt had refused to sell the land, and now they were going to make the deal without her. I was a pawn in Delany's scheme to get the lakefront property he wanted. And Erskine was going to pocket the money for it. With Davie as hostage, I was helpless in the situation—and they knew it.

"That's one of my offices," he said, pointing across the street to a one-story building with a big sign hung across it, *Delany Lumber and Flume Company.* "My business has grown with the town . . . before I moved most of my operation to Glenbrook, I had the largest business around Tahoe City. At one time I was supplying lumber from the area for Virginia City, Carson City, and a lot of mining towns in between."

"But you need more land," I said curtly.

"Oh, not for timber. As I told you before, I'm interested in seeing Tahoe Lake developed as a resort. The railroad will bring people into the area, and soon there'll be roads leading to different parts of the lake. More steamers, sailboats, and fishermen," he laughed. "And to think we're right here at the beginning, Anna. What an opportunity to—"

"To get ahead of the other land sharks, and grab up all the property for yourself," I snapped. "And it doesn't matter how, does it?"

He looked surprised. "I make an offer for a piece of

land and if it's accepted, I buy it. There's nothing underhanded in the transaction."

"And a little strong-armed persuasion is not frowned upon?"

"What are you implying? If you have an accusation to make, please make it."

For an instant, I almost released the fury that was raging inside of me, but I thought of Erskine's warning and swallowed hard. Davie's safety depended upon my silence. Venting my anger on Delany was pure idiocy. I was sure everything had been arranged to sell him some land. All they needed was for me to sign the papers. Erskine had sent me to Tahoe City, and the prosperous lumberman was personally conducting me to the judge's office to take care of the matter.

Suddenly Delany jerked me to a stop. "If you have something to say, say it! We can stop this whole thing right now. This is a business deal, profitable for both parties. I acquire a parcel of land, and your aunt gets a reasonable price for it."

"All nicely arranged, isn't it? How could anything be underhanded about such an arrangement?" I asked sarcastically.

His eyes narrowed. "You needn't act the injured party with me. Talk about an opportunist, Miss McKenzie. In less than a few weeks you have gained complete control of your aunt's assets. Pretty shrewd maneuvering on your part, wouldn't you say!"

"What—?"

His eyes had hardened. "Everyone knows your aunt has had little contact with the outside world in the last ten years. If Erskine hadn't looked after her, she'd probably be dead by now. He's not the most pleasant of men, but he's loyal. He tells me that you took over the house—and your aunt. And now all her holdings are in your hands." His stony eyes met mine. "I didn't realize what a shrewd, calculating mind lay behind those innocent honey-brown eyes."

I slapped him.

Black fury flared in his eyes. His expression was granite.

Gawking spectators giggled.

For a moment I thought he might slap me back, but slowly his mouth curved in a mocking smile. "I apologize for my impertinent remarks . . . to such a lady."

Heat like a flame surged up into my face. His apology was a worse insult than his accusations. Instead of coldly countering his insinuation that I was after my aunt's assets, I had reacted without thought. My behavior had been inexcusable . . . impulsive . . . childish—a mature woman used words, not fists! Steadily meeting his mocking gaze, I replied, "And I apologize for mistaking you for a gentleman."

He laughed fully then. "First round to you, Anna. Shall we declare a temporary truce?"

I didn't have a choice . . . not at the moment. How cleverly he had put me on the defensive! By spreading the lie that I had surreptitiously arranged to handle my aunt's affairs, Delany and Erskine could easily make me out to be a money-grabbing relative who was selling off Aunt Minna's land. I had never felt so helpless in my life. With Davie and Aunt Minna held as hostages to my behavior, I had to do as Erskine had instructed.

"Judge Hackerman's office is up there." Delany

pointed to some outside steps rising to the second floor of a log building. A post office and barbershop were located on the ground floor.

I lifted my skirts and mounted the staircase ahead of Delany. We reached the landing, and he opened the door to a small, musty office that was crowded with bookcases, black leather furniture, and a rolltop desk loaded with papers. The judge swung around on a swivel chair at our entrance, peering at us through tiny round glasses perched on his nose.

"Good afternoon, Judge," greeted Delany. "I've brought Miss McKenzie to sign the papers for her aunt."

"Ah, yes," the old man breathed heavily, nodding his pink head. "How nice to see you again." He held out to me a withered hand which felt cold and flaccid in mine. "Well, well, please sit down. I have the papers here somewhere." He started fussing with the stacks on his loaded desk.

Delany offered me a straight-backed chair that creaked when I sat down in it. He remained standing, leaning against one of the bookcases, and I felt his eyes on me as I sat there stiffly with my hands clasped in my lap. Despite my determination to ignore him, I was poignantly aware of the way his masculine physique filled up the small room. I wanted to squirm under his gaze, and I didn't understand the quick, hot excitement that sped through me in his presence. He was an unscrupulous opportunist. Even if he didn't know the extent to which Erskine had gone to ensure my cooperation, he was ready to benefit from it.

"Here we are." The judge held out a sheaf of papers to me. "Everything is ready for your signature. I've drawn

164

them up according to the instructions Erskine passed along to me. I hope you find them in compliance with your wishes, Miss McKenzie."

My wishes! I wanted to laugh. I knew nothing about the arrangements that had been made. Erskine and Delany had decided everything, and I was nothing more than a pawn on a chessboard, moved about at their will. The description of the land meant nothing to me. I didn't know where the property was or if the price offered was a reasonable one. Not that it mattered . . . Aunt Minna would never see a penny of the money. Erskine would be waiting at Blackbriar House to take it from me.

The expression on my face must have made Delany ask, "Is there something wrong? I hope you haven't changed your mind."

Was there a warning in his tone? I couldn't be sure. "No," I said in a neutral tone. "I'll sign." I wasn't going to endanger Davie's life for a piece of property. And Aunt Minna had brought this on herself. She had set herself up to be cheated when she allowed her caretaker to take over.

The judge dipped a pen and handed it to me. I signed everything he put in front of me. After the last paper, a smile crossed his wizened face. I wondered how much he had made on the deal and how much he had charged for arranging for the transfer of authority from Aunt Minna's hands to mine.

He handed the papers to Delany, added his signature, and then gave them back to the judge. "You have the money in the safe, Judge?"

The old man nodded, then walked in a hunched position over to a large black safe set in a corner. He opened it and brought out a leather bag. "Cash. That's what you stipulated, wasn't it?" He peered at me. "Mr. Delany arranged to have this transferred from his Sacramento bank."

He handed me the bag of money. "I would suggest you deposit it at the Wells Fargo office or some similar establishment."

"No. I'll take it with me." Erskine's order rang in my ears. *Bring me back the money.*

"Aren't you going to count it?" asked Delany.

"No, I'm sure I can trust you," I said with a sarcastic edge to my tone.

The judge's forehead wrinkled in a frown. "You shouldn't be wandering around with that much money on you. Why don't you leave it in the safe until morning? I'll give you a receipt for it, of course."

"Thank you, but I'd rather keep it with me." The bag contained ransom money which I must give to Erskine as soon as possible. I dared not think what would happen if I returned empty-handed.

I stood up and slipped the leather strings of the bag over my arm. "Now, if you will excuse me, I'm tired and would like to find some accommodations for the night."

"I reserved a room for you at the Lake House," said Delany. "Mrs. Mallory runs a clean place and serves decent food."

"I thought I would stay at the Timberline Hotel," I said, remembering that Randy had mentioned it. "I heard it was expensive—but good."

"Not for an unchaperoned lady," he said flatly. "You'll stay at the Lake House."

I flared at his dictatorial manner. What right did he

166

have to tell me where I should stay and where I shouldn't? He had his property. I didn't have to kowtow to his every wish. I faced him with my chin jutted. "I'll stay where I choose. Please tell me how to find the Timberline."

He opened his mouth as if to argue the matter, and then closed it. Tension snapped between us.

"I'm sure that Mr. Delany will look after you," said the judge in his wheezing voice.

"I'm sure he will," I echoed coldly. "After all, he may want to buy more of my aunt's property." My frigid glaze challenged him.

"Are you planning on selling all of your aunt's assets?" he countered just as coldly.

"How much are you planning on buying?"

"No more—at the moment. But I'll let you know if I change my mind."

"I'm sure you will."

The judge cleared his throat. "Good day, then, Miss McKenzie. Give my best to your aunt." Was there a mocking edge to his voice?

How deftly all three of them, the judge, Delany, and Erskine, had managed to get their share of Aunt Minna's assets. They had found a doddering old judge to make everything legal. I wondered how much his fee had been to declare Aunt Minna incompetent. Without a doubt, my signature on the papers would hold up in any court. Who would believe that I had been coerced into selling off her property? With the judge and Lyle Delany spreading rumors that I was a greedy niece who had been instrumental in declaring Aunt Minna incompetent, who would believe the truth?

I looked at the two men and knew I was in the midst of enemies more suave than Erskine, but probably just as deadly. "If you'll excuse me, I'll be on my way. Where is the Timberline Hotel?"

"I'll take you there," said Delany shortly.

"Don't bother. I can find it."

He held the door open for me, and there was nothing I could do but leave the judge's office with him.

"Are you always so obstinate, Miss McKenzie?" he inquired as he accompanied me down the steps.

"Only when someone thinks he can order me about."

"Is that the impression I give?"

I turned to face him. "At this moment, Mr. Delany, I don't care to discuss my impressions with you. It doesn't really matter what I think. Now, if you will direct me to the hotel, I'll bid you good day."

Smiling, he took my arm, and I couldn't disengage myself from his guiding touch without creating a scene. The heat of his hand burned into my arm. The smooth rhythm of his legs brushing my skirts was disconcerting. He seemed to be taking advantage of the narrow sidewalk to walk as close to me as he could. I was furious that he was giving everyone the impression that we were the most congenial of companions. I knew the gossips would be delighting over the story that I had slapped Lyle Delany's face. I had never felt so much on display in my life.

In a stony silence we left the main street and walked up a narrow road between thick stands of trees. At the top of the hill was a sprawling structure that was half-saloon and half-hotel. Even before we reached it, I was having misgivings about staying there.

Delany watched my expression. I vowed I wouldn't give him the satisfaction of sensing my growing uneasiness.

Horses tied to hitching posts whinnied as if to remind their owners that it was time to leave the saloon. Bawdy music blared above the sound of laughter and tinkling glasses. Swinging doors were in constant motion as men came in and out of the saloon part of the building. The hotel side was less boisterous, but as we passed curtained windows, I peered inside and saw only men sitting in the lobby smoking. There was no sign of any women or families.

"This is a hotel, isn't it?" I questioned Delany.

"Yes, but the saloon next door dictates the kind of patronage the Timberline enjoys. I tried to tell you . . . but you have to find out everything for yourself, don't you?"

I felt like a fool, and I could have killed Randy for getting me into this situation. Why would he recommend it? I suspected that Timberline was too expensive for his seaman wages and he didn't know that it catered to rowdy saloon customers.

"Are you ready to take my recommendation and stay at the Lake House, as I proposed?" Delany demanded.

If I'd been alone, I would have instantly decided against staying at the Timberline, but Delany's manner was so patronizing and his tone so threaded with amusement that I knew he enjoyed seeing my stubbornness make a fool out of me. My mind raced for a way out that would leave my pride intact. I was certain that no one would approach me in his company. Once I had registered and was safely in my room, I would be able to spend the night in privacy and comfort.

"Don't be ridiculous," I retorted with spirit. "I'm perfectly capable of taking care of myself in a public hotel."

With that pronouncement, I swept through the door with a haughty lift of my skirts. I thought I heard him chuckle but I wasn't sure.

A pasty-faced man with straggling gray whiskers was behind the desk and greeted Delany by name. The clerk let his eyes slide over me in a way that fired the ends of my red hair.

"The lady needs a room," Delany told him.

He grinned. "Sure thing. I have one at the same end of the building as yours, Mr. Delany. Just across the hall, in fact."

My eyes widened and I swung on him. "You're staying here?"

His blue eyes twinkled. "Most lumbermen do when they're in Tahoe City. Built quite a reputation as the place to stay.

The clerk nodded. "Good food, drinks, and . . ."

I was certain he was going to say "women," but I didn't wait to find out. I turned on my heels and walked out of the door with my back as stiff as a ramrod. How dare he compromise my reputation like that! I was certain he had pretended to oppose me just so I would make a fool out of myself and give everyone the impression that I was his fancy woman.

Rage made me almost blind as I stumbled down the narrow road, almost losing my footing in the steep incline banked by thick trees on both sides. Suddenly the shadows came alive.

I screamed as a man leaped at me. I struggled against him as he knocked off my bonnet and then caught me on the side of the head with a blow that sent fireworks exploding in my skull. I fell to the ground. He reached under me, grabbed an end of the leather money bag, and pulled. With life-and-death tenacity, I hung on so that he dragged me along as he yanked to get it loose.

He gave me a kick in the side and I cried in pain. But I didn't let go! Even though it felt as if my arm were being jerked out of its socket I didn't let go of the money bag.

Suddenly the pressure eased.

With the force of a charging bull, Delany plowed into the man's stomach and then land a punch on his jaw. The two of them went crashing back into the trees. My assailant was broad through the shoulders like a rhinoceros, with arms that looked thick as piano legs. The black-bearded man battered Delany's head against a tree trunk; I thought the lumberman would slip senseless to his knees at any moment.

I tried to get my weak legs under me, but the blow to my head had affected my equilibrium.

The black-bearded man staggered back as Delany managed to bring a jaw-cracking blow against the side of his face. As the man wavered, Delany jumped on him, bringing him to the ground. In a rolling mass of arms and legs, they fought. I couldn't tell who was winning, and I watched helplessly as they beat upon each other. Then suddenly my attacker was on his feet, running away through the trees, leaving Delany wavering to his feet and touching his bleeding lip.

I stood unsteadily on my feet as Delany turned to me. "You all right, Anna?"

171

Suddenly I was in his arms, sobbing and trembling, and pressing my cheek against his steely chest. His arms cradled me with a gentleness I wouldn't have thought possible. I could feel the rapid rise and fall of his breathing. The strong, firm length of his body pressed against mine was the sweetest warmth I had ever felt. A strange excitement crept deep within me. I seemed to change as he held me, a bewildering metamorphosis into a woman with frightening desires.

"I'm sorry," I blubbered. "I should have listened to you."

His lips touched my forehead in a whispery kiss. "It's all right, Tiger," he said. "Everything's all right."

And at the moment, for one brief instant in time, I believed him.

Chapter Twelve

The Lake House was just off Tahoe City's main street, a large, two-storied log building on the waterfront. Meg Mallory took one look at us and put a plump hand up to her round cheek. "Heavens be praised!" she gasped. "Did a mule team run over the two of you?"

Delany gave a wry laugh. "More like a ten-ton skunk." He kept his arm around my waist as we followed the landlady into a large, homey kitchen smelling of hot bread.

"Sit yourselves down and tell me the story while I finish getting supper ready for my boarders." She eyed my tear-streaked face. "A cup of tea laced with a wee drop of brandy would be putting some color back in your cheeks," she declared, quickly placing a steaming cup in front of me. She grinned at Delany, "And you'd be liking yours without the tea, I'll wager." She poured him a generous drink.

I sat across from Delany and wasn't surprised when he stretched his hands across the table and squeezed mine. "You hung in there in good shape."

"I wasn't going to let him have the money if he pulled my arm off!"

He laughed. "I'll choose you for my side anytime."

"I think you're going to have a black eye," I said, feeling guilty that it was my fault he'd gotten into a fight.

"My badge for rescuing a fair maiden." He grinned. "Besides, I need to stay in condition." He rubbed his jaw. "I can't take it on the chin the way I used to. At one time I would have had that skunk laid out on the ground with one punch." He grinned. "I have a feeling that I may get in condition if I hang around you long enough."

"I don't understand. Who was he? How did he know about the money bag?" Suspicion flared. Had someone arranged to take it from me?

"If you remember, the judge tried to persuade you to leave the money in his safe. Waltzing out of his office with a leather bag swinging from your arm is a pretty good advertisement that you've just completed some kind of transaction. Blackbeard was probably lounging about, saw us leave, and followed us up the hill. When you came rushing down alone, he saw his chance and took it. I'm just sorry I took a couple of minutes bantering with the clerk or I'd have been there sooner."

"I suppose you had a good laugh at my expense," I said, heat easing up from my throat as I remembered the clerk's knowing smile. "You should have warned me what kind of hotel that was."

"Would you have listened?"

My smile was sheepish. "Probably not, but you should have tried. And I don't mean by giving me orders. That just riles me . . ."

"So I've noticed."

Meg bustled in and out of the kitchen, laying out a long

174

table in the dining room for the evening meal.

I met Delany's eyes over the rim of my teacup. Smile lines crinkled around them as he held my gaze. I found myself surrendering to their warmth. He set down his drink, reached over, and took my hand again. "Feeling better, Annie?"

I nodded. No one had ever called me Annie. I knew I should inform him in brisk tones that my name was Anna, but as his fingertips lightly touched my skin, my objections to the nickname dissolved. I knew that my face was as dirty as my dress. I had lost my bonnet—it had been crushed beyond repair as the thief dragged me over the ground. Rebellious curls brushed my cheeks and forehead and hung low on my neck. I must look dreadful, I thought, and found myself laughing weakly, a weird reaction to all that had happened.

He laughed with me. "That guy thought he'd grabbed hold of a wildcat, for sure. You weren't going to give up that bag if he dragged you all the way to Glenbrook."

"And you were knocking him about like a punching bag." I couldn't keep the admiration out of my tone.

He sobered. "When I saw the guy roughing you up, I was afraid I wouldn't get there in time. I don't usually wear my gun, but sometimes a man needs one in these parts. I should have known you'd give him a fight." He studied me as if trying to reach into my mind and draw something out. "I don't understand you, Annie McKenzie."

I drew my hand away. "What is there to understand?" My guard went up. The warmth that had arched between us was gone, leaving an empty chill in its place. This was the man who had conspired with Erskine to get my aunt's land. He had used me, and if I didn't watch out, he would have my emotions in such a tangle, I would begin to trust him.

His eyes held mine with a piercing intensity. "Sometimes, there's a hardness in your glare that could kill. Like right now. Angry. Haunted. Guarded." He leaned toward me. "What have I said that warranted sending daggers into my heart, Annie?"

I wanted to launch a volley of accusations at him, but Davie's safety depended upon my silence. One word in the wrong place and Erskine could reap his anger upon my helpless brother. "My name is Anna," I said stiffly. Lifting the cup of tea, I kept my eyes away from his face.

"You could call me Lyle," he said in a teasing tone. "That might make us friends."

"Friends?" I looked at him then. "No, I don't think so. Your ambitions won't end with the property you have just acquired from Aunt Minna. I suspect that you already have your eye on more of her land. Am I right?"

He leaned back in his chair. "Is it so wrong to acquire property at a fair price from someone who wants to sell?"

"Wants to sell? Or is forced to sell?"

"You're the one who signed the papers," he reminded me. "You could have refused."

Did he really believe that? I couldn't tell.

"In any case, I don't think friendship is the correct term. We will never be friends, Mr. Delany."

"Don't be too sure, Annie." He gave me a slow smile. "I have a feeling that our association is just beginning."

Was there a promise or a threat in his words?

Meg bustled back into the room. "Well, now I suspect you'd like to freshen up a bit," she said to me.

"She'll need a room for the night," Delany said,

standing up.

"Of course." She raised a speculative eyebrow. "I could put you up, too?"

"Thanks, but I'm already registered at the Timberline." He turned to me. "Well, I leave you in good hands. Maybe I'll drop by in the morning before you leave."

"There's no need," I responded, hoping that my response was neutral, hiding a foolish impulse to be grateful that I was going to see him again.

"Good night, Annie. Sleep well." Before I knew what he was doing, he bent over and laid a kiss on my forehead.

I must have turned all shades of crimson. My feelings were in such a muddle I couldn't sort them out.

Meg eyed me after he left. "Ain't that Lyle Delany something else?" There was an avaricious gleam in her eye, like that of a gossip about to enjoy a delicious morsel. "You two seemed to be sparking pretty good, you know what I mean. Holding hands and all. I'd say that cupid rascal has let go an arrow or two in this direction." She beamed the way people do when they see a courting couple. "Lyle's sweet on you, that's for sure."

"No, he's not," I said much too quickly.

Meg laughed. "I've known Lyle nigh on to six years now, and I've never seen him hover over anyone the way he does you."

"I imagine that he's spread his attentions around," I said primly, remembering how the women in town eyed him—and me.

"Oh, he's not been one to spend cold winter nights alone, that's for sure, but he's never lost his heart to anyone." She winked at me. "But he's taken with you."

"Not with me—with my aunt's property," I retorted before I could think.

Something in my tone raised Meg's eyebrow. She started to say something more and then stopped. "Well, it isn't any of my business, that's for certain. Come along and I'll show you your room."

She led the way upstairs. The bedroom Meg gave me was at the front of the house on the second floor, overlooking the lake. A clean, sweet-smelling room was furnished with a deep featherbed, hooked rug, solid oak dresser, wardrobe, and a high-backed rocking chair by the window. After a quick bath down the hall in a tub filled with hot, soapy water, I put on my flannel gown and faded robe and sat down in the rocker. Meg had promised to bring me up a tray after her boarders were fed, and I thanked her for realizing that I wasn't up to any socializing.

My head ached, and there was an ugly bump above my ear where the robber had hit me. An ugly burn around my wrist had been caused by the deadly grip I had kept on the leather strap when he had tried to jerk the bag away from me. I had a bruise on my side where he had kicked me. Thank God, I had saved the money. Returning to Blackbriar Bay without it would have caused Erskine to explode with the fury of a maniac. I trembled just thinking about it. I had paid Meg out of the bag and then hidden it behind the wardrobe. I didn't think the robber would try again. Lyle was probably right about what had happened. Thank heavens, Lyle had followed me down the hill. Lyle? When had I started to think of him as Lyle and not Mr. Delany?

The memory of his protective arms around me and the hot thrill of feeling his lips touching my forehead brought a new rush of heat through me. Downstairs in the kitchen, I had foolishly reacted to his touch and had almost forgotten that his interest in me arose out of the desire to own Aunt Minna's land—certainly not from any sincere interest in me.

He had gone back to the Timberline, where he was well known. The clerk had made that clear. More than one woman had shared his room, I was certain of that. He was a man to get what he wanted, one way or another.

A firm knock at the door jerked my thoughts away from the commanding Lyle Delany.

Meg bustled in with a tray perched on one ample hip, a ready smile on her lips. "Here you be. My, my, you look different with your face clean." She chuckled. "I declare, the two of you were a sight, all right." She handed me the tray. "Mind if I sit down a spell?" Without waiting for my nod, she plopped down on the edge of the bed. "Whee, my feet are the size of gunboats at the end of the day." She raised a quizzical eye. "So you're Minna Brown's niece?" Her tone was an invitation to chat. "Didn't know she had any relatives. None of them ever showed their faces around here before. I bet she's glad for the company." She eyed me with open curiosity. "You don't have any more family?"

Briefly, I told her about my father's recent death that left Davie and me homeless. "You know Aunt Minna?" I asked, deciding to use the landlady's curiosity to answer some questions of my own.

"I wouldn't say 'know' is the right word. If you mean am I a friend of hers, the answer is no. She and her husband, Horace, used to come into town now and again when he was alive. She was a pretty thing, with her hair the color of yours and a pleasing, quiet way about her. I never thought she looked happy, though. Her husband was old enough to be her father, and he treated her like a child. After he died, I heard she went a little off her rocker. And got old."

"Her hair's gray now," I said. I almost added that she had turned to drink, but caught myself in time. "She's . . . ill."

"Too bad. That man Erskine was the only one she'd allow at Blackbriar House and he ran everybody off. I guess you get along with him all right?"

I thought about Davie and fought an urge to tell her everything that was going on at Blackbriar. Instead, I said, "He seems to be in charge."

She nodded. "I guess you'll be changing all that. I heard that the judge had you sign some papers so you can take care of her affairs. I bet Erskine didn't like that."

"As a matter of fact, he arranged it."

"He did? That's surprising, ain't it? I mean, why would he want you to take over?" She shook her head. "There's no understanding men, is there?"

I pretended to concentrate on the delicious slice of roast beef I had lifted to my mouth. Apparently Meg was not a woman who could stand a conversational vacuum. She chatted about meeting Lyle and his father about ten years earlier in the small town of Truckee, about fifteen miles north of the lake. "It was a booming place for a while. Rumors about strikes as big as the Comstock brought prospectors pouring in. Never did turn out to be a bonanza, but Lyle's father set up a trading post and cleaned up. After the rush, a lot of people like my folks and the Delanys migrated down to Tahoe City. Lyle went into the lumber business after his pa died. Done quite well for himself, too. He's a businessman, that one. Going to be rich someday." She winked at me. "He knows how to go after what he wants."

"Yes, doesn't he," I echoed dryly. The first time I met Lyle Delany he told me he wanted to buy the land Aunt Minna owned at the southern tip of the lake—and now he had it. Unless I could get Davie and myself out of the situation, there was nothing I could do to prevent him from getting all my aunt's property. Erskine got the money, Delany got the land, and when there was nothing more to sell—then what?

I must have blanched, for Meg said anxiously, "You look peaked. Are you sure you're not hurt? Lyle said that varmint treated you rough."

"I'm all right. Just a tender spot on my head."

"All kind of riffraff preying on innocent people nowadays. Don't know what the world's coming to." She sighed. "Sometimes I think the human race will never amount to much. Well, I guess I'd best be getting back to the kitchen. I've got a girl helping me, but she needs a lot of watching. Sure you don't want to eat any more?" she asked as I held the tray out to her.

"No, thank you. It was very good. I appreciate your bringing the tray up to me."

"No trouble. I enjoyed our little chat." Then she laughed. "Kinda close mouthed, aren't you?"

"I . . . I don't have much to talk about."

"Don't you? Wanna bet?" I heard her chuckling as she made her way down the stairs.

The next morning, I retrieved the money bag from its hiding place and took out enough for my return fare on the *Tahoe Queen*. Then I pinned the money bag to the waist of my petticoat. I had learned my lesson: I wasn't going to leave the bag in plain sight. I brushed off my grown, braided my hair into a coil at the nape of my neck, and lamented the loss of the bonnet that Mrs. Greenberry had given me. For a foolish moment I thought about taking a couple of dollars from the bag and buying another one, but the memory of Erskine's glowering instructions soon quelled that idea. No, I didn't dare spend any of the money. An urgency to get back to Blackbriar, give Erskine the money, and rescue Davie from his clutches was like a spring tightening within my chest, making my movements quick, my steps hurried.

Meg was already setting out breakfast when I went downstairs. "Sleep well?" she asked me as she made a place for me at the dining room table.

"Yes," I lied. The truth was that I had lain awake in the dark most of the night, making and discarding plans. I had finally come up with one that seemed to hold the least threat of failure. I looked at the idea from every angle and decided I had no choice but to try the plan as soon as possible. Satisfied, I had turned on my side and finally fallen asleep.

Meg introduced me to the other boarders who came down to breakfast, but I didn't enter into any of their conversation. An older woman and her husband were busy talking about a lame horse that had kept them in Tahoe City longer than they'd planned. A young couple talked in quiet tones, and a couple of men exchanged views about the way railroads were cheating everybody out of their land. Everyone ate quickly and left the table loaded with dirty plates and empty platters.

I had just finished my sausage and biscuits when I heard Lyle's voice in the kitchen. His deep laughter floated into the dining room. My hand suddenly trembled, and I quickly laid down my fork. A reaction that bordered on pleasure was quickly routed as I took myself in hand. I had told him there was no need for him to come by in the morning. I could manage quite well on my own.

"Mind if I join you?" he asked, sliding into an empty chair beside me.

"I've just finished," I said, touching a napkin to my lips.

"Then have another cup of coffee. Did you sleep well?"

"Yes," I lied a second time. "And you?" My eyes traveled over his tanned face, smooth and smelling of a shaving tonic. His hair glistened with a recent washing and drifted forward on his forehead. He wore a blue cambric shirt that deepened the blue of his eyes, and fawn-colored jacket and pants that hugged his firm, hard body.

"Well, what do you think?" he grinned at me, raising one of his tawny eyebrows. "Do I pass inspection?"

Heat swept up into my face. "An improvement over last night," I said crisply, trying not to return his smile but failing.

"I might say the same."

We both laughed then and the air was cleared. He ate his breakfast with a young boy's enthusiasm, and I was intrigued with the way a half-dozen flapjacks and as many biscuits disappeared.

"Have to keep up my strength," he quipped, seeing my astonishment. "Never know when I might get in a fight."

I chuckled and then sobered. "Thank you again for coming to my rescue."

"That's my specialty—rescuing damsels in distress. Call on me anytime."

If only I could. If I had not seen him with Erskine, or if he had not been the buyer of my aunt's property, I might

183

have succumbed to his charming smile and the warmth of his gaze. But I dared not trust him. If my judgment was wrong, Davie could suffer for it. "I'd better go, I don't want to miss the steamer. I'm anxious to get back to my brother. I've never been away from him this long." Accusation was in my tone. "I wouldn't have come if I had had any choice."

"The judge insisted that the papers be signed in his office . . . I don't know why," Lyle said.

He lied. Without the danger of Davie being held as hostage, I could have refused to go through with the sale. I suspected that the three men were in it together, Erskine, the judge, and Lyle Delany. The knowledge made me sick to my stomach.

I said very little as we walked down to the wharf. I had my money ready, but before I could hand it to the same grizzled-face little man, Lyle handed him a ten-dollar bill. "Two tickets . . . one for Glenbrook . . . one for Black-briar Bay."

My face must have registered surprise, for he laughed. "I have business in Glenbrook. I hope you don't object to my company for part of your journey."

I didn't know whether I should voice any objections or not, since they didn't seem to matter. With a firm guiding hand on my elbow, he ushered me up the gangplank and into the long cabin, choosing the same bench that we had occupied before.

"Just like old times," he quipped, his eyes twinkling at me. "Only today you're even prettier without that ugly bonnet covering up your wildfire hair."

I instinctively touched a hand to the weighty twist on my neck and firmed the pins holding it.

"I like it better hanging on your shoulders . . . the way

it was last night." His tone softened. "I didn't know how feminine you were until I held you close . . . without any starch in that lithe body of yours."

The memory of me clinging to him brought a rush of embarrassment. "I was frightened . . ." I said by way of an apology for my lack of self-restraint. "I apologize for my forward behavior."

The grin that curved his lips made matters worse. "Don't expect me to apologize for mine." I knew he must be remembering the kisses he had placed on my forehead and the way I had pressed against him.

I was relieved to see Randy standing in the doorway. I flashed him a smile and waved, secretly pleased when I felt Lyle stiffening at my side.

"A friend of yours, I gather," he said.

Randy's smile wavered when he saw who my companion was. Dislike registered on his face. He gave me a returning wave and then disappeared on deck. I felt let down. I needed Randy to help me with the plan I had worked out.

"What's the matter, Annie?" demanded Lyle, seeing my disappointed expression. "Surely you don't have amorous feelings for a gawky guy like Randy Bowles. He'll never get more than two dollars together."

"Money isn't everything," I snapped. "Trust counts for much more. And integrity. And many other things that you wouldn't know about. He's a better man than you'll ever be."

"Really?"

A chilled edge to his tone should have warned me, but like the spillwater over a dam, I couldn't stop. "All you care about is getting your hands on more land. You don't care how."

"I bought your aunt's land for a reasonable price. I didn't steal it."

"There are different ways of stealing." I bit my lip to keep the tears from spilling. I knew that in another minute, I would endanger Davie's life by screaming accusations at Lyle.

"Are you calling me a thief?"

I swallowed back my anger. "No. The term is too mild for men like you and Erskine. You don't have to pretend to be the good guy, watching over me, seeing that I deliver the money as promised."

He surprised me with a bitter laugh. "If anyone's a thief, my dear, it's you. In a few weeks' time you managed to get control of your aunt's property, and trying to pretend you are the injured party is very amusing."

I raised my hand to slap him, but he caught my wrist. "The first slap was free . . . the next one will cost you," he warned.

Furious at him and at myself, I jerked away and swept out of the cabin with as much dignity as I could manage. I found a private corner half-hidden by stacked kegs and crates and stood at the railing, trying to get control of my rampaging emotions.

The suave Lyle Delany had my feelings on a seesaw. One minute I was ready to throw myself into his arms, the next I wanted to slap his conceited face. What was the matter with me? Why couldn't I detach myself from emotions that befuddled my thinking? My thoughts were still thrashing about a few minutes later when the *Tahoe Queen* pulled into a small logging settlement. A few men boarded the steamer while the crew rushed to load cords of wood.

I was grateful for a cool breeze that bathed my heated

face. Without a bonnet, I knew my nose would peel and the freckles across my nose would dance brightly from sunburn. At the moment, I didn't care. My appearance was the last of my concerns at the moment.

"Well, lookee who's here!" A slurred voice from one of the arriving passengers swung me around.

I felt as if someone had punched me in the stomach. "You—!"

"Yeah. Me." Zeke's yellowed grin and foul breath assaulted me. "I knew I'd run into you at one time or another. We have a little score to settle, you and me."

I tried to move past him, but he blocked my way and grabbed me. His fingers bit deeply into the soft flesh of my arms.

"No, you're not going anywhere, bitch. Not till you pay up." He shoved me back against the railing. "Know what I mean, sweetheart?"

"Let me go," I gasped, jerking my head to one side to avoid his foul mouth. He clamped his hand on my jaw and shoved my head back so that I couldn't move it. I thought my neck would break from the pressure he put on it.

"Now, let's have a kiss, bitch. A nice—" He let me go with such force that I didn't know what had happened.

Zeke gave a gurgling sound, and I saw that Lyle had caught him around the neck with his arm and had jerked him back. Zeke's face turned red as he tried to get free of the hold Lyle had on his neck. He gasped for breath and tried to remove Lyle's arm, which was a like a vise shutting off his air. Zeke's eyes grew white in his head as Lyle brought him to his knees.

"Don't kill him," I cried when Lyle didn't loosen the deadly strangle. Zeke's limp body and Lyle's expression frightened me. "Let him go. Let him go!" I shrieked.

Lyle removed his arm and Zeke slumped to the floor. He gasped for air and touched his hand to his throat. Then he raised murderous eyes to Lyle and started to his feet. Before he got his balance, Lyle grabbed him and lifted him up against the railing, and then, with one quick shove, he sent him tumbling over the side.

A loud splash sent water spraying high into the air. I looked down and saw Zeke disappear, and it was a horrifying long moment before he came splashing back to the surface. He struck out swimming as if a shark were after him. Fortunately, the steamer was still close enough to the shore for him to reach land safely.

"Are you all right?" Lyle asked me. The hot strength of him radiated through me as he touched my arm.

"I . . . I think so." I wanted to lean into his virile body, lay my head against his chest, and fold his strength around me. Stiff pride made me subdue such feminine weakness. I wouldn't let him know how devastating Zeke's attack upon me had been. I knew that if I trembled, he would put his arms around me—and I couldn't take that. Not again! Not when I feared that he had already manipulated me toward his own ends. And yet if he had reached for me, I doubted that I could have kept my composure. Fortunately, he gave me the moment that I needed to calm myself. "Thanks for your help. I'm not sure I could have handled him by myself," I said evenly.

"Another friend of yours?"

"He was on the stage from Rocky Gulch. He made my life miserable the whole trip. Forced himself upon me at every stop. Zeke Stone is his name. I'd hoped I'd seen the last of him." I raised my chin. "I bloodied his nose just before I left Glenbrook."

188

He chuckled. "I might have known. Well, you certainly keep a protector of damsels busy. I'd better keep myself in condition if I'm going to be around you very much." He offered his arm. "What do you say we go back inside and have some coffee?"

We had reached stairs leading to the wheelhouse when Randy came barreling down, taking two steps at a time. "Did you see some fellow fall overboard?"

Lyle shook his head solemnly. "No."

"There's someone swimming away from the boat toward shore," Randy insisted.

Lyle smiled innocently. "Maybe he forgot something."

Chapter Thirteen

The steamer chugged along the Nevada side of the lake, passing Carnelian Bay and Sand Harbor, and stopping at small lumber camps to leave and collect mail and passengers. I must confess that the journey to Glenbrook passed very quickly. I was grateful for Lyle's company as the cabin filled with more rough-looking men at every stop. My encounter with Zeke had shaken me more than I cared to admit. I wondered if some of the men worked as loggers for the Delany Lumber Company. Several tipped their hats to Lyle as if he might be their boss. Once more I felt a host of curious eyes upon me, and I felt terribly on display. Randy continued to glare as if he thought I might be needing his protection at any moment. Having two men looking out for me made me feel good, and I found myself laughing easily as Lyle entertained me with Indian legends.

"Indians living around the lake believed that the Great Spirit created it as the bottom half of the sky. An inverted bowl. They called it Lake of the Sky." An apt description, I thought, looking down into the lake and seeing the blue

191

of the sky and white clouds floating across it.

"They believed that the Great Spirit filled the woods with animals so that every living creature could live in harmony: grizzly bears, mountain lions, and the eagles and the deer. He told the Indians to eat fish and berries and be happy. The legend says they were, until an unhappy brave invented the bow and arrow and began killing animals and Indians of other tribes."

"Paradise lost." I nodded, saddened that mankind had not been satisfied with the bounty which the beautiful lake offered. "Man is never satisfied," I said, thinking aloud.

"And therein lies progress," he countered. "On the whole, life is better because of man's discontent."

"I wonder."

"Dissatisfaction is not always bad."

"Unless it's another name for greed."

"Perhaps the two go hand-in-hand," he proposed, and then a smile tugged at the corner of his lips. "Let's change the subject or we'll be fighting again."

I couldn't help but chuckle at the way he put out his hands in a gesture of surrender. He had the power to disarm me to the point where I almost let down my guard.

"Oh, I nearly forgot," he said, drawing a small package out of the inside of his jacket. He handed it to me.

"What is it?"

"A pamphlet. Remember I said that I'd try to get some material from Gallaudet College? I was hoping they'd send some books, but maybe this will help."

I eagerly broke the string and loosened the wrappings around a small booklet, *Talking with the Deaf.* My eyes fastened eagerly on the pages as I quickly turned through them. Sketches! Hand signs! Depicting everything from single letters to whole phrases. Everything had been organized into learning patterns, giving me a wealth of new information. Such joy rushed through me that my eyes welled up with tears. "Oh, thank you . . . you don't know how much this means to me."

My reaction obviously embarrassed him. "It's nothing . . . really . . ."

"It's everything. If I can teach Davie letters . . . he can read and write. Don't you see? I can open up a whole new world to him."

His voice was suddenly husky. "How lucky Davie is . . . to have someone like you pouring out such love to him."

"He means everything to me."

"Yes . . . I know." The way he said it made me stiffen. Had he been the one to suggest Davie as hostage?

The steamer's shrill whistle put an end to the poignant moment. Lyle rose to leave. "You'll be all right?"

"Of course."

He lowered his voice. "I'm glad you have the money bag in a safe place. When I had my arm around your waist, I felt it."

The blunt statement brought warmth into my cheeks. How crude he was to admit his hands had discerned my hiding place. I realized then he was as eager as I was for me to get the money safely to Erskine. I would have given anything to fool them both and head for Sacramento with the money bag. But of course there was Davie. I had to content myself with a crisp, "Thank you for rescuing me . . . twice."

"I'll make certain I see you on my next visit to

Blackbriar Bay," he promised.

"You'll be coming back . . . for more land, I suppose," I answered testily.

"No. I'm only interested in acquiring lakefront property at the southern tip of the lake. Except for Blackbriar, the rest of your aunt's property extends up Chimney Canyon, rocky and barren land—not suitable for much of anything right at the moment."

"You mean you bought the only good piece of property that she has?"

"The only one . . . besides Blackbriar which, of course, includes the bay and island, making it very valuable." He raised an eyebrow. "But I'm sure you know all that. You wouldn't have any trouble finding a buyer for it."

My heart sank. Was Blackbriar next on Erskine's list? He wouldn't hesitate to strip my aunt of everything. "It's a prize property," said Lyle watching my face.

My instant anger thickened the air between us. I didn't know whether he was accusing me of intending to sell my aunt's home, or was warning me that he intended to buy it. "Good day, Mr. Delany."

"Sometimes your eyes snap as hotly as the flaming color of your hair, Annie. By the way, I think your nose is sunburned. Tsk, tsk. Are those freckles I see?"

I launched a dagger look that should have withered him, but he only gave an infuriating chuckle and bid me goodbye. He left the boat. I watched him through a window as he moved in a graceful, masculine stride away from the dock. Under the edges of his hat, blond hair fell in casual waves to the collar of his leather jacket, and I remembered how it had tumbled on his forehead after the fight. He was a paradox: protective, caring, and often tender, and yet unscrupulous, and hard as steel. I watched his commanding, arrogant figure stride across the street as if he owned every inch of it. When he disappeared into a nearby store, the world seemed smaller. Such foolishness, I chided myself, fighting a feeling of abandonment. He must have protected me because he wanted to make certain that nothing happened to cancel the deal he had made with Erskine. Nothing more. Being charming was a part of his nature. I imagined that a good many women had thought themselves special in his eyes when, in truth, his attentions were selfishly motivated. I knew all of this, but it didn't help.

I sat there waiting for the steamer to continue its trip around the lake and a deep emptiness settled upon me. I doubted that I would ever see Lyle Delany again. He had the land he wanted and would have no further cause to use me for his own gain. Good, I lectured myself . . . I had more important things to think about.

Randy came by and told me that the *Tahoe Queen* remained at Glenbrook for nearly forty minutes while cargo was unloaded and loaded. "You could go ashore and stretch your legs a bit," he suggested.

Forty minutes was long enough to walk to the Greenberry cabin and say hello, but I didn't want to leave the steamer. The dangers of walking alone with so much money on me kept me in the cabin waiting for the steamer to continue its journey around the lake.

Now that Delany was gone, Randy was his friendly self again. "Did you have a good stay in Tahoe City?" he asked. "Did you get a room at the Timberline?"

"No. I stayed at the Lake House. The Timberline didn't seem right for a single woman."

"Really? Gosh, I'm sorry. People are always talking about it and I thought . . ."

"It's all right. No harm done." I wasn't going to make him feel more guilty by telling him about the attack on me. "Meg Mallory has a very nice boardinghouse on the lake. Everything worked out well." I was surprised at how even my voice was. "Now I'm eager to get back to Blackbriar." My stomach tightened. *Davie . . . Davie . . . please be all right. . . .*

"After we leave Glenbrook, we'll be heading around the lake to the California side, and you'll soon be home again."

Home? The word was like a nettle stuck in my throat. *Prison* was more like it.

"What's the matter?" Randy asked. "You look frightened. Isn't your aunt good to you? Everybody says she's kind of batty."

"She drinks."

"No wonder she can't keep a housekeeper. I'm surprised Erskine puts up with it. It can't be easy working for somebody like that. I know . . . my father was a drunkard. I was glad to get away, I'll tell you. But he's dead now, and my mother needs my help. As soon as I've saved a little bit more, I'll be going home. Almost got enough." He smiled happily. "Won't be long now."

"I'm glad for you."

He shook his head. "Can't be very pleasant for you and your brother. Too bad you don't have someplace else to go."

Getting away was the hurdle I had to face first.

"Randy, if I arranged for Davie to get aboard the *Tahoe Queen*, would you see to it that he got to Meg Mallory's safely?"

He looked puzzled. "Sure. Be glad to, but—"

"Don't ask me anything more. If you could somehow arrange for the *Tahoe Queen* to stop at Blackbriar Bay in three or four days, I'll try to have Davie ready to board."

"All right." He smiled. "Don't worry. I'll take care of the kid."

"Thank you."

The steamer blew a warning whistle. A few last passengers scurried aboard before the engines started thumping and the boat moved out into the lake, leaving Glenbrook behind.

"Well, I've got to check some bills of lading before we get back to Tahoe City." As Randy hurried away, I was surprised to see the grumpy man who took tickets coming toward me.

I smiled at him, uncertain why he was glaring at me. What had I done now? Lyle had bought my ticket. Was there something wrong?

"You're Annie McKenzie?"

"Anna McKenzie," I corrected him.

"Close enough. This was sent aboard for you," he said in a grouchy tone that told me he didn't appreciate being used as an errand boy.

"There must be some mistake . . ." I began.

"No mistake." He thrust a hat box into my hands. I opened the lid and lifted out a lovely blue velvet hat. A brim that dipped over one eye and was decorated with velvet flowers and a wide ribbon bow in the back. I had never seen anything so lovely. There wasn't a card, but I knew who it was from.

The old man shuffled off, and I felt curious eyes on me and on the fashionable hat I held in my hands. For a moment I couldn't get control of the emotions that surged through me. I wanted to feel indifference, perhaps anger, or at the very least, indignation. Instead, I entertained a warm feeling that defied interpretation. Lyle had left the boat and bought me a hat to replace the bonnet that had been ruined in the fight. The gesture had probably meant little to him, but to someone who had never in her life received such a gift, it caused utter confusion. I'd never owned a real lady's hat. Mrs. Greenberry's cast-off bonnet had been luxurious compared to my faded calico sunbonnets. I fingered the soft velvet, touched the exquisite flowers, stroked the satin ribbon that would hang jauntily down the back of my head.

I felt utterly foolish as I put the hat on my head, tipping the brim over one eye, and shoving the matching hatpin through my thick hair to hold it. A perfectly ridiculous thing for someone like me to be wearing.

Much to my surprise, my eyes were misty. Don't be a ninny, I scolded myself. It's a woman's hat—nothing more. I took myself in hand. Lyle Delany would find that it took more than a fussy hat to change my opinion of him and his assocation with Erskine.

As the steamer chugged around the lake, a mounting uneasiness grew within me. My thoughts fled ahead of the steamer. I left the cabin to pace the deck nervously. Surely Davie would be all right. Erskine wouldn't want to lose the hold he had over me. Anger mingled with anxiety, and I was almost beside myself with worry when we finally entered Blackbriar Bay and passed the small rocky island rising in the middle of it.

My eyes anxiously scanned the weathered pier. The old rowboat and Erskine's skiff were there, but an eerie deserted gloom surrounded the dock and the ugly unpainted house. Thick stands of pine trees sent dark shadows against the roof and walls. Clean panes of glass from my window-washing efforts reflected the afternoon sunlight like unseeing eyes. An evil miasma hovered in the air. I felt a sinister foreboding that was almost palpable. When Randy lowered the rope ladder I scrambled down it as if another moment's delay would put Davie in mortal danger.

I scarcely heard Randy's parting promise to see me in three days' time, my mind was so filled with concern over my little brother. Lifting my skirts, I raced toward the house. Breathless, I bounded through the front door, and immediately Erskine loomed up in front of me in the small hall.

"So yer back!" His bloodshot eyes swept over my new hat. "Spending me money, were ye?" He gave me such a violent shove backward that I almost lost my balance.

"No," I gasped, "Delany bought it for me."

"Oh, he did," he smirked. "Gave him a good night's tumble for it, did ye?"

I wanted to dig my nails across his face. He laughed at my fury. "Give me the money."

I swallowed to put some moisture in my mouth. "Not until I've seen Davie."

He shoved a drunken leer into my face. "And who be ye to be making conditions? If I'm a mind to, I'll snap yer neck with one hand—"

"But you won't!" I said defiantly, amazed that my voice hid the trembling inside. "You *need* me. Don't you think that I'm not onto your little scheme to steal everything Aunt Minna owns."

"Ye'll do as I say—"

"Only if Davie is unharmed. If he's all right, you'll get your money. If not—!"

"The idiot's well enough," he growled. "I'll give ye five minutes to give me the money. If ye try to trick me, I'll see ye both at the bottom of the lake."

"Where is he?"

He gave a jerk of his head toward the stairs. "Go see for yerself." His drunken laughter followed me as I bounded up the stairs two at a time. The attic room door was open—and the room was empty.

Don't panic, I counseled myself. Erskine was just playing games. I stamped on the floor. *Davie.* His name choked in my throat, and I knew it was a waste of breath to call him, but I couldn't help myself. "Davie!" In response, a high-pitched bark reached my ears. Rags!

"Rags, where are you? Here, boy!" I couldn't pinpoint the direction of the puppy's bark. Close by, I thought as I went out of the attic room, which was the only one I knew about on the third level.

"Rags!"

The muffled bark was close. But where? Frustration spilled hotly through me. There had to be another room. In the crazy labyrinth of added halls and rooms, I didn't know where to start. I went back down the steep steps leading to the attic room and then stopped when I reached a sharp turn.

The landing was scarcely more than two feet wide, but

200

as I stood there, my head cocked for listening, I was positive that I heard the puppy's bark coming from the wall. A doorknob that I had never noticed betrayed a half-sized door. I opened it like a cupboard. I poked my head through it and saw a ladder that led up to a trap door.

"Davie! Rags!" I crawled through the narrow opening and climbed up the ladder. The dog's whimpering bark came through the cracks of the small trapdoor, and when I shoved it upward, Rags licked my face with smothering, moist enthusiasm.

I saw Davie then, curled in the army blanket, sound asleep. "Thank God," I breathed. A slanted roof made standing up impossible, and I realized that Erskine had put my brother in the cupola that had the weathervane mounted on it. The space was empty except for some old newspapers which Davie had used to make firemen hats and paper boats. Unable to hear the dog's barking, he was still asleep.

I gently touched him, giving him a big smile as he opened his eyes. As if he were not surprised at all that I had come back, he sat up, smiling. The puppy bounded all over us, tugging and nipping while we hugged each other. *He was all right.* The short confinement apparently had not destroyed his usual complaisant, trusting nature. As if he knew I wouldn't let anything happen to him, he had spent the time making paper hats and boats and playing with Rags.

He looked at my hat, grinned and made a sign, "Pretty."

I laughed and blinked rapidly to keep tears of relief from spilling out the corners of my eyes. We climbed down the ladder and went to our attic room. I took off my hat and removed the money bag from the waist of my petticoat. With Davie's hand in mine we went downstairs to the front room.

"So ye found the little bugger," said Erskine with a laugh.

"You heartless animal—keeping him confined in a little space like that!"

"A good place to keep him out of trouble. He had the mutt to keep him company."

Aunt Minna was sitting in her usual chair, her eyes glazed, and a pitiful frown covered her face. "What do you want?" Her forehead furrowed as if she were trying to remember who I was.

"She's yer niece, you fool!" swore Erskine. "And she's been taking care of business for ye. Haven't ye, honey?" He held out his hand for the leather bag. He drew out several packets of green bills. "How much did ye spend?"

"Just a couple of dollars . . . for my lodging. Delany bought my steamer ticket."

He raised his ugly spiked eyebrows. "Sweet on ye, is he?" Erskine grunted in satisfaction. "Ye signed the papers like the judge wanted? Was there any trouble?"

"It went just as you and Delany planned," I said coldly.

He eyed me with an ugly twist to his lips. "Maybe he got a better deal than he expected."

"I don't know what you're talking about."

His laugh made me feel dirty. "A man doesn't buy presents for a wench unless he's paying for services rendered." He swaggered over to me, a nasty curl to his lips. "Maybe I'll see what he got that was worth a fancy hat."

202

"You'd better keep your hands off me—if you want me to keep signing papers." I glared at him. "I don't think you're stupid enough to ruin your chances of cashing in on the rest of my aunt's holdings."

The avaricious gleam in his eye dissolved the lust that had been there a second before. "I'd have ye if I had a mind to," he warned, "but seeing as how Delany's got a fancy for ye, I'll let him enjoy himself—for a price." Erskine's yellow-toothed laugh turned my stomach. "From now on, no hats, just money, ye hear? And don't try to hold out on me." His eyes held a lewd glint as they swept over me. "I'll have to thank Delany for helping me see I got meself a money-making trollop. Yep, I was blind. That fancy hat made me see what a golden goose is nesting under me roof. On some nightly trips over to one of the lumber camps, ye'll give the boys some of yer fiery pleasure—and I'll rake in a few silver dollars."

"Over my dead body," I growled.

He laughed. His eyes slid to Davie staying close at my side. "I wouldn't be talking of dead bodies if I was ye."

His meaning was clear. My heart twisted as if it were in a vise. Whatever the cost, I had to get Davie into a safe place as soon as possible. He must have seen the calculating glint in my eyes. He shook a threatening finger at me. "Ye'll do as I say or else!"

I grabbed Davie's hand and we retreated to the kitchen. The extent of Erskine's evil overwhelmed me. He would enjoy turning me into a whore as a way of lining his own pockets. Look what he'd done to my aunt! Turned her into a mindless slave lost to the rotgut gin her body craved. I felt helpless and defeated when it came to trying to find a way to wrestle her from his grasp. In spite of everything, a sense of stubborn resolution settled on me. I had to find a way. The photograph of the young girl in my father's watch had laid some kind of charge upon me. The tragedy of her lost love and my father's part in her unhappiness added to my obligation to protect her as much as I could. Now that Erskine could strip her of her property through me, I feared for her life. And yet at times he seemed almost fond of her.

Sometimes in my loneliness I gripped the watch tightly, drawing a mysterious healing from it. The gold casing of the watch felt warm in my hands, and the precious metal seemed to have recuperative powers. Renewed by this link to my father, I vowed that I would save Aunt Minna in spite of herself.

More than once Erskine carried Aunt Minna up to bed when she was in a drunken stupor. At mealtimes, he yelled at me to take her breakfast or supper as if he cared about her. This kind of behavior was at odds with his mean selfishness. Maybe there had been something tender between them in the past. The thought was an unpleasant one. How could my aunt have taken up with the likes of Erskine? He seemed to encourage her drinking, making trips up to the moutain still to get her more bottles of rotgut whiskey. How could Lyle Delany be in league with such a man?

On the night of my return to Blackbriar House, I took the hat from the cupboard and held it in my hands as I sat on the floor in front of the window. The lake was washed in moonlight, gleaming like a shimmering sculpture, and stars twinkled like a million spearpoints on the water's surface.

I slid my fingertips over the soft, silky ribbons and

touched the flower's plush petals. A peculiar warmth filled my heart. Erskine had tried to sully the gift, but he had failed to cheapen it with his crude remarks. A deep need which I didn't understand made me cling to the belief that Delany had bought it for me because he wanted to make me happy. Was it possible that he felt the same kind of bewildering stirrings as I did when we were together? And what should it matter if he did?

My mind wrestled with a frightening suspicion that the deep, hurting pain within me was caused by a horrible truth—I was in love with a man who would willingly be partners with a man like Erskine. Both of them were using me to get what they wanted.

Tears dropped on the velvet hat, and I didn't bother to brush them away.

Chapter Fourteen

Davie was receptive to the flood of new signs which I took from the booklet that Lyle had given me. Instead of changing the ones which we had developed ourselves, I simply expanded them to incorporate new concepts. I added new ones as fast as Davie was able to absorb them. He seemed to think it was some kind of game, not work, and his eyes sparkled as his fingers flew with longer and more involved conversations. His world expanded as names for objects found identification and he glimpsed a relationship between written symbols and the objects themselves. I knew he would make great strides under a trained teacher. Many times I felt frustrated and baffled as I struggled to bridge the gap between concrete objects and abstract concepts. Thank heavens for Davie's placid personality, I thought more than once. Another child might have rebelled against my feeble efforts, but Davie seemed happy with whatever progress we made.

I'd laugh and ruffle his hair, and he'd give me that wonderful sweet smile. There was much I couldn't tell him. I tried to prepare him for my plan to put him on the steamer by himself. I knew that Randy would keep his promise about arranging for the *Tahoe Queen* to stop for Davie as I had asked. Getting my brother away from here seemed the only way to assure his safety. No telling what Erskine might do to him the next time he had him in his clutches.

On the morning of the day I expected the *Tahoe Queen* to stop, I set Davie in front of me and painstakingly tried to communicate to him the plan I had devised for getting him away from Blackbriar House. "The boat will take you to a nice lady. You will stay with her—"

He reached out and stopped my hands. "You, too," he signed.

"Later. You go first."

He shook his head. Not very often did he get a belligerent set to his lips, but this was one of those times.

"You have to go, Davie."

He settled unblinking eyes on me.

I knew that Erskine's explosive anger could settle on him at any moment. I had to get him away. "You must do as I say. You could get hurt if you stay here."

His hands slashed the air. "You, too."

I shook my head. How could I explain to him that Erskine needed me to carry out his thievery? If Davie wasn't at Blackbriar House, I would have a chance to outwit Erskine without endangering my brother's life.

"You must run to the boat when I tell you I hear the whistle. Understand?"

Slowly he nodded.

"Good. I'll keep Erskine's attention on me so you can get away. You must, Davie."

His little chin was set and his mouth was held in a rigid

line. Most of the time he was pliable and easy to handle, but the McKenzie stubbornness ran through his veins. This was one of those rare times that his belligerence threatened to ruin everything I'd planned. "You must get on the boat this afternoon. Promise?" I put a firm hand on his shoulders, looked deep into his eyes. "Promise?"

He finally nodded.

"Good boy." I pressed him against my chest, kissing the top of his tumbled red hair.

He pulled back and pointed to Rags.

"Yes, you can take him."

Some of the rigidity went out of his shoulders, and I knew he would do as I said. I tried not to show my nervousness as we dressed and went downstairs.

All morning my mind raced with myriad nervous "what-if" questions. What if the boat didn't come today . . . or any day? What if Randy hadn't taken me seriously? What if Erskine suspected something and grabbed Davie before he could get to the boat? What if—! My nervousness increased with every passing hour. I burned myself on the stove, spilled coffee grounds, and developed an excruciating headache at the back of my head.

At noon, I set lunch out in the dining room for Erskine and Aunt Minna as usual. Usually my aunt ate very little and was silent during the meal, but today I heard the two of them shouting at each other.

"I don't want her here," my aunt screeched.

"She stays!" I heard Erskine's fist come down on the table. "I told ye, I have plans for her."

"What kind of plans?"

"Ye'll be seeing . . . when I'm ready."

She snorted. "I've been watching you sniffing around her. Makes a body sick, Jem, the way she's made a fool out of you!"

"Nobody makes a fool out of Jem Erskine. Not her. Not ye. Not anybody! Ye got that, woman?"

"There's no privacy with her sneaking around. The way she looks at me makes me want to puke."

"She's a damn sight better as a housekeeper than ye've ever been. And she cooks something besides charred meat. No skin off your back having someone else doing yer work."

"She watches me like a hawk. Hides my bottles, too. Watches every drink I take with that hangdog expression of hers. I don't want her around. Get rid of her and that brat, too . . . or I will."

"The devil ye will, woman! Ye'll do as I say! I need her more than I need ye—and don't ye forget it. If I come back tonight and she's gone, it'll be your hide."

Come back tonight! Erskine was going somewhere! If he left before the *Tahoe Queen* made her afternoon stop, both Davie and I could flee on the steamer!

The next hour was the longest. Erskine finished his lunch and went outside. With every minute, a breathless eternity, I waited to see if Erskine was going to leave in his skiff. In order to keep an eye on the dock, I started cleaning the front of the house, and I sent Davie upstairs to watch out the attic window. Because of the cluster of pine trees hugging the house, I didn't have a clear view of the dock. When Davie came bounding down the stairs and into the front room with a smile on his face, I knew Erskine had left.

"Why is the dummy waving his hands like that?" my aunt demanded. She was wandering around the room restlessly, no bottle in sight. I wondered if Erskine had taken away her ration of whiskey. No matter how many bottles I emptied, there always seemed to be more making their way into the house.

"Davie wants to go for a walk," I said quickly.

Her eyes narrowed. "Hike up the hill and bring me back a bottle."

I wanted to argue with her, try to persuade her to give up swilling whiskey all day and night, but I knew it wouldn't do any good. She already resented my efforts to keep drink from her. Hating myself, I nodded. "Sure. I'll bring you back a bottle."

I scooted upstairs to collect my father's watch and stuff things in my canvas bag. Davie sat on the bed with Rags and watched me. When I had finished, I nervously glanced out the window and gasped a cry of relief. I saw the steamer just entering the bay.

Randy hadn't let me down! The *Tahoe Queen* was going to stop!

I motioned to Davie. He grabbed the pup and we hurried out of the attic room and down the stairs—and then stopped. I couldn't believe my eyes. Aunt Minna blocked our way on the second floor landing. She stood there, pointing Erskine's rifle up at us. "You two ain't going nowhere."

"Aunt Minna, you have to let us go," I pleaded. "You don't want us here. I heard you tell Erskine to get rid of us. Now's your chance. You won't have to put up with us any longer. I know how much you hate us."

"No, you don't," she said.

I felt myself pale under her malevolent glare. The hatred she felt for my father had been transferred to us. We must be a constant reminder of the beloved man she had lost because of my father's interference. He had ruined her life, and she hated us for it. "I'm sorry, Aunt Minna, but Davie and I aren't to blame for your unhappiness."

"I'd as soon see you at the bottom of the lake, but Jem would break my neck if you're not here when he gets back."

"Come with us, Aunt Minna. Get out from under Erskine's control. Live your own life!"

She gave a bitter laugh. "You're as crazy as that brother of yours."

I heard the warning whistle of the steamer. I was desperate. "We're going, Aunt Minna," I said in a firm voice, eliminating the pleading tone I had used before.

I took a step downward.

She raised the rifle. An expression of eagerness crossed her face. *She wants to shoot me!*

Davie read her expression as well as I did. Frantically, he pulled on me, and I backed up the stairs, keeping my eyes on Aunt Minna's face. For a horrifying moment I thought she was going to shoot me even as I retreated step by step. She had a glazed eagerness on her face like a hunter closing in on his prey.

At the top of the stairs, I shoved Davie into the room and shut the door. I heard her diabolical laughter. Then a shot vibrated loudly and a splintered hole broke through the door just above my head. "Next time it'll be your face!" she yelled.

We cowered in the attic room. Then I heard her

retreating steps.

Frantically, I ran to the window. Through a mesh of needled branches brushing against the house, I glimpsed the bow of the steamer and heard another demanding toot of his whistle. It was leaving.

No! No! I waved frantically, praying that Randy might see me high up in the attic window of the house. My prayers went unanswered. The *Tahoe Queen* chugged away from Blackbriar Bay until the boat was nothing more than a speck out on the lake.

Davie tugged on my skirts. His hands slashed the air. "It's all right. Don't be sad. I didn't want to go." He was obviously relieved that he was staying.

I wavered between a smile and sob. How innocent he was. He could accept Aunt Minna shooting at us with his usual placidity. Obviously his joy at not having to leave me outweighed any concerns he had that we had nearly been shot.

I didn't know what time Erskine got back that night; I was too sick at heart to care. The splintered hole in the door was a shocking reminder that my aunt had been ready and eager to shoot my head off. Could she be as evil and mean as Erskine? Had she been emotionally tortured for so long that her brain was as twisted as her caretaker's? My heart ached for the pathetic creature she had become. Even looking at her picture in my father's watch could not soften the memory of her eyes as she'd pointed the gun at me.

Davie's silent world protected him from some of the harshness that went on around him, and he trusted me to keep him safe. I tried to clear my mind of the failed plan and devise another one.

Erskine taunted me the next day with our aborted escape. "Ye thought Auntie would let ye waltz out of here pretty as ye please, didn't ye? Instead, ye almost got yer head shot off." His barrel chest shook with laughter, and his mouth was moist with mirth. "Wish I could have been here to see yer face when Auntie was ready to splatter yer brains."

"You've made her into something as vile as yourself," I snapped. "Poisoning her with drink. Controlling her with threats. Someday she'll turn a gun on you!"

His eyes snapped with amusement. "Will she now? Yer not as bright as I thought ye were. No siree, ye ain't got many brains under that mop of fiery hair. Thinking I'd let ye make a fool of me."

"Why don't you let us go? You got all my aunt's money, and you've sold the lakefront property."

"Ain't finished with ye yet. And when I am . . ." His ugly mouth curved in a smile that chilled the marrow of my bones. "Ye'll be the first to know."

"You'd never get away with it . . . killing us. People would ask questions." Delany might be willing to go along with Erskine to get the property he wanted, but he was not a killer. "I've made friends," I said haughtily.

"And ye don't think I'd be supplying the right answers to yer . . . friends?"

"They're not dumb."

"And ye be thinking that I am?" His black eyes snapped. I knew he was baiting me and enjoying every minute of it. He was beyond any kind of sane reasoning—and I feared my aunt was nearly as demented. Her irrational, drunken behavior defied any hope I had of persuading her to rebel.

"I think you're in league with the devil," I said without flinching under his smoldering gaze.

He grinned as if I'd given him a compliment. "And ye'd do well to go on thinking it."

I tried to stay clear of him and Aunt Minna as much as possible in the days that followed, my mind always sorting and grasping any means of breaking free of the vicious trap that had snapped shut on us.

We needed a boat. It wouldn't do to try and steal Erskine's skiff, I reasoned, as I knew nothing about sailing. I'd capsize the craft if I ever got it away from the shore. A rowboat I could handle. I thought of the old one turned upside down on the dock. Unless the cracks were caulked, it wouldn't float more than a couple of minutes. A raft might be the answer, if we managed to build one. But how would Davie and I propel it through the water? Impossible with the lake as deep as it was. Besides, I had watched Erskine come and go in the skiff. He was an accomplished sailor, and trying to outmaneuver him on the water in any kind of boat would be the height of folly.

There had to be another way—if I could only find it.

Erskine kept gloating over the way my aunt had done his bidding. "She doesn't give a tin plug about ye or the kid. Just as soon shoot yer head off as look at ye." He smirked. "Ye have me to thank for a roof over yer head. About time ye learned to be grateful for me setting ye up pretty. Between the two of us, we can turn a nice piece of cash, partner."

"I'm not your partner. And I want no part of swindling my aunt!"

He laughed and spit tobacco on my nice clean kitchen floor. "A wee bit late for ye to be spouting off like that.

Everything's all legal-like. And yer name's the one that's all over them papers. Yep. Everybody knows who's selling off Minna Brown's property." He winked at me. "Lots of talk going on. Ye've got yourself quite a reputation around here. Course I'm helping it out a bit, telling what a money-hungry wench ye are, coming here and getting control of everything." A deep belly laugh shook his chest. "Yep. Folks around here ain't thinking too kindly of Anna McKenzie, taking advantage of a poor unhappy woman the way ye have."

I set down the skillet I was scrubbing because the urge to bring it down on his hard head was almost overpowering. I knew I would never get the best of Jem Erskine with physical force. Somehow I had to outmaneuver him, but he was as wily as a saw-toothed tiger, and his claws were just as sharp. Spreading lies about me would keep anyone from looking into the truth of the situation. I wondered if Lyle Delany had heard his share of the gossip. I remembered how he had accused me of profiting from my aunt's properties, and that thought made me feel sick. From what Lyle had said, except for Blackbriar House, the rest of Aunt Minna's property was in a rugged canyon, not much good for anything. I doubted that Erskine would arrange a sale for Blackbriar unless someone like Lyle Delany offered him more than his greedy soul could refuse.

That afternoon Davie and I hiked to the highest point of the rocky hills surrounding the bay. The view was spectacular. I could look down at the bay and see the house like a child's toy set in the middle of the trees. The boathouse and chicken coop were miniatures, and the rock sepulchre was a tiny pile of rocks.

216

Davie pointed to a dark spot way out on the lake. He said "boat" with his hands and grinned, pleased that he could share this moment with me. He pointed to high puffs of clouds and quickly made a movement of his hands which I had taught him meant "floating." I had illustrated the sign by floating a piece of wood on water, but Davie's quick mind had made the transfer. I hugged him with delight. He was capable of transferring concepts—a sign of high intelligence. Somehow, someday, I had to give him the chance to educate himself as far as his mind could take him.

From this vantage point high above Blackbriar Bay, I strained to see something besides evergreens stretching away in every direction. The beauty of the untouched wilderness was lost on me. Perhaps someday, roads would lace the boundaries of the lake, but that day had not come. Hiking out of the region with Davie was impossible. Wild animals roamed the hills, and I had found the bloody carcass of a fawn not far from the house where some predator had enjoyed a feast. The distance between isolated camps was too great for an unarmed girl, boy, and a dog. We could perish before we ever reached another place of habitation. I sat down on a rock, a defeated slump to my shoulders.

I felt Davie tugging at my arm. His frown was questioning. I was his anchor, his hold on reality. When I wavered, his world shook. I was ashamed of my weakness. For his sake, I had to keep my self-control and present an optimistic front. We would have to take each crisis as it came. How could I even imagine what evil twists Erskine's mind could take?

"Come on!" I jumped up and forced some bounce into

my steps as we walked along the lake, picking up bits of driftwood and floating them on the water. Davie threw a stick for Rags to fetch. The bottom-heavy pup tumbled and rolled in the dirt, making us laugh with his clumsy and enthusiastic antics. He returned to us with the stick in his mouth like a warrior returning with spoils. Rags was the best thing that could have happened to us. Thank heaven he had stubbornly followed us that first day.

My spirits rose. We returned to the house, strengthened by laughter and a loving closeness. Maybe Erskine would leave us alone until the money ran out.

The hope was folly, as I discovered the very next night, when the vile man came into the kitchen and made me a part of his next diabolical plan.

Chapter Fifteen

I was in the kitchen cleaning up the evening dishes when Erskine came in. My heart started racing, and nervous sweat formed on my palms the way it always did when he was near.

"Send the brat up to bed," he ordered, jerking his head toward Davie, who was sitting at the table eating a leftover biscuit.

I stiffened. "Why?"

"Don't ask questions!" he bellowed. "Do as I say, or I'll throw him up the stairs meself."

Davie darted over to my side, not understanding what Erskine had said, but instinctively reacting to the vehement expression on his face.

I knew that Erskine would carry out his threat, so I led Davie out of the kitchen. "Go to bed," I signed at the bottom of the stairs. "Stay there . . . don't get up. Understand?"

He nodded, but didn't move.

"It's all right. Do as I say." I turned him around and gave him a playful pat, scooting him up the stairs. He looked back once, and I smiled reassuringly. Rags was probably upstairs asleep on the bed already. If they stayed there, they might escape Erskine's wrath. What was happening? *Why does he want Davie out of the way?*

"Get back in here!" yelled Erskine from the kitchen.

"You don't have to shout," I said with as much poise as I could muster when I returned to the room. "What do you want with me?"

He took an old mackintosh off a hook by the back door and threw it at me. "Here! Put it on. This, too." He tossed me a rain hat with a droopy brim.

"Why? Where are we going?"

"Out on the lake. Where in the hell do ye think?"

"Now? At night? What for?"

His twisted smile chilled my blood. Was he going to drown me, as he had threatened? What if I refused to go?

He read my thoughts. "Do as I say, or I'll throw ye over me back like a trussed-up carcass."

Don't panic, I warned myself. "I want to know where we're going," I said in a firm voice, as if I were dealing with someone who might give me a rational answer.

"And I'll be telling ye when I'm ready. Are ye going to put on the coat, or do ye need some help?" He made a threatening movement toward me and I backed up. The thought of his hands on me was enough to make me slip into the voluminous raincoat. I buttoned it up with trembling fingers.

"That's better." He smiled in satisfaction.

What was he going to do with me? I doubted that he would offer me a hat and coat if he were going to toss me overboard. But where were we going? The evil excitement in his eyes brought back the threat he had made about taking me to a lumber camp. Surely he wasn't going to give me over to men like Zeke for their pleasure! What should I do? How could I thwart him? I knew he was capable of unbelievably barbaric treatment. He had destroyed Aunt Minna over the years, and now he was ready to twist me and my life to suit his ugly purposes. If I walked out that door with him, there was no telling what would happen. Maybe I would never come back! Terror must have leaped into my face, for he laughed. "Scared, ain't ye? Not so high-and-mighty now. I'll take ye down a peg or two. Put on the hat. That blazing hair of yers will show up like a beacon in the moonlight. Cover it up!"

With trembling fingers, I shoved wayward strands of hair up under the crown. I pulled the hat down on my head. Was this some kind of disguise? Why did he want me covered up from head to foot?

He growled approval and gave a curt nod toward the door. I hesitated, and he reached out and gave me a shove.

An instinct for self-preservation made me want to call out to Aunt Minna for help, but I knew she would never interfere. It was hopeless. Even if she'd been sober, which she seldom was, she wasn't any match for Erskine. He would knock her around as easily as he did me, and she had already been trained to obey.

There was no one to help me. Whatever happened, I was on my own. He hurried me down the path to the water's edge, and we walked out on the long pier to the end, where the skiff bobbed waiting. I didn't want to get into the frail craft with him. I lurched backward.

"Get in!" he snarled as he grabbed me and shoved me down into the boat. My terror rose to such a peak that I lost all control. With a cry, I lunged at him, catching him off balance. The boat dipped. He went down on his knees.

I leapt forward, then scrambled madly away.

He lunged after me. "You blasted—!"

The next instant, he caught the back of the mackintosh with one of his giant hands. I screamed. Like a fish caught on a line, I writhed and twisted, trying to get away. With a diabolical laugh, he jerked me back. I lashed out. My fingers raked his face. His mirth dissolved in a burst of swearing. "Goddamned wildcat!"

The blow he landed on my jaw brought an explosion of fiery pain behind my ears. Instantly, a wave of weakness engulfed my body. Crumbling like wet paper, I felt my arms and legs lose all rigidity. My head fell to one side on a neck that wasn't strong enough to hold it up as he threw me back in the boat.

A whirling vertigo spun in my head, and my ears rang with the clash of cymbals. I felt the boat get underway. It was several minutes before the punch he'd given me wore off. I stared up at a sky, a gray canopy overhead. Ghostly cloud vapors warned of a night rain, but a million spear-tipped stars stayed in position, firm and reassuring. For a strange moment I was detached and at peace. My mind registered an undulating, rolling movement, but at first my fuzzy brain handled the sensation without recognition and without fear. Then a spurt of memory shattered my detached perspective. Terror leaped like a waiting tiger. Erskine! He was taking me somewhere in his skiff.

I could see Erskine's huge frame silhouetted against the darkening sky. Even though my crumpled position was uncomfortable, I dared not sit up. I feared any movement that would bring his attention upon me. My cheek scraped against the side of the boat as it moved swiftly through the water, and my nose filled with the dank odors of wood and hemp. Spraying water came into

222

the swiftly moving craft and laid a wet chill on my face. I was grateful for the enveloping mackintosh and hat.

My mind raced. None of it made sense. Where was he taking me? He handled the skiff as if it were an extension of himself. Sometimes the boat seemed to rise up out of the water as he deftly turned the sail about to catch the wind. I lay inches from his feet on the floor of the small boat. A wash of despair surged through me. Was he taking me out in the middle of the lake to dump me overboard? And what about Davie? What if I didn't come back? Davie had been making wonderful progress, but he was still dependent upon me to interpret the world for him. After all, he was only eight years old, too young to make it on his own, even without a handicap. Whatever I must suffer at the hands of Erskine, the price would not be too great if it allowed me to keep Davie safe.

The skiff cut through the water with an agility that would have been enjoyable if its rapid motion had not been taking me faster and faster to an unknown destination. Why had Erskine talked about my hair showing up in the moonlight? He had insisted upon the hat and the mackintosh—not because he wanted me to be comfortable, I was certain of that. More likely, he didn't want anyone to see me. Why? If he was going to offer me to a bunch of lumberjacks, my identity would be clear enough. There would be little concern who I was if he turned me over to a bunch of crude, rough men who would lustily use a woman and then toss her aside. Zeke's leering face rose in my mind's eye. How he would delight to have me in his clutches! What if Erskine handed me over to someone like him?

I would have to save myself, somehow. Begging Erskine to change his mind was futile. I knew him well enough by now to realize there was no appealing to his conscience—he didn't have one. And if I didn't cooperate, Erskine would carry out his threats to Davie.

Desperation made killing Erskine seem to be the only answer. *Unless he kills me first.* But he wasn't going to dump me in the lake. At least not right away, I realized on some calm, rational level. By now, we were miles away from Blackbriar, a safe distance for him to safely dispose of me, if that was his intention. No, he wasn't going to throw me overboard just yet. I was certain that he had other plans for me—at least temporarily.

Summoning my courage, I sat up. The lake was luminous in the moonlight. A dark line of trees and mountains stretched along the rim of the lake, and the shoreline seemed to be coming closer and closer. Erskine was going to bring the boat ashore! Where? I couldn't see any lights or recognizable landmarks. He headed straight for a rocky promontory jutting out into the water. But where were we? There was no sign of habitation . . . not a lumber camp or settlement, I was certain of that.

I turned my head in every direction, but I couldn't tell where we were. I remembered that Lyle had said it was easy to be disoriented at any point around the lake because the shoreline all looked the same. Sky, earth, and water blended together in the gloom of night and made me dizzy as my eyes swept over the shadowy landscape. I had no idea how far we had come or in what direction. In contrast, Erskine seemed to know exactly where he was as he maneuvered the skiff to shore.

Relief that the spot seemed uninhabited was diluted by new worries. He hadn't brought me here for any loggers' pleasure, but why *had* he brought me to this deserted spot on the lake? I strained to hear the sounds of human voices. Nothing. Only the high wailing of wind through the crowns of trees broke the night's waiting silence. The rain clouds had thickened, and I felt a soft drizzle on my face.

"Get out!" He ordered harshly. "Any more of yer foolishness and I'll knock yer head three ways to Sunday."

I climbed out, trying to manage the cumbersome coat and my full skirts without letting them touch the water rippling over the edge of white sand. I stumbled a few feet away from the lake's edge. The urge to flee was quickly lost as I viewed the surroundings. Piles of rock rose high against craggy cliffs, and huge boulders formed a point reaching out into the water. There was no sign of human inhabitants in this rugged rock outcropping. The landscape stretched before me, stark and craggy. Why had he brought me to this isolated place? To kill me? That didn't make sense. He could have thrown me overboard into the depths of a lake reputed never to give up its victims.

"Don't just stand there!" he bellowed at me. "Grab some of these bags. We got a long hike ahead of us." He thrust four or five leather bags into my arms. They were so heavy I nearly dropped them. "Blast it all. Hold on to 'em," he swore at me.

I staggered from the weight. Each bag was heavy enough to be filled with rocks. "What's in them?" I demanded. "I can't carry them . . . they're too heavy!"

He suddenly loomed over me. "Ever see a pack mule move under the bite of a whip?" I couldn't believe it when he cracked the air with a snap of a bullwhip he'd stuck in his belt. "Thought ye might be needing a little persuasion. Now move!" He pointed toward a break in the rocky cliff. He picked up twice as many bags with ease.

I staggered forward, expecting to feel the sting of his whip on my back. He laughed as he followed me and then strode ahead of me. "Ye'd better keep up," he shouted back over his shoulder as he led the way up a canyon away from the lake. A light night mist had settled upon the ground and gave a shiny patina to rock walls rising high on both sides. He must have known the terrain well because he never hesitated. Up and down, between rocks and along a small stream, we made our way in the darkness.

Veils of cloud floated like gray specters over the cliffs as we struggled upward. Without the mackintosh, I would have been soaked to the skin from a soft drizzle that made the air thick and moist. Wet earth and slippery rocks made each step uncertain as I climbed over the uneven ground. I slid and stumbled and nearly wrenched my ankle a dozen times. Before we had gone very far up the craggy canyon, my muscles protested with a cramping pain that made me bite my lip with each step.

Erskine kept a good distance ahead of me, calling back from time to time to lash me with a foul tirade. I knew that he would beat me senseless if I threw away my burden and tried to escape from him. He knew the rugged territory; I didn't. I wouldn't have a chance of getting away. The bags grew heavier and pulled on my back and shoulder muscles with every step. The excruciating physical discomfort dominated my thoughts.

He finally stopped and ordered me to wait for him as he went ahead. I slumped down on the ground and smothered a groan as I let the heavy bags drop from my arms. I leaned my head back against a boulder and closed my eyes. At that moment, my only thought was to find relief for my aching body.

The respite was brief. He was back before my breathing had even returned to normal. "All right. Git a move on."

I fumbled with the bags and let one drop. "I can't . . ."

He swore as he picked up the bag. "Move."

I saw that some of his bags were gone. We walked and climbed and hiked in a never-ending nightmare that seemed to go on forever. The pattern never varied. We would stop and he would disappear. When he came back, we would hike some more. The only thing that changed was the number of bags we carried. One by one he took the leather pouches from me. The rain clouds had moved on after a brief shower, leaving behind a wet chill that went bone deep.

Once I almost followed him to see what he was doing with them, but I was too exhausted. Even the nearby howl of some wild animal failed to bring about any excited response. If I had come face to face with some black-eyed bear, I couldn't have run away. I was just too tired.

Just as the first silver wash of dawn warned of the night's end, Erskine took the last bag from me. Then he handed them all back to me—empty. "Let's git moving. I want to be back on the lake before it gets too much lighter."

I didn't know what he had done with the heavy contents of the bags, and I didn't care. The physical torture my body had endured outweighed everything else at this point. Besides, the fact that he had used me as a pack mule seemed insignificant beside the knowledge that I had escaped the ugly fate I had feared.

On our return trip back to the lake, I stumbled and

bruised myself with almost every step along the rocky gulch. Impatient with my clumsiness, Erskine swore, jerked me along, and shoved me down rocky inclines. He treated me callously every step of the way, showing no concern for my pain or the torture inflicted upon my exhausted body. Once he laid his whip across my back and I nearly fainted from the pain.

"Git moving! It'll be light soon."

Fighting back tears, I let anger fuel my exhausted body. When we reached the boat, the horizon was losing its dullness to a luminous dove gray. "We should have been away an hour ago! Blasted weakling!" He swore at me. "Slowing us down to a snail's pace." With a growl, he gave me an angry shove into the boat.

I collapsed without protest as he pushed the boat out into the water, handling the rigging so that we were soon skimming across the lake.

Huddling in the old raincoat, I shivered from exhaustion and the early morning chill. I realized I had lost the hat somewhere along the way. A branch of a thorny bush had jerked it from my head. My hair was hanging wetly on my shoulders, and my arms and face were scratched and bruised.

An unearthly haze like a ghost's breath spread over the lake. The reflection of the skiff in the water was a bony black skeleton. Caught in the throes of exhaustion, I closed my eyes. The next instant I was sailing away with the devil, flying across the water to the portals of hell. In the fiery torment, there was no escape from the grappling hands laid upon me. I felt clothes taken from my body, rough hands biting into my soft flesh.

"No—!" I screeched, flailing with my hands.

"Blast it, wildcat," he swore, quickly moving out of my reach.

I realized with a start that I was sitting in a kitchen chair. He must have carried me up from the boat and was removing the wet mackintosh when my nightmare made me lash out at him.

"Git me some breakfast," he ordered. "All that work gave me an appetite."

I staggered to my feet and walked wearily toward the hall.

"Where ye going?"

"To bed."

"What about me breakfast?"

I didn't even answer him. I groaned with every step as I made my way up to the attic room. Every muscle cramped as I stretched out beside Davie. I ignored Rags' welcoming kisses bathing my face.

I was back, all in one piece. At that moment, everything that had happened seemed like a bad dream. Surely I had not spent the night as a beast of burden. Tomorrow it would all make sense. Tomorrow, when I could think. . . .

Chapter Sixteen

The next two weeks passed in a blur as exhaustion gave way to aches, fever, and weakness. I could barely drag myself around the house as I did my kitchen duties and watched after Davie. We dispensed with his lessons. My head was too heavy to hold up. Except when Erskine had something for me to sign, he came and went without paying me much attention. I was too sick to read the papers he shoved in front of my blurry eyes. "Sign!" he bellowed, thrusting an inked pen into my hands.

I scribbled my wobbly signature without protest. I was too drained physically and emotionally to fight his threatening orders. I didn't know what our midnight excursion had been all about—and I didn't care. My healthy body had betrayed me, and my mental powers ebbed away, along with my physical strength.

Aunt Minna spent her days in various stages of inebriation, and I kept to the attic room as much as possible. I worried about Davie as he spent more and more time away from the house. Despite my orders for him to stay near, I knew that he and his dog were extending their roaming territory. After one of their jaunts, his hands flew as he tried to describe the waterfall and beaver's dam they had seen that day. When I asked how far away they were from the house, he just shrugged. I worried that something would happen to him as he scampered around in his silent world. He would never hear the growl of a wild animal, the roar of a rushing stream, or the approach of someone's footsteps. I knew his love of water and feared he would try swimming in the lake. I always watched him carefully when I let him bounce around in the water at the lake's edge. His deafness added to the risk any small boy faced with playing alone without adult supervision. Because conversation was so limited, Davie had been raised without the usual daily warnings that most normal boys receive. Nagging didn't come easy with signs. Each situation had to be handled as it arose, and I worried that a test would be given first—and the lesson too late.

I awoke from one of my naps to three small trout dangling in front of my face. Davie's face glowed with boyish pride as my nose wrinkled from the fishy smell. Rags bounded about as if he'd had something to do with the catch. I smiled weakly and sent Davie outside to gut the trout for supper.

Sometimes I slept the whole afternoon away, unable to fight off a debilitating lethargy, shivering and sweating in the throes of chills and hot flashes. Even in childhood, I had rarely succumbed to a winter cold. Illness of any kind was a stranger to me. I was frightened as the strange malady took me with revenge. The physical weakness I felt shattered my emotional fiber, and tears flowed down my cheeks without the slightest cause. In my feverish sleep, I was plagued with nettled dreams, sometimes fleeing from a nameless terror, often lost in a labyrinth of tunnels, or poised on the edge of a rocky chasm, waking with a cry as I fell into the vaulting emptiness. Erskine was always in the nightmares, terrifying me, filling my mind with endless torment.

After seven days, the illness ran its course, leaving me weak and bone weary. On the eighth afternoon, I awoke from a nap with loud voices vibrating in my ears. At first I thought I was in the midst of one of those torturing nightmares, but as I sat up, I realized that the voices were not a figment of my imagination. *They were coming from downstairs.*

Erskine's booming roars were mingled with another voice. *Lyle Delany!* He was here—downstairs! Tears of relief flowed into my eyes. I jerked to my feet so suddenly that I had to catch the edge of the washbasin for balance. Without giving a thought to my tangled hair or mussed dress, I stumbled down the stairs, praying that my weak limbs would not give way under me.

The angry exchange was coming from the front room, and I was breathing in short gulps when I reached it. I wavered in the doorway, touching the door frame for support. Erskine and Lyle stood in front of the fireplace, facing each other. Aunt Minna was sitting in her usual chair, a bottle clutched in her hand, her expression one of sloppy amusement as she viewed the angry exchange.

"I know that there's no gold in that canyon. I've been all over that area a hundred times," said Delany angrily.

Erskine shrugged. "Maybe ye didn't know what to look for."

"Hell, there's enough ore samples scattered up and down Chimney Gulch to blind a blind man. And they didn't get there by the grace of God, either."

"What are ye accusing me of?" bellowed Erskine, clenching his fists in a threatening manner.

"You know damn well! The cry of 'Gold' has brought half the miners at the Comstock Lode rushing up here with mules, picks, and shovels. That whole canyon is filled with prospectors, all paying you a fortune for a parcel of land that's utterly worthless."

I must have gasped, for everyone's eyes swung to the doorway. Delany's gaze traveled over my disheveled appearance, and his expression tightened as he looked from me to my aunt. I was horrified by the expression on his face . . . *he thinks I've been drinking like Aunt Minna.*

"Good afternoon, Miss McKenzie," he said, as if we were strangers—as if I'd never had his protective arms around me, as if we'd never spent hours talking together and never shared that bewildering rush of intimacy when he looked at me.

"I . . . I've been sick," I stammered. My legs suddenly felt too wobbly to hold me. I found my way over to the nearest chair and sat down.

"Have another little nip, dearie," smirked Aunt Minna, holding out her bottle. "It'll put some fire back in you."

Erskine's eyes turned wily. He saw the expression on Delany's face. "Tests a man's patience to put up with the likes of them two, Mr. Delany. McKenzie blood runs to drink. Look at 'em. Turns a man's stomach, don't it?"

"Stop it!" I screamed at him. "It's not true." My anguished eyes swung to Lyle. "You have to believe me. I've been sick . . ."

"But not too sick to take part in a scheme to salt Chimney Canyon. You had me fooled. I misjudged you completely," Lyle said.

I fought to put some meaning into his accusation. "Salt—?"

"Don't play the innocent with me." His eyes were as hard as arctic ice. "There's bits of gold ore scattered all over Chimney Canyon. Low-grade ore—but gold nevertheless. And it wasn't there when I was up Chimney Canyon before. Someone salted the ground, someone who has been selling off pieces of worthless land . . . you, Miss McKenzie." It was hard to believe he'd ever called me Annie. There was nothing but hard disdain in his voice and his glare.

I tried to put some indignation in my tone. "You have to believe me!" I protested, reacting to the scorching fury of his gaze. "I had nothing to do with it!"

He laughed at that. "Oh, you didn't? Isn't that interesting? I suppose you were never near the place."

"I—"

"Don't bother denying it!" he snapped. "I found this caught in some brush at the foot of the canyon." He drew something out of his jacket pocket and tossed it to me. "I believe you lost this."

"Tain't hers," said Erskine quickly, his threatening gaze swept my face.

My heart sank like a lead weight. Caught in the ragged brim of the droppy rain hat were several hairs—long ones, deep red and touched with a glint of copper. Mine. I remembered how I had cried out when the hat was jerked off my head by a jagged twig. I had left my calling card as clearly as if it were my name printed in ink. There was no denying that the snaggled red hair belonged to me.

"You were in Chimney Canyon, all right," Lyle said, watching my face.

I couldn't deny it, but it wasn't the way he thought.

"He made me do it!" I cried, defending myself.

Erskine laughed. "I'm hired help. That's all. She's the one pulling all the strings. Got herself put in charge of Minna's property. She's the one who's been signing all the bills of sale."

My aunt nodded. "That's right . . . she's stolen everything . . ." she slurred her words and blinked her glassy cold eyes at me. "I haven't trusted her from the beginning. I knew she was trying to bleed me blind."

"Turning a pretty penny for herself," smirked Erskine.

"That's a lie! It's not what you think. I—"

"Don't be believing her wild tales." Erskine moved closer to my chair.

Lyle looked at Erskine and then at me. "All right, Anna, I'm ready to listen. What's going on here?"

Before I could answer, Erskine growled, "I've been telling her she ought to be careful. Watch her step. Take care of herself and her little brother." The veiled threat was loud and clear. Erskine would make Davie pay for any accusations I made. He had shut my mouth as effectively as a gag wrapped around it. I didn't dare put Davie's life in jeopardy.

"Anna . . . ?" Lyle waited for me to respond.

I swallowed my accusations. What if I told him everything and he didn't believe me? How could I gamble with Davie's safety? I couldn't . . . at another time, I might have had my wits about me and could have defended myself, but the horrible hoax Erskine had perpetrated stunned me. My illness had left my brain foggy and my body weak.

When I didn't speak, Lyle nodded. "That's what I thought. Well, I'll give the three of you credit . . . overnight you managed to turn a worthless gulch into a

236

bonanza for yourselves. Spreading ore samples around like setting out honey for flies. By the time the men realize there's no gold in that canyon, you'll have made a tidy sum."

A new wave of sickness enveloped me. Ore samples . . . that's what had been in the heavy sacks. I knew now what Erskine had done with them. He had scattered them all over the canyon, seeding the hillside, making it appear to be rich in gold ore, when in fact there wasn't a dusting of gold anywhere in that area.

"You can't prove nothin'," glared Erskine. "And ye don't have no call to come here and throw around yer lies."

"Lies? I think not. I think I've hit the nail squarely on the head."

"Git off this property. Yer trespassing!"

"Gladly." His tone was curt. "I had hoped that I was wrong about all of this—but I see now that I wasn't." His eyes met mine. "It isn't often I'm played for a fool."

"It's not what you think," I said with stiff lips.

"Isn't it?" His gaze raked my tangled hair, unkempt dress, and slumped body. "Please forgive the intrusion." He started toward the door.

I made a move to follow him. Erskine clamped his hand down on my shoulder. "No, ye don't," he growled softly to me. Then he shouted after Delany, "See that ye don't step on this property again—less ye want to be warmed by a barrel of buckshot."

The front door slammed. Like a devil's roar, Erskine's laughter vibrated through my aching head. I closed my eyes against the memory of Delany's scathing eyes. For the first time in my life, I wished I were dead.

"He won't be back," Erskine grinned at me. "I think

yer admirer thinks yer a drunk like Auntie."

"He'll have the law after you—"

"Not me—you! He took the hat with him . . . for evidence." He smirked. "If he shows it around, he could stir up a lynching mob—once it gets around what ye've done."

I didn't have the strength to fight him. I stumbled back upstairs, threw myself across the cot, and let the tears come. Lyle believed Erskine. He thought I had engineered the hoax to sell of my aunt's worthless property. The rumors that Erskine had spread around me had been fueled by the discovery of the hat I had worn. Lyle had proof I had been in the canyon. In any case, the papers I had signed made me responsible for selling the worthless land. I could deny my involvement with my last breath—but who would believe me?

My strength came back slowly. Fleeting glimpses of my face in mirrored surfaces were those of a stranger. My cheeks were gaunt and hollow, and tired lines ridged the corner of my mouth. My complexion had an unhealthy transparent cast to it, and my eyes were sunken into my pallid face. A loss of weight caused my clothes to hang on me, but my appearance was less of a concern than my lack of energy. Not only was my physical endurance at low ebb, but my spirit was like a ship shattered upon a reef. Fragmented and torn, I couldn't pull myself back into one piece. I could see why my aunt had turned to drink as an escape from her tormented days and nights.

Erskine loomed up at my side when I least expected it. I endured his touch on my arm or hot breath on my neck with indifference and repulsion. "Leave me alone," I'd tell him again and again, but my response lacked its usual fire.

He laughed when I refused to respond to his goading insults. "A stuck pig has more life in it than ye do. Guess I'll have to liven ye up a bit. We should be celebrating, after all. You should see the way men have poured into Chimney Gulch. Sinking holes all over the place. Fighting and killing each other." His smile was moist with satisfaction.

I shut out his jeering voice. Even though I had been an unwilling party to the deceit, I felt heavy responsibility for it. My father had been a prospector, and I knew too well what sacrifices were made by a man and his family, including the poverty, the back-breaking toil, and broken dreams which dominated their lives. It was costly enough in human life when there was a chance of making a good strike, but when trickery had taken away even that chance, the situation was beyond human decency.

Lyle Delany had every right to be appalled. The callous deceit was deserving of the condemnation in his eyes. But I was an innocent party to the scheme! Couldn't he see that? Why was he so quick to judge me? Even though the hat and the strands of red hair were evidence that I had been involved in the seeding, he shouldn't have condemned me without knowing the circumstances. A self-righteous judge, he had come to Blackbriar already convinced of my guilt. My appearance had added to the conviction that I was no better than my drunken aunt and her disreputable caretaker. In fact, Lyle readily accepted me as the brains behind the vile seeding of my aunt's property. My face flamed with embarrassment when I remembered how slovenly I had looked. But I had been ill . . . why couldn't he see that? He had accepted the situation at face value. I had not thought him so rigidly judgmental and condemning. The memory of his gentleness was like salt in a wound. Anger mingled with disappointment.

Several times I tried to talk to Aunt Minna about the horrible trickery that had cheated poverty-stricken men of their last dollar. "We have to do something about it. We can't let Erskine get away with it. Aunt Minna, please help me."

"Help you? And why should I? I've been watching you play up to Erskine like a cheap trollop ever since you got here."

"Play up to Erskine!" I echoed, staring at her with utter disbelief. "You don't believe that, Aunt Minna. I loathe the man. He's evil. Look at what he's done to you."

"You better watch your mouth." She glared at me with raw hatred.

"Aunt Minna, he's evil." I refused to back off. "You've got to see Erskine for the devil he is. I know he's been with you for a long time, but once he has every penny of yours, he won't care what happens to any of us. It's not just me and Davie," I warned. "Can't you see your life's in danger?"

She laughed as if enjoying a private joke. "You're a fool. A scatterbrained fool. Can't see what's right in front of your nose. Jem'll never hurt me."

"Of course he will. Don't you see, he's already managed to get the money for the lake property, and now he's sold all your land up Chimney Canyon. The ony thing that's left is Blackbriar House—and he'll get that away from you, too."

She sat there, a pathetic figure flushed with drink, her

hair stringing like a witch's around her bloated face. Thank God, my father wasn't here to see what had happened to that pretty redheaded girl who had meant so much to him. He had loved his sister so much that he had ruined her life trying to protect her. If only he had let her marry the boy she had loved, the woman I saw drinking herself to death might have had a different fate. I felt that I had failed my father by not helping Aunt Minna overcome these dire circumstances. "There's nothing I can do," I said aloud, as much for my own ears as hers. "Nothing."

"Jem's smarter than you," she agreed with a wobbly nod of satisfaction. "Ain't a smarter man around."

The pride in her voice brought a cold shudder trickling up my back. She must love the horrid man. Why else would she defend his ruthless treatment of her? I didn't understand any of it. With Aunt Minna blinded to his evil schemes, I didn't see why he needed me to sell off her land. She was obviously willing to turn everything over to Erskine—even her life. Why did he need me to sign the papers? The question kept nagging at me, as if I were looking at a picture hanging crooked, knowing that if I could look at it straight on, I would see an entirely different picture.

As my physical strength returned, so did my determination to find a means of escape. Any help for my aunt must come from the outside. My hopes took a leap forward when I saw Erskine working on the old rowboat. I smelled hot piñon sap and I knew he was caulking the cracks. Even though I had rowed a boat only once in my life, I was ready to grasp at any chance to steal it and try to make our way across the lake. I kept a secret vigil on the progress Erskine was making getting the boat

241

lakeworthy. When he turned it over and started working on the inside, I knew that he would be shoving it into the water before long.

My best chance to get away in the boat would be at night . . . sometime after Erskine returned to the house. Davie and I would have to be waiting outside, ready to slip down to the dock after he made his way upstairs to bed. Unlike my aunt, who was a creature of habit— always in bed before midnight and never up until mid-morning—Erskine came and went in erratic patterns. I never could tell from one night to the next where he would be . . . in the boathouse, somewhere in the rambling house, or coming back from a trip in his skiff.

The day I saw the rowboat in the water, I knew that the time had come to get away in it. Before I could lay any plans, an unexpected sight greeted my eyes a day later when I looked out the attic window and saw a boat approaching the bay. Someone was coming!

I slipped downstairs. I could hear Erskine and Aunt Minna in the front room, engaged in one of their bombastic conversations. I slipped out the back door, looking for Davie and calling, "Rags! Come here, Rags."

If they were anywhere close, the dog would come running with Davie at his heels. I called again and waited impatiently. No sign of either of them.

I'd have to collect them later. I couldn't delay. I must seize the opportunity to meet whoever was coming to Blackbriar.

I circled the house, and as I ran down the path to the dock, I squinted my eyes and searched the bay. Empty . . . no sign of a boat. It couldn't be! From the attic window, I had seen the small craft entering the sheltered bay. Where had it gone?

242

I ran to the edge of the dock. My frantic gaze swept the azure water—then I saw it. Instead of coming straight for the dock, the single occupant of the craft had beached it on the east bank of the bay. A fisherman? A sightseer? Someone exploring the lake? Lifting up my skirts, I ran a familiar path along the water's edge where Davie and I had taken our walks. I knew I could get to the stranger's boat in a few minutes.

My mind raced with what I would say to him. It mattered not to me who the stranger was or why he had come. In my desperation, I had to throw myself upon anyone who would help us get away.

My lungs burned as I raced over rough ground and wet sand. I rounded the last mound of rocks spilling down to the water and saw the boat where I had expected it to be. The man was a few yards from the water's edge.

I yelled, waved, and ran forward.

He spun around at my voice. A wide brimmed hat hid his face until I was almost upon him. Then his crooked nose and thin-lipped mouth brought instant recognition. *Zeke!*

I tried to spin away—but he had me. "No, you don't!" His yellowed teeth flashed in a broad smile. "Well, if this ain't a surprise. Running to meet me with open arms, were you?"

I struggled against him, but his arms were like a steel vise around me. His foul-smelling breath quivered my nostrils, and the sight of his ugly face poised close to mine churned my stomach. "You—!" I gasped.

"Yes, me. You thought I'd forgotten all about you bloodying my nose and that bastard Delany throwing me overboard, didn't ya? Well, the whole thing's been festering inside me. That goddamn Delany fired me from

243

logging crew, he did. Let me go just because of some cheap skirt. But he owes me . . . and you owe me. I swore I'd get my hands on you if I had to camp out here all summer." He smirked. "But here you are. By God, I've come to collect my debts."

I shoved against his chest as his hand fastened on the front of my dress. With one vicious jerk he ripped it to the waist. His mauling hand fastened on a breast, squeezing it with such force that I cried out in pain.

He laughed as he threw me to the ground and pinned me in the wet sand with his body. "Time to pay up, wench."

Chapter Seventeen

His hands were all over me. Grappling. Squeezing. Bruising. Fired with lust, he ravaged my mouth with moist, foul kisses that left my lips bleeding. I twisted under him, trying frantically to free the arms he had pinned above my head. "You beast!" I gasped, turning my face away from his savage mouth.

"Treat me like dirt, will you? I gave you a chance to be friendly. But no, you just spit on me. Not good enough for you. By God, now we'll see if you're worth the taking."

Pinned by his legs stretched across mine, I was taking the brunt of his whole weight. My breath came in strangled gulps. "Get off me!" I cried, sickened by the taste of his tobacco-stained mouth.

"Tried to make me look the fool. Nobody gets away treating Zeke Stone like scum. Nobody. I'll show you a thing or two."

"You can't get away with this!"

"You ain't going to stop me . . . not this time. And by the time I get through with you, you'll wish you'd paid me a little attention when you had the chance." His mouth descended on mine again. I caught his lower lip in my mouth and bit as hard as I could.

He jerked back, blood spouting from the bite. He let go of one of my arms and slapped me with his broad hand. "You goddamned bitch!" With a vicious thrust, he swept my legs apart and pulled up my skirt. As he moved to loosen his trousers, I pulled a leg upward and caught him in the groin.

The unexpected onslaught of pain he felt gave me a moment to twist free of his weight. My arm was free for only a second, but I grabbed up a handful of sand and threw it in his eyes. Blinded for a moment, he raised his hands to his face. His eyes were red and watering as he tried to rub them.

His body slipped to one side, and I would have been free of him if he hadn't reached out and grabbed the folds of my skirt. The worn fabric of my dress and petticoat tore as I jerked away from him. Then, hampered by the cloth that tangled around my legs, I stumbled and fell.

With a triumphant bellow, he lunged at me but didn't move fast enough to trap me on the ground.

I rolled away, got up, and ran. He was after me in a second. If the lake's edge had been smooth, I might have outrun him, but the shoreline was rough and uneven. Rocks that had tumbled down to the water's edge eliminated any edge of sand as they collected along the water.

Trying to keep my tattered dress from tripping me, I clamored over a mound of loose rock, scraping myself on jagged edges and bruising my arms and legs in a frantic flight to get away from him. My dress hung open to the waist, and my hair fell in a tangled mass around my face. I gulped air into my fiery lungs as I forced energy into a body that was still weak from my recent illness.

His long stride was closing the distance between us.

I scrambled over the top of a rock spill, slid down the other side, and went almost to my knees before I regained my balance. With a triumphant snarl, he lunged at me once again.

I had no choice but to flee out an outcropping of rock extending out into the lake. The footing was so rough that he caught me before I had taken a dozen steps. With a clenched fist he rocked me backward with a blow to my chin. "Goddamned slut!"

I staggered and spun around, dizzy and disoriented. In a desperate effort to escape him, I backed up. The next thing I knew, I was falling.

Water hit me with the shock of a hundred icy fists. My arms flailed outward as I went down. The depth was only a few feet over my head, but my drenched skirts wrapped around my limbs like mummy windings. The weighted cloth pulled me down until my feet touched the bottom. I shoved upward, gasping for air, floundering, unable to keep from floating farther and farther away from the shore. Every time I went under, the bottom of the lake was deeper. Soon I would be unable to push back to the surface.

I was going to drown.

The realization stabbed me with panic—not for death itself, but for Davie's fate without me to protect him. I summoned my last ounce of strength and bobbed to the surface. Through watery eyes, I saw Zeke in the water, reaching for me, and I felt his arms miraculously holding me up to life-giving air.

At that moment, I wanted life more than escape from

the ravishment of my body. I realized that I would accept what degradation I must to survive. I didn't fight Zeke as he brought me back to the bank.

He tossed me down on the sand. "You'd better be worth it," he snarled. Wet clothes molded his body, and I saw the hardening of his groin and felt lust radiating from him like a banked fire. The fight had only increased his appetite. I had heard stories of men who beat their women to increase their gratification. Zeke was obviously one of them.

He stood over me, and his legs looked like two mammoth trunks as I looked up through waterlogged eyelashes.

His mouth twisted in a satisfied leer. "I like a bit a fire when I tumble a woman."

My strength was gone. He could do what he wished. Deliberately, he loosened his trousers at the waist, but before he could drop them, a shot rang out.

Zeke's eyes widened. I watched the expression on his face freeze. Then he fell forward in slow motion. Right on top of me!

A red, sticky wetness flowed out of his body and spread out all over me. Zeke's bulging eyes stared unseeing inches from mine. Pinned by his weight, I screamed as Erskine's hand reached down and jerked the dead man off me.

I thought I was going to faint. My stomach sent bitter gall up into my mouth. Warm blood coated my breasts and trickled down my neck.

"I ought to blow yer head off while I'm at it," he swore at me. The rifle in his hand radiated heat. He unleashed a torrent of angry insults, calling me every degrading name he could think of.

The insults washed over me. I didn't care. I stared horrified at Zeke with his glassy eyes and sagging mouth. I wavered to my feet. Strangely, I had no feelings of remorse for the dead man who lay crumpled at my feet, despite the fact that he had not let me drown. At one time I would have dissolved into tearful hysterics at the sight, but no more. I had aged years in the last few weeks.

"Ye were planning on running off, weren't ye?"

How long ago that seemed. I brushed drenched strands of hair from my face. "Not with him," I said honestly.

Erskine's gaze traveled over my torn clothes, and he gave a grunt. "Looks like he manhandled ye a bit."

I couldn't tell if there was an edge of admiration in his tone or a touch of cold fury. "I saw ye on top of the rocks. Grabbed my gun and came after ye." Suddenly his rifle was leveled at me. "I ain't aiming to lose me golden goose just yet. Now hie yerself back to the house."

"What . . . what about him?"

"Come dark, I'll dump the bastard in the lake. You know his name?"

"Zeke Stone. He was on the stagecoach with Davie and me and . . . and he wouldn't quit bothering me."

"Ye probably led him on, sneaking bitch that ye are. Wouldn't put it past ye to invite him here."

"He came here to even a score." I didn't tell him how Delany had dumped him in the lake.

"Well, he picked the wrong place. He'll be meat for fish come nightfall."

"But what if Zeke told somebody he was coming here?"

He grunted. "And what if he did? T'ain't no skin off my nose if he turns up missing. I'll tow his boat out in the middle of the lake and sink it along with the body. Who's to say he's been here?" His eyes narrowed. "Unless ye've a mind to tell 'em."

I shook my head. And then I smothered a hysterical laugh.

"What's so funny?"

My laughter turned into smothered sobs. *Me and Erskine, conspirators.*

"Git back to the house," he ordered harshly. "And see to it that ye don't end up in the lake with your friend Stone." There was nothing but cruelty in his eyes. He would have shot me as easily as he had Zeke if it had been to his advantage.

That night, I watched Erskine row out of the bay into the lake with Zeke's boat bobbing behind. The hope that had been born when I first saw it that afternoon was a mockery to the horror that had followed. I knew what lay motionless in the bottom of the boat. Zeke would disappear and never be sorely grieved by anyone. This thought brought tears of pity to my eyes, and I said a prayer for the man who would have used me callously for his own pleasure.

Perhaps the fact that Erskine had saved me from Zeke made me less anxious about getting away. As long as he had need of me, I was safe. I didn't know what he had planned now that all of Aunt Minna's land had been sold except Blackbriar House. Surely he would take his time and let all the rumors settle before he forced me into signing any more papers. When Davie and I made a break for freedom, I wanted to be certain that Erskine would not be able to bring us back at the point of a gun.

It seemed to me that he watched me more closely than ever. Several times I caught his eyes on me, lingering on my breasts and hips as if remembering the torn dress and the clinging wet cloth that shamefully molded my figure. Several times the raw lust in his eyes was more terrifying than his anger.

I kept out of his reach and picked up a knife or a poker when he tried to put his hands on me. His gutteral laugh was mocking, as if he were only waiting for the right time to enjoy himself. He seemed, in the meantime, to enjoy seeing a flash of fear in my eyes.

I waited for the authorities to come and ask about Zeke's disappearance. Maybe his friend, Clyde, who had been on the stage, would make some inquiries. What if Zeke had told someone he was coming to Blackbriar House? Would anyone believe my story? In a settled town or populated area, a man couldn't just disappear without a ripple of concern and inquiry. But this was not a civilized section of the country . . . not yet. As settlers put down roots and the railroad brought in more and more elements of society, law and order would follow. But at the moment, I knew in my heart that no one was going to be concerned with the disappearance of a drifter like Zeke Stone.

I had other worries, too. Surely, there would be some repercussions to Erskine's scheme to make people think there was gold in Chimney Canyon. I feared that a mob of angry prospectors would arrive in force with firebrands and guns. The disdain in Lyle's face mocked the feelings I had for him. Even on my worst days, I had protected a tiny bit of warmth that overtook me when I relived the moments with him. Now that was gone. Even the sight of the pretty hat could not revive my spirits. Better forget about Lyle Delany. The scorn in his eyes had been void of any of the gentle feelings he might have felt when he called me "Annie."

When I asked Erskine what was happening in Chimney Canyon, he laughed and slapped his leg. "Ye ain't going to believe this. With all that digging going on, somebody ran into a vein. All hell broke loose. Some men sold their claims for twice what they paid for them. Quite a stir it caused. A lot more men poured in and ate dust before the ore proved too poor to be worked."

I felt sick.

He watched my face, seemingly pleased with my reaction. "Yep, after a few futile tries to find a richer vein, everybody picked up and moved on. Tahoe's gold rush just petered out." He laughed as if enjoying a joke.

I could picture the deserted scene. Tumbled shacks littering the hillside, trash heaps, dry wooden fumes used to float the ore, quiet rockers that creaked when separating ore and rock. Dead dreams. I had seen and felt them as my father had moved us from one gold strike area to the next. Always hoping, always sacrificing. Always failing.

"I hear Delany's about to open his lodge." Erskine peered at me. "Putting a lot of money into the place. Wouldn't be surprised if he turns a pretty penny for himself." As if Erskine knew the sound of Lyle's name was like a nail in my side, he seemed to find devilish glee in telling me all the details of the Delany Tahoe Resort. "Advertising in the San Francisco papers, he is. Going to open on Labor Day. All kinds of rich sons-of-bitches are expected. A lady or two, I hear. Wouldn't be surprised if Delany is courting one of them. Course, she'd have to be rich . . . and proper-like."

I knew he was baiting me, but it still didn't stop the hurt. The remembered disdain in Lyle's eyes had not dimmed, nor had the memory of his touch. Fool that I was, I felt a spurt of jealousy knowing that he was using that same charm on other young women more deserving than me.

The month of June passed without incident, but a startling new relationship between me and Aunt Minna seemed to mark a change in our daily patterns. My aunt's drinking eased off, and she began to play cards on the dining room table. Solitaire, at first, and then she asked me if I knew how to play poker.

Startled, I nodded. "My father taught me."

"Good. We'll use coffee beans for chips." Her eyes sparkled with more life than I had seen since my arrival.

Too startled to question this unexpected overture, I happily brought the jar of coffee beans and played cards with her.

She was a good player, much better than me. Not that I cared about winning or losing . . . the chance to have an opportunity to relate to her in any fashion was better than none. A deep sense of loneliness began to fade as I played cards with her almost every afternoon. Even though my aunt remained withdrawn from any personal overtures, I was encouraged to think that in time we might find some ground for becoming friends instead of adversaries.

I chatted as we played, keeping one eye on her expression as I tried to share intimate anecdotes with her about her brother. "He said you loved to ride horses. Do you remember the pony called Dolly?"

She would sometimes grunt in reply or ignore me completely. My attempts at conversation seemed to have little effect upon her cold indifference. Her responses were usually curt and at times strangely off the subject. Her memory was sharp enough when it came to a poker hand, but I feared that her excessive drinking had dulled Aunt Minna's mental faculties. More than ever I felt a deep sense of responsibility for her.

I wondered if my father had seen her on one of her good days. According to Trapper it hadn't been many months ago that he had stopped at Blackbriar House. I wondered why he hadn't told me about the visit. Surely Aunt Minna must not have shown him her worst side or he would never have sent us here. Or maybe he knew she needed help and thought I could do something to make her life happier. I felt guilty that I had been able to do so little for her, but maybe I was making slow progress. At least, I liked to think I was.

As the days of summer brought a languid sweetness to the hillside, Davie and I spent hours away from the house. I watched Erskine work on the rowboat, and, as if he realized I had my eye on it, he kept it under lock and key in the boathouse. He used the skiff as he came and went from Blackbriar House.

Then, one day, he shoved the rowboat into the water. I was watching him from a spot down the lake a few yards where Davie and Rags were splashing in the water.

Much to my surprise, he bellowed my name and motioned for me to come to the dock. What could he want? Did he want to gloat about the repair job on the rowboat? Or taunt me about my secret hope to steal away in it?

I left Davie and the pup and walked back to where he waited.

"Git in!" he ordered.

"What—?"

"Ye heard me. Don't think I haven't seen ye eyeing my work on the boat. Watching . . . and waiting." He gave a laughing grunt. "Well, ye can try it out. We'll take a little row down the lake. See if it stays afloat. Git in."

"Davie, too?"

"Hell, no. The dummy stays here." He cackled. "Just the two of us. Ye've been thinking about stealing the boat. I'll make it easy. All ye have to do is wrestle it away from me." His eyes gleamed. "A bit of warning, though— if ye return without me, your auntie will take care of the boy before ye set one foot on the ground."

He was like a cat setting up a mouse for malicious play. Cruel and heartless, he relished the fear that lurched up in my eyes when he threatened Davie.

He grabbed my arm in a painful twist. "'Tain't good manners to refuse me polite invitation. Git in the boat or I'll throw ye in head first."

Davie had seen Erskine grab me, and he came running. I had no choice but to do as the tyrant ordered. "All right," I said. "Let me go. I have to tell Davie where I'm going."

"Well, tell him," he spat.

"I have to use my hands."

He hesitated and then dropped his arm.

"How long will we be gone?"

He smiled. "Not long. Be back sometime tonight. Tell the dummy we're taking a little trip."

A clammy chill invaded my body. A little trip? Out to the middle of the lake? *Would I be coming back at all this time?*

enough by now to realize there was no appealing to his

Chapter Eighteen

I sat in the bow of the boat as Erskine rowed away from
Blackbriar Bay. Davie became a small, lost figure as he
stood on the weathered pier, watching us cross the bay
and move out into the lake. He had begged to come with
us but I shook my head. "I'll be back in a few hours," I
had signed, praying that I would be able to keep the
promise. I wanted to hug him and hold him close, but I
knew such behavior would increase his own fright. "Play
with Rags. Stay away from Aunt Minna. Understand?"

He nodded. I settled a brief kiss on his cheek and
climbed into the boat. I had no idea what devious plans
Erskine had for me. Since the night we had gone to
Chimney Canyon, I had been waiting for his next move.
My stomach tightened with tension and my hands were
sweaty as I held onto the sides of the boat.

Erskine's powerful arms moved the oars in a sweeping
rhythm that sent the craft skimming over the water. His
thick body rippled with bulging muscles. He rowed with
an animal fierceness that seemed without thought or
mental effort. Beads of sweat formed on his brow, the

deep purchase of the oars in the water strained his arms and shoulders, and an expression of raw pleasure coated his ugly frame. A kind of manic pressure drove him, as if he were testing himself, the boat, or me.

If the boat had sprung a leak that distance from the shore, I doubted that even his mammoth arms could have propelled the craft to the bank fast enough to keep it from sinking. The recently caulked seams appeared to be holding, I thought as I anxiously watched the bottom of the boat for any sign of water.

I purposely kept my eyes away from his face. Some warning instinct told me not to let him read the mounting terror that every stroke of his oars brought deep inside me. He wanted to see me cower and tremble, but I felt that my only hope was to meet his threats with defiance. On some level, I knew that the goal of his malicious sport was to break my spirit, and I vowed that I would draw my last breath before I broke down and begged for his mercy.

He had not given me time to put on a sunbonnet, so my head was bare and the sun touched my skin with reassuring warmth. I was wearing my blue wool dress because it was the only change I had since Zeke had torn my other day dress off of me. At the moment, my attire was of slight importance. The beautiful day was at odds with the dark desolation within me. The lake spread around us like a shimmering mirror, reflecting the sky and drawing deep tones of the underwater rocks to the surface in breathtaking mosaic patterns.

As Erskine rowed farther and farther down the western side of the lake, my taut nerves began to ease. If Erskine intended to throw me overboard, I saw no reason for him to put so much distance between us and Blackbriar House. No one on the faraway shore would be able to see his murderous act. Even though I strained my eyes, I saw no other crafts dotting the water.

When he piloted the boat closer to shore, I saw only a sheer, forbidding precipice that rose hundreds of feet in the air with water lapping against its sides. He laughed when he rowed the boat so close to the sheer cliff that I could have reached out and touched the smooth rock.

He yelled with glee. "Look down!"

I leaned my head over the side of the boat and gasped. The water was so clear that I could see that the giant precipice went straight down hundreds of feet to the bottom of the lake. The waterline blurred, creating a sensation of being drawn into the watery depths. I jerked back, dizzy and shaken, my chest suddenly tight.

Erskine laughed as if pleased with my reaction. For a moment I thought he had brought me to this special place for his evil deed, but he didn't linger near the cliff. He began rowing again and I breathed easier. My gaze traveled to the highest point of the rock, eight or nine hundred feet in the air, and wondered if anyone had ever climbed to the top. A good place for a lighthouse, I thought, wondering if there would ever be enough boat traffic on the river to warrant one.

This thought brought me to unbidden thoughts of Lyle Delany and his plans to make the lake a bustling resort. We must be getting close to his property, I thought. Almost at the same moment, I saw the *Tahoe Queen* steaming ahead of us toward the southern tip of the lake. I expected Erskine to turn the boat around quickly in retreat. Instead, he only chuckled. "Well, well, seems like everyone's heading for Delany's Resort."

I knew then how he delighted in dangling freedom in front of me, knowing that I dared not make a move that would anger him. As if reading my thoughts, he smirked. "Guess we could take a breather. You probably want to say hello to your admirer." Like a cat dangling a piece of cheese, keeping razor-sharp claws ready, he taunted me with the fact that I could say nothing that would endanger Davie's safety.

He pulled the rowboat to shore, a short distance from where the lake steamer was docking. Excitement raced through me. Randy was on that boat. Maybe I would be able to arrange something with him. I tried to keep my expression masked, but I feared the wild pulse of my heartbeat showed in my neck. Erskine could see every flicker of my eyelids.

"I left word with yer aunt to shoot the boy if ye go back without me," he said, as if seeing hope leaping into my eyes. "She'll blow his brains out before ye make it to the house." He laughed at my horrified expression. "If ye want to keep that dummy all in one piece, ye'll act happy as a coon in a tree around everybody we meet."

An apt metaphor, I thought. A victim in a tree, trapped, unable to escape, guarded by a snarling, jagged-tooth beast who would relish sinking his teeth into my flesh at the first opportunity.

We approached a long, narrow dock and boat slips built for crafts of all sizes. A new sailboat had the name *Lyle's Retreat* on the bow, and I knew who was the owner of the sleek craft. For a moment I let my fantasy run free, imagining him standing in the bow, wind whipping his silver blond hair, his legs planted in a firm stance as he steered the boat across the mirrored waters.

"Git out," ordered Erskine when he had brought the rowboat to dock.

Without hesitation I gathered my skirts and stepped

out. I heard hammering and men's voices coming from a clearing not far from the lake's edge. Looking about, I saw a two-story lodge with a wide veranda taking shape. Several small cabins on the lake front were already finished, and smoke rose from the chimney of one of them. Delany's cabin? What would he do if he saw me here? Suddenly my mouth was dry and my heartbeat had quickened. He had looked upon me with disgust and repulsion the last time. I remembered how he had dismissed everything I said as lies. The hat and my red hair had condemned me in his sight. And he had readily interpreted my illness as drunkenness. Anger surged through me. I didn't care if I never saw him again, but the lie dissipated in a wash of nervous anticipation as I searched a group of workmen for that silver-blond head and fringed deerskin jacket. When I didn't see his familiar figure, my gaze swung back to the lake steamer.

Randy was bounding down the gangplank with his hands full of mail. He stopped short when he saw me.

"Hi!" I waved in greeting, expecting his wide, full grin in return. Instead, he glared at me with a hatred that was like a vicious jab in the stomach. I should have been warned by Erskine's gleeful chuckle, but I hurried over to him. "What is it, Randy? What's wrong?" This couldn't be the amiable young man who had shown me such friendliness.

"Don't play the innocent with me!" he growled. "All this time, hiding your goddamned greedy heart behind a friendly smile."

I swallowed hard. "What are you talking about?"

"As if you didn't know. You took me in, all right. And a bunch of others, too. Spent all my savings on a stake in that gulch of yours. Nothing but rock. No gold ore—

except what was put there. If you was a man, you'd a been tarred and feathered by now."

A hurricane wind shook me. Oh, no, not Randy. Not the hard-earned money he had planned to take back home. "It's not what you think," I protested in horror. "I'm innocent, you have to believe me."

Erskine bellowed, "'Course she is. Innocent as the driven snow." A sly, crafty look belied his words. He couldn't have thrown more guilt upon me if he'd tried. "Ye have anything to say to Miss McKenzie, ye say it to me," he blustered.

"I have nothing to say—to either of you." Randy brushed past us.

Erskine gave a deep chuckle. "Seems a bit riled, don't he?"

I wanted the earth to swallow me up. Randy, my only friend, the only one I felt I could call upon to help me—now was my accuser. He believed the lies spread around about me. My name must be a curse on everyone's lips.

"Let's go back," I said, starting to walk away.

Erskine grabbed my arm. "No, not yet. There's a couple of fellows I want to see." He motioned up a path toward the unfinished building.

I walked woodenly beside him as the steamer gave a warning toot behind us. My thoughts were like nettles scratching me with hurtful pricks. Randy was the one person who had liked me. And trusted me enough to sink his hard-earned money in the gold rush that Erskine had perpetrated. Now he hated the sight of me. I couldn't depend upon him to carry out any plan to get Davie away from Blackbriar House. My last link with help from the outside had been destroyed.

We reached the unfinished lodge, and Erskine strode

over to a group of men laying logs on one side of the building. He took a flask from his pocket and passed it around, laughing and swearing as the men stopped their work to take a turn at the bottle. I wondered what vile trickery he was up to now. He never did anything without a reason.

I wandered along a wide veranda that hugged the sides of the new lodge.

"Take care!" he called to me in a warning tone that said clearly, "One false step, one careless word, and ye'll never see yer brother again." There was gloating in his eyes. He knew that I couldn't escape the leash he had on me. The apparent freedom he had given me was a farce. He could reel me in any time he wanted, and he knew it.

I bit my lip in frustration. Leaning up against the porch railing, I stared out on the lake. Lyle had picked his location well. In the distance, tall timber cupped the lake's edge like the dark pile of a velvet carpet. A pearly mist softened the expanse of water and sky, and brilliant hues of aquamarine and deep indigo blended together artfully. Closer to shore, emerald water lapped lazily upon white sand. My warring emotions were soothed by the scene, and I began walking around the veranda, looking into the unfinished lodge and speculating about the floorplan.

When I came around the west side of the building, I didn't see him for a moment. Then a movement below stopped me. Shirtless, his bronze torso gleaming in the sun, Lyle was working in a small clearing, pulling at brush, bending and carrying, piling the debris in piles. He raised an arm and wiped his forehead with his arm. As he did so, his gaze fluttered upward and he saw me.

For a moment neither of us moved. He looked stunned,

as if he didn't believe his eyes. My heart leaped like a startled bird and beat wildly. I was breathless when there was no reason for it.

"Is it you?" He walked slowly toward me.

I tried to lighten the moment. "I'm not a ghost," I said with a feeble smile. As his eyes swept over me, I chided, "Ghosts don't have red hair."

He swung over the railing in a smooth leap and suddenly he was beside me, looking straight down into my face. His forehead furrowed, and his eyes were searching mine. A quivering muscle in his cheek betrayed his agitation. "What are you doing here?"

The demand was less than gracious. "Just looking around. You're going to have a nice place when it's finished. I'd like to see the rest of it," I said boldly.

He reached out and tipped up my chin, searching my face. "You must have given up drinking . . ."

"It was easy," I snapped, "since I never started."

"Last time I saw you—"

"I was ill! Not drunk. If you'd taken the time to touch my forehead, you would have known why I was weak and trembling. You were ready to condemn me—and you did. You didn't want to listen to any explanations."

He dropped his hand. "No, I guess not. I was too riled up. Still am," he warned. "That was a dirty business . . . making it look like there was gold in the canyon."

"Please. Let's don't talk about it, not now." These few minutes with him were too precious to waste on something that couldn't be changed. A swirling pattern of golden hair upon his bare chest led my eyes downward to the low waist of his pants. I felt heat rising in my cheeks as I reacted to his nearness. A scorching heat sluiced through me.

We stood there for a moment without speaking. His breathing deepened to match mine. Whatever was happening between us disturbed him as much as it did me. "Annie . . ." he whispered my name, in a tone that was almost a plea.

If we had not been standing in the bright sunlight, with the sound of men's voices just around the corner, I would have gone into his arms. All rational thought fled, all sense of decorum. I wanted to run my hands over his glistening skin, feel his length pressed against mine, and give my mouth up to his in wanton abandonment.

He must have read the desire in my face. "When you look like that, you could tempt Adam himself." A wariness shone in his frown. "What is it you want from me, Annie?"

I forced my eyes away from his. "Nothing." I swallowed. "Unless you want to show me around the place."

A slight pause. "I'll get my shirt."

He swung over the railing again, retrieved a plaid shirt from a tree stump, and buttoned it as he came back to the porch. "There," he said with a wry smile. "I apologize for my state of undress. I'm used to a lumber camp with no women around."

Even with his shirt on, he exuded a physical magnetism. I saw wisps of curly hair at his open neck, and my mind filled in the rest on his broad chest. I drew my eyes away from him and began walking back the way I had come. "I peeked in the windows. Looks as if everything is coming along nicely," I said in a conversational tone which denied the bewildering stirrings inside me.

"The usual problems. Scarce materials . . . unexpected delays. But all in all, I'm rather pleased." The eagerness in his voice was obvious. He touched my arm in a guiding pressure. "I'll show you the ground floor. The upstairs rooms are just framed in." He led me through an open doorway into the unfinished building. "This is the main hall."

"What a spectacular fireplace!" Dominating one wall and built of native stone was a fireplace with a raised hearth, nearly eight feet wide and rising to the high ceiling.

He laughed at my expression. "Beautiful, isn't it? I hate little bitty fires that puff and smoke and pretend to throw out heat. I decided to build one that could handle a couple of nice-sized logs. What do you think? Will this one do the job?"

"It should warm one's toes—and everything else, if you've a mind to stand with your back to it," I quipped. He laughed. "My thoughts exactly. Come on . . . I'll show you the dining room and kitchen."

Our footsteps echoed hollowly on the unfinished planked floor as we toured a large room that offered a spectacular view of the lake. Lyle exuded so much enthusiasm that I found myself caught up in it. Even though there was nothing but bare walls in the dining room, I pictured linen-covered tables circled with high-backed chairs, and golden pine walls lined with sideboards offering steaming, aromatic dishes, and I could imagine the voices of guests floating up to the high-beamed ceiling.

"And now the kitchen." He swept me into a large room that had been divided into work areas and several pantries. "I fashioned it after a hotel restaurant I saw in San Francisco. I even stole their cook. He'll be here to serve up the finest culinary dishes. No beans and mutton on my menu."

"Sounds wonderful."

"I'm planning a gala affair when I open the doors for business. I've already received some reservations—a couple of bankers and their wives." He laughed. "They want to see what I've done with their money, I guess."

"I think you've made a good investment," I said honestly. "I'm sure that most people would love to spend some time at Lake Tahoe."

"Most people?" He caught the slight emphasis on the word. "Why do I have the feeling that doesn't include you?" He put his hands on my arms and turned me around. "Why don't you tell me why you have that haunted, angry look in your eyes all the time?"

"Because I can't."

"Is it Erskine?"

I kept my eyes focused on some point beyond his chin. Careful, some inner voice warned. I desperately wanted to release all the pent-up fear and terror that I held inside, reach out for his strength, and pour out the truth. And then what would happen? If Lyle believed me, he would act. He would confront Erskine with my accusations—and Davie would be in danger. Even if Lyle managed to detain Erskine, I didn't doubt for a moment that Aunt Minna would carry out his orders to harm my brother if I returned alone. I had seen the crazed look in her eyes the day she had shot a hole through the attic door. No, I couldn't chance it. I firmed my chin and looked him straight in the eye. "There's nothing wrong."

"I don't want to believe that you are the selfish, conniving bitch that you seem to be. I can't get you out of my mind even when I'm away from those lying lips and guileless eyes."

"Maybe you ought to trust your feelings," I challenged.

"How can I? You show up here, turning them upside down. I can't make sense out of the way I feel about you."

"How do you feel about me?"

He was silent for a long, long painful moment. "I don't know. God, I wish I did." He suddenly jerked me to him, and his mouth descended upon mine. Almost angrily, he took possession of my lips, kissing me hungrily, building a searing fire within me. I lost control of my senses. Exploding desire blotted out all reason. There was no reality but winging emotions that made me want to stay in the circle of his embrace. His lips trailed hotly over my cheeks and buried themselves in the soft crevice of my neck. "Annie . . . Annie," he murmured. "What am I going to do about you?"

The anguish in his tone brought at once a flood of guilt and happiness. He *did* care for me. Even when he thought the worst, he couldn't deny the feelings that swept between us. I drew away from him and opened my mouth to try and explain, but the words never left my throat.

"So here ye be," boomed Erskine behind us as he strolled into the kitchen. "Well, now, ye got quite a place goin' up here, Mr. Delany. Yes, sir, quite a place. Me and Anna just had to come and take a peek." His eyes glistened with hidden pleasure, and I wondered why he was pleased to see Lyle and me caught in a moment of obvious intimacy. "I guess Anna told ye the good news."

Lyle frowned. "Good news?"

"Yep. Seems as how her aunt has decided to sell the house. Course, everybody knows ye've been wanting to get your hands on it. Now's yer chance, ain't it, Anna?"

My stomach took a sickening plunge.

"What are you talking about?" demanded Lyle.

My heart sank. I saw it all now! Erskine had brought me here to make it look like I was selling off the last of Aunt Minna's property! Denial lunged up, but Erskine's eyes narrowed in warning, choking the words in my throat. *Ye better be keeping yer mouth shut,* his look said. I wanted the floor to rise up and swallow me.

"Anna thought she'd be giving ye first crack at it," Erskine told Lyle with a wink.

"Oh, so this is a business call?" said Lyle, an arctic frost in his voice. "And where's Mrs. Brown going to live?" Lyle's cool eyes swept over my face. "If you sell her house out from under her, Anna, what will your aunt have left?"

Erskine answered quickly. "Oh, she's fixing to buy a little place in Tahoe City. Ain't that right, Anna? Be better for everybody. Blackbriar House is all run down and worth a lot more to somebody like yerself. That little bay will be a popular place for vacationing visitors."

As Erskine continued to press him, my thoughts sprang ahead. Once Blackbriar House was sold, Erskine would have no more need of me. He would have turned all Aunt Minna's property into cash. And he wouldn't need Aunt Minna, either. I didn't know how he would do it, but the ink would scarcely be dry before he disposed of all three of us, I was sure of it.

"Well, I'm afraid your trip has been for nothing," said Lyle curtly. "I'm financially extended to the limit for my present project." He looked directly at me. "I'm afraid you'll have to use your charms on someone else, Miss McKenzie. Although I appreciate a shrewd speculator as much as anyone, I always keep business separate from personal feelings."

"Lyle . . . please understand . . ."

"Oh, I do. You thought you'd come here and soften me up. You and your partner . . ." His eyes slid to Erskine. "You thought you'd turn a nice profit on the old lady's land. I don't know how you two have managed to get your hands on it but if I wanted to buy Blackbriar House, I wouldn't add another dollar to the offer because some pretty gal was cozying up to me." His eyes were hard as flint. "Now if you'll excuse me, I have work to do." He stomped out without a backward glance.

Erskine grunted. "Hard-nosed bastard, didn't he?" Then he chuckled. "But I seen the way he was lookin' at ye. Doing a little sparkin', weren't ye?" He gave a dirty laugh. "He'll come around. We'll see to that. Once ye find a way into his bed . . ." He chuckled gleefully. "Yep, we're goin' to land him, all right. A fish may circle a hook for a while, but sooner or later, he'll take a sweet morsel in his mouth—and wham! We've got him! Yep. Delany's swimmin' close to the bait already." His laughter echoed loudly in my ears.

"I won't do it."

"'Course ye will, honey." His smoldering eyes lacked the mirth in his deep chuckle. "Now let's get going. We'd better get back and see whether or not your drunken aunt has already blown yer brother's head off. Sometimes she goes off the deep end, ye know. Wouldn't be surprised if we find ourselves a bit of a mess."

I pulled away from his touch and walked woodenly back to the boat, sick at heart . . . and worried. My lips still burned with the warmth of Lyle's kisses, but a deep chill had invaded my body. My soaring spirits had crashed to earth, but my heartache was set aside by a bigger worry. I had left Davie unprotected, at the mercy of an unstable woman who was capable of anything when she was drunk.

Erskine rowed away from the shore. I didn't look back. My thoughts were centered on one prayer. *Please, God, don't let anything happen to Davie.*

island in a gradual slope. The next moment I was standing
tiptoe in the water. I arched my head to keep my nose

Chapter Nineteen

Lost in my thoughts, I didn't notice that the sunny day was losing its brightness to a stormy evening as we rowed back to Blackbriar Bay. Light in the sky quickly faded as high thunderhead clouds raced down the mountain slopes into the valley, spreading a blanket of darkness over the lake. I sat in the bow of the boat and noticed very little, keeping my eyes lowered on some point at my feet as I listened to Erskine's satisfied taunting.

"Turns a man's stomach to see the way ye was throwing yerself at Delany. I've seen doxies eye a man the same way who are worth the money slipped in their garter. Ye don't even have the class of a first-rate whore!"

His taunt failed to raise me. His words could never hurt me the way Lyle had with one look that reduced me completely. He believed I had been trying to soften him up, using the attraction between us to persuade him to buy Blackbriar House. The moments of ecstasy had turned to ugliness. Already suspicious of me, Lyle had not seen through Erskine's maneuvering, and because

273

of Davie, I had been unable to defend myself. How cleverly Erskine had made me out to be the one in charge! In everyone's eyes, I was the greedy one, ready to sell my aunt's home out from under her; I had been the instigator of the fraud perpetrated in Chimney Canyon. Remembering Randy's angry accusations, I knew that no one would believe my innocence in this new scheme. No one. Least of all, Lyle Delany.

We had reached the middle of the lake when the wind came up, whipping the lake into rolling swells that caught the rowboat in deep troughs and spilled water into its bottom. Huddled against sprays of water, I clung to the sides, fighting against a feeling of nausea as we rolled and dipped. The lake had turned an ugly gray, reflecting the lowering, shroudlike clouds. The rising wind seemed to be blowing from all points of the compass at the same time. The lake's surface was like a cauldron, rising and falling as whirlwinds sped across its surface. I prayed we would make it back before the center of the storm hit.

Erskine worked the oars feverishly, trying to find purchase in the churning water as he sent the boat crashing over rising swells. Hull timbers groaned so loudly that I feared all the caulked seams would break open again. Lightning forked the blackened sky and thunder like the roll of cannonballs cracked the air with deafening peals. In a matter of minutes the earth and sky had turned black. And in the midst of the raging wind, Erskine threw back his head in wild, ecstatic laughter. His black hair whipped around his face, his eyes shone with crazed brightness, and he yelled against the wind as if he were Lucifer himself, commanding the devils of hell to rise up and join in his maniacal glee. He was the embodiment of primeval evil rising out of every dark, festering pool, a Lucifer with forked tail who planted in every man the seeds of destruction. The forces of evil converged in him.

Every sweep of his mammoth arms made the boat shudder, and I feared that he would turn it over in some diabolical challenge to the elements. My hair whipped about in wild abandonment. The first spatter of rain hit my face. I couldn't tell if we were still heading for Blackbriar Bay or if the boat had been driven off course by the rising storm. What if we didn't get back? Davie! Like a searing poker, fear stabbed at my chest. Had Erskine been telling the truth? Would Aunt Minna carry out his orders to harm my precious little brother if we didn't return?

"Better be saying yer prayers," Erskine yelled at me, his face glowing with saturnine pleasure. The background of churning black water and ugly heavens harmonized with the explosive darkness within him. From his mocking taunt and laughter I realized that the challenge of pitting his strength against the elements was familiar to him and that he had weathered storms like this, delighting in skirting a watery edge to death. His twisted glee was being fed by watching my terror, so I jutted my head at a defiant angle, raised my face to the whipping wind, and kept my expression as bland as I could.

Every minute became a torturous eternity. I swallowed back terrified screams when the boat listed so far to one side that I could barely mantain my hold on the sides. Somehow I managed to keep the cries trapped in my throat. The rain was thickening minute by minute. Black thunderheads moved over the rim of mountains, closer and closer. With the force of an overturned bucket, the sky was threatening to open up in a downpour that would surely sink us. I wanted to shriek at Erskine to head for shore, but I knew he would only delight in my panic-stricken pleas.

He threw back his head and yelled. Forked spears of jagged lightning rent the sky. My ears filled with the sound of his laughter, the crescendo of thunderbolts, and wild waves hammering against the boat.

"The devil takes his own!" laughed Erskine.

I closed my eyes and prayed. They were still closed when we swept through the mouth of the bay. Suddenly the waters grew smoother. I opened my eyes as we sailed by the small island and reached the long pier which held the boathouse.

We had made it! For a moment, my terror refused to release its grasp. I knew then that I had never believed I would see land again.

I scrambled ashore, shutting out the sound of Erskine's laughter. Lifting my drenched skirts, I ran up the path to the house and burst in the front door.

One quick look in the parlor told me it was empty. I silently screamed Davie's name as I ran down the hall to the kitchen. For a moment I didn't see him, and I was about to turn on my heels and dash upstairs when the top of his head rose from beyond the table. The vibration of the floorboards had communicated my entrance to him.

"Davie!" I rushed over to him. He had been sleeping on a braided rug I had put near the stove. The impression of the pattern was on his cheek. I threw myself down beside him. "Are you all right?"

Reading my lips, he nodded, giving me his sweet smile. Then his expression changed to puzzlement as he viewed my streaming hair and clinging damp clothes. "You're wet," he signed.

I nodded, motioning to the window. Sheets of rain ran in silver streaks against the pane. For a moment Davie watched the rain and lightning, remaining oblivious to the thunder, which he could not hear. The clamor of the threatening elements did not reach him. Thunder was only seconds behind a white tracery of lightning that would undoubtedly leave some trees split and blackened. I breathed a prayer of thanksgiving that I was safely back.

"Where's Rags?" I asked.

Davie pointed. Then he clapped his hands.

At the sound, the puppy came tumbling from a corner of the kitchen where he was relishing a bone with his tiny teeth. His tail-wagging little behind made me laugh as I defended myself against his enthusiastic biting, licking, and jumping welcome. My chuckles were close to tears as a warm pink tongue bathed my face with kisses. Relief made me weak and slightly giddy. I hugged Davie. Everything was all right. He was safe. Sitting in the warmth of the fire, inside the weatherbeaten house where the storm couldn't reach us, I felt my frayed nerves begin to knit.

Erskine must have stayed in the boathouse, I reasoned, and shivered picturing his maniacal delight in sounds of the hammering rain upon the roof, and the vibrations of crashing thunder rattling the weathered boards. He'd revel in the deafening onslaught, laughing and bellowing at crashing waters pounding on the dock. With sickening certainty I knew that the evil man's mood was much like the violent fury of destructive forces that destroyed and killed. He would be as impersonal as the storm when the time came to wreak his pleasure and destruction upon us.

"Where's Aunt Minna?" I asked, suddenly filled with

new fear.

Davie shrugged.

"She must be upstairs. You poke up the fire in the stove and add some wood," I told him with my hands. "I'll check on Aunt Minna and then make supper."

Surely my aunt would resist Erskine's efforts to sell Blackbriar House. This had been her only home for years. I could tell that changes and additions had been made to it as time went by. She must have a great deal of herself invested in the house.

When I reached the second-floor landing I could hear her wheezy snores. Even before I reached her bed, I knew she was stone drunk. Looking down at her slack mouth, her puffy cheeks, and her pasty complexion, I felt my disappointment mingled with fresh anger. I wanted to shake her shoulders and yell at her. She had been doing so much better. Why did this have to happen, just when I needed her help to outwit Erskine before it was too late and he didn't need us anymore? He would kill us all as soon as he cheated Aunt Minna of her last dollar. Our time was running out.

"Aunt Minna, you've got to help me," I blubbered, sitting on the edge of her bed, as close to tears as I could come without them pouring down my cheeks. I took her hand in mine. It was cold and clammy to the touch, and I tried to rub some warmth into it. I knew that if she was awake, she would lash out at me with her vitriolic tongue and demand another bottle. All my efforts to show her affection had been harshly rejected. Life had twisted my aunt into a hard and uncaring person. Her life was centered on the drink she clutched in her trembling hands. Except for playing cards, I had found nothing that could break through her selfish demeanor and establish any kind of rapport between us. Lying there with her mussed gray hair and unkempt appearance, she looked years older than my father. The deep lines around her mouth were drawn downward as if a smile were foreign to her lips. And yet she had once been young and happy. I had stared at the photograph in my father's watch a thousand times, reminding myself that once upon a time Aunt Minna had been a laughing, carefree young girl. I had to do my best to save her from the greedy man who had bent her to his will.

The rain did not pass over as quickly as most sudden mountain storms. The bad weather lingered, settled in, sweeping moisture into the area so that it rained steadily until the earth was drenched, streams overflowed, and the lake rose, flooding low areas at its edge.

A heavy gloom permeated the house, casting deeper shadows into the rooms and halls and settling such shadowy darkness in the house that we kept kerosene lamps and candles burning in an attempt to alleviate the gloom. The air was chilled and dank; even wood fires did not keep the cold from seeping into our bodies. Davie and I were trapped inside and were unable to escape its desolate rooms.

I thought a lot about Lyle Delany and his new resort. Even though the heartache was sharp, I relived those moments in his arms. In my mind I wandered through the rooms again, picturing a fire in the huge stone fireplace. Soon the room would be filled with guests, lounging about in comfortable chairs, laughing and talking, and enjoying the pungent smell of pine logs. Men would enjoy their pipes and women would sit in companionable circles doing needlework or gossiping. And there would be one young woman who would raise her eyes when Lyle entered the room. She might be a daughter of one of the bankers he had mentioned. He would bow politely and offer his arm for a walk on the veranda. I could picture them strolling down to the lake's edge. She would smile and raise her face to his—and he would kiss her. Spirals of hot desire would make her weak, and her arms would wrap around his neck. Her fingers would thread the thick, tawny waves of his hair. Then he would brush his lips against her hair and—! *Stop it!* The cry came deep from within me.

During the rainy days, Davie and I spent more time on lessons in the kitchen. In the light of a flickering candle Davie bent his head over his paper and pencil, laboriously tracing the letters I had patterned for him. Even though he didn't know the sound of my name, he began to recognize A-N-N-A as belonging to me and D-A-V-I-E to him. If only he had a knowledgeable teacher he could make ten times the progress, I lamented as my feeble efforts seemed more trial-and-error than anything else. At least we had something constructive to do and working with Davie kept my thoughts from the tortuous maze of what to do to protect ourselves from Erskine.

It was impossible to avoid him. Kitchen chores kept me working at the stove and worktables, and I suffered his mocking, leering eyes as he sprawled in one of the chairs and taunted me.

"I seen the way Delany was looking at ye." He smirked. "Wanting to be putting his shoes under yer bed, he was."

I kept silent.

"Ye should be thanking me for taking ye to see him."
He laughed coarsely.

I kneaded the bread dough as if it were his head I was pounding with my fist. I vowed that his dirty mouth wouldn't get a rise out of me.

"A tumble with a fiery redhead ought to be worth a coin or two." He matted his thorny eyebrows. "Course, if ye were able to get Delany interested in buying Blackbriar House, I wouldn't be thinkin' about turning ye over to someone like Zeke Stone."

My hands were trembling slightly as I put the dough in a pan and stretched a piece of cloth over it. Zeke's name brought back the humiliation of his assault and the narrow escape I'd had from being raped.

"Ye should be thanking me for saving ye from that bastard. I've got yer best interests at heart, I have." He grinned. "I'm thinking ye need to show a little gratitude." His lewd smirk climbed up my skin as he reached out and jerked me over to his chair. "Let's see what you got to offer."

He would love to see any sign of weakness. I flared on the attack. "I've carried out every one of your cheating schemes. Keep your hands off me or you'll lose your golden goose, I promise you."

I jerked away and he just sat there and laughed. "First things first. There'll be time enough to tame ye proper-like . . . after ye persuade Delany to buy this house."

"Aunt Minna will never sell," I countered. "You may have her under your thumb about everything else, but this is her home and she'll fight to keep it."

"Yer sure about that?"

"Yes, I'm sure," I said with more confidence than I felt.

"Woll, I reckon we'll just have to see about that, won't

281

we?" His mocking smile settled a chill upon me.

I knew there was a crisis when I heard him bellowing at Aunt Minna. "I'm telling ye the hill is like a mudslide. There ain't no help for it. I found the still turned over and washed halfway down the hill. No chance of setting it up again until this confounded rain stops."

"But I need a drink," she whimpered.

"Then go out in the rain and dig for a bottle. I'm telling ye, there's none left. No, I haven't got some hidden away. Blast it all, ye go through a bottle of rotgut like it was spring water!"

"It's your fault!" she lashed out.

"Oh, is it now? Don't forget ye can be thanking me for taking care of ye and yer cravings. Without me, where would ye be?"

"Please don't be mad, Jem. I hate it when you're angry with me." The pleading in her voice made me sick. "I know you'll take care of me."

"Course I will." His voice softened. "I'll see if I've got a couple of drinks in the boathouse . . ."

"Oh, thank you . . . thank you, Jem. You're a good man." Her groveling blubbering was sickening.

I heard Erskine stomp out of the house and was surprised when he returned in a few minutes with three dead chickens.

He threw the soggy fowl on the table. "Stupid things drowned. God damn this rain. The chickenhouse is washed away, and the whole hillside likely to start sliding if this blasted rain doesn't stop."

The lack of fresh eggs would be a real hardship, I thought. The smell of wet feathers was strong enough to turn my stomach, and I didn't relish the task, but the birds had to be plucked and cooked right away. Our food supply was getting back to where it had been when I first came. Only a small portion of the deer carcass remained, and there was no chance of success fishing in the high waters.

I set Davie to work plucking feathers with me, and as we worked on the chickens, I thought about the conversation I had overheard. One fact looked promising: if Aunt Minna was deprived of her whiskey, she might be rational enough to understand that Erskine was going to sell Blackbriar House out from under her. Once she accepted the truth, and if she cooperated, we could devise a plan to thwart him. She had to realize that all of us were safe as long as he failed to sell the last of her property. Once it was all gone— I pushed the thought away, determined to enlist Aunt Minna's help as quickly as I could.

The chance came the next afternoon when she wanted to play cards. Her moods became more cantankerous as her supply of whiskey was shut off, but I was encouraged by the clear, steady glare she gave her cards and her brisk movements as she shuffled.

I wasn't certain where Erskine was, so I leaned forward and said in a conspirator's whisper, "Aunt Minna, you have to listen to me. Erskine is making plans to sell your house."

"Don't be an idiot," she snapped.

"It's true. You have to believe me. The other day, when Erskine took me away in the boat, we went to see Lyle Delany, the man who bought the rest of your lake property. Erskine offered him Blackbriar House. He's going to sell it, Aunt Minna. Your home."

"Why would he do a thing like that?" I thought she was secretly laughing at me.

"For money. What else? He's taken everything else from you. Don't you see, Aunt Minna? He's robbed you blind . . . and when there's nothing left, he'll have no reason to care what happens to you."

"Jem will always care what happens to me," she said with exasperating firmness. "He always has . . . and he always will."

"No, you're wrong . . . he's evil. He'll kill all of us when he's ready." I grabbed her hand. "You, too, Aunt Minna. He's after your money. Don't be fooled by his lies. He's shrewd and cunning and . . ."

She gave a deep chuckle. "He's some man, isn't he?"

I couldn't believe it. Nothing I said about Erskine was getting through to her. She was blind to his true nature. Whatever the ties were between them, they were strong enough to withstand any attack I could make on Erskine. "You have to believe me. He's evil, a murderer—"

"I told you before, I won't have you bad-mouthing my—" she stopped before she said the word.

Lover? I wondered.

"I didn't ask you to come here," she snapped. "If I hadn't sprained my ankle, you'd never have got inside the door. I told Jem it would be better all around if we got shut of you and that stupid boy."

"How can you talk like that? Your own flesh and blood! Davie is a wonderful little boy. What kind of woman are you to let Erskine bring you down to his level? A cold-hearted, evil—"

She reached over and slapped my face so hard my ears rang from the blow. "That's for you and your high and mighty ways!" she screeched. "I'll take Jem Erskine over

284

the likes of you and your father any day!"

I fled upstairs and threw myself on the attic bed. I didn't know what I was going to do. Sunlight was breaking through the clouds, and I knew that time was getting short. If Delany didn't buy Blackbriar House, somebody else would.

Davie came in, patted my shoulder, and then gently laid his cheek against mine.

"Davie," I held him close. "What are we going to do?"

Chapter Twenty

The next day a waterlogged earth began to dry under the bright light of a brassy sun. From the crowns of ponderosa pines, needles dripped silver droplets like sparkling dew, and cedar trees that had been bent over with the weight of soaked branches began to straighten. The air was filled with a perfume so redolent of spice that it made me heady with its freshness.

The waters of the bay and lake shimmered in the sunlight, shedding iron gray tones for delicate shades of purple, violet, and cobalt. Erskine left in the skiff to get needed supplies. I knew he would be gone most of the day, and I felt the heavy despondency of the last few days lighten.

Aunt Minna thrashed about her room looking for a hidden bottle and not finding any. I had scoured her room for bottles and had emptied at least four of them. She called my name, but I didn't respond. I could hear her throwing things about and knocking over furniture. She was in a wild mood, and I wasn't about to give her a chance to vent her anger on me again.

As soon as my kitchen chores were done, I signed to Davie, "Let's take a walk. I'll fix a lunch."

He smiled and picked up his piece of wood and rolled-up fishing line. "Fish for supper?" he asked with his hands.

"Good idea. But let's take a walk up to the waterfall first," I answered back. Tons of water vaulting off the high cliff would be beautiful with all the extra rain.

Davie watched as I wrapped up some pieces of chicken and slices of bread. The puppy whined at the back door, understanding on some intuitive level that we were going somewhere. He sat down on his rounded bottom and cocked his head, waiting for us to make a move toward the door. When we came out, he danced around in a circle, barking and wagging his tail.

Davie laughed at his antics and once again I thanked the day the ugly little stray had come into our lives. How desperately we needed the laughs he gave us.

"It'll be wet," I said, looking at our worn shoes and wishing for boots. The hill would be muddy. We'd have a job cleaning our shoes when we got back, but there was no help for it. The walk would be worth it.

As we started away from the house, I couldn't believe the sight. Like a gully washer, the recent rainstorm had poured down the rocky slopes, carrying dirt and stones and uprooting shallow-rooted plants. Piles of stones and debris had been washed up against the house. The dilapidated chicken run had been washed away completely, and all over the hillside saplings had been bent over, uncovering their roots.

Walking was difficult on the waterlogged hillside. Rags and Davie bounded ahead of me with the exuberance of youth, slipping and sliding on the wet ground. Trying to

288

keep up with them was no easy task. Several times I had to put my hands out and touch the ground to maintain my balance. The exercise, the fresh air, and the carefree joy of my companions overrode a growing anxiety that Erskine might return that very day with a buyer. As I stopped and looked back over the roof of my aunt's house to the breathtaking beauty of the bay and the lake beyond, I knew that there was no place on earth any lovelier.

I could have been perfectly content here, I thought with a sad ache. If Aunt Minna had taken us with any degree of love and affection, Davie could have grown up here, strong and healthy, and the three of us could have been a family. If Erskine hadn't been in such a position of power, I might have had a chance to win over my aunt. He'd poisoned her mind with lies and her body with whiskey. Sadly, Aunt Minna's hatred of my father had been extended to Davie and me. I pitied her but still believed I could save her from herself and from Erskine's clutches if I only had more time. Time. How many days and nights were left to me? Once I signed the papers on Blackbriar House, there would be no reason for Erskine to let me live. Aunt Minna seemed to be my only hope. If she could only realize that he was planning to sell her home, I believed she would turn on him. By the time the truth penetrated her befuddled brain, it would be too late.

I pushed my heavy thoughts aside, determined to enjoy the beauty that surrounded us. We reached the waterfall and sat on a warm boulder to watch the mesmerizing sight of water dropping hundreds of feet off the high precipice like a stream of diamonds. The water fell into an emerald green pond and sent a spatter of jewels into the air. Just watching it, I felt something deep inside me expand. I couldn't have put the sensation into words, but the beauty of the scene reached my soul and healed some of the pain. I sat in silence beside Davie as crashing waters vibrated in my ears and a sense of peace invaded my heart. I reached over and squeezed his hand. He smiled in response. No hour spent in church had ever been more replenishing.

We took our lunch slowly, eating all the bread and all but a couple of pieces of the chicken, which I wrapped up and put back in my pocket. I knew better than to waste any food. We drank water from the pond by cupping our hands.

Davie begged to play in the water and since his shoes were so dirty, I let him roll up his pant legs and splash and jump about like a little frog. He was drenched to the waist when I finally called a halt to the water play. I promised we would come back another time and let him paddle about.

We left the scene reluctantly. There was such beauty and peace here, high on the hillside, and such dark hell awated us in the house below, I thought, as we made our way back down the hill.

When we reached the place where the stone sepulchre had been built on the hillside, I saw that the rains had disturbed one side of it, washing away some of the rocks. The wooden cross had fallen sideways. Once more I wondered why no headstone had been placed on the burial mound. Maybe Horace Brown hadn't wanted one, I thought, wondering what kind of husband he had been to Aunt Minna.

I motioned for Davie to help me staighten the cross. As frisky as ever, Rags bounded up on the mounds of rocks as if playing king of the mountain. He poked his nose into the rocks we were piling on top to brace the cross.

"Get down, Rags," I ordered.

He tumbled down the side, loosening another spill of rocks.

I scolded him and stooped to the ground to retrieve the stones and put them back. Before I could straighten up, I nearly fainted.

Showing in the mound of dirt and rocks was a mass of human hair, red and curly. *McKenzie red!*

The roar in my ears was as loud as the waterfall had been. Truth, like a piece of pottery thrown against a wall, shattered in a thousand pieces—and then came together in perfect harmony. For a moment my breathing stopped. My mind raced. It was not Horace Brown who lay under the pile of stones but a redheaded woman.

"My God . . . it can't be." But I was sure it was. I sank to the ground in sudden weakness. The body that lay under the mound of rocks was Aunt Minna. The woman I had called by that name was an imposter . . . she had to be. Her behavior had never been close to that of anyone related to Davie and me. She had laughed when Erskine called her "Auntie." All my attempts to get her talking about the past had failed—because she wasn't the young girl in the photograph and knew nothing about our family. Erskine had pretended she was mentally unstable to cover up any slips she made. How could I have been taken in so completely? I had been trying so hard to love and accept her that I had ignored a thousand clues. From the first, the woman and Erskine had let me think she was Minna McKenzie-Brown, when in truth my aunt must have already been dead and buried underneath these stones when I arrived.

My mind raced backward. I had called her Aunt Minna when I helped her into the house that first day. Now, I understand why she had not wanted me around after her ankle got better. It must have been tiring for her, pretending to be someone she wasn't. I didn't know what relationship she had with Erskine. She had always defended him against any of my accusations. Now I knew why: she was involved in the deception with him. The two of them had arranged it. My aunt couldn't have been dead very long. I was certain my father had seen his sister when he'd talked to her a few months back. He would have recognized an imposter. Who was the woman? Not a wife, I didn't think, since I hadn't picked up any matrimonial exchanges between them. Nor any romantic innuendoes, even though the woman had always defended him—more like a member of his family. A sister, perhaps? Or just someone he had brought in? I wondered then if she could have been the housekeeper who Randy had told me about that first day on the boat. He had said that the last housekeeper had not stayed long. But maybe she had. Maybe she was still here . . .

For a moment the breadth of the deception swamped my thoughts. They had fooled the judge into thinking that my aunt was no longer capable of handling her affairs—hence the power of attorney was put into her niece's hand. What could be more legitimate than that? The judge had never seen my aunt, so he accepted the drunken woman without question. Now I knew why Aunt Minna couldn't sign away her assets—*because she wasn't Aunt Minna!* Erskine would have had trouble trying to sell the dead woman's property. Maybe they had intended to forge my aunt's signature but when I came along, he had a blood relative to do it for him.

How they must have laughed at my efforts to "save" Aunt Minna! All the time the woman had been ready to kill Davie and me whenever Erskine gave the word. Even now, they must be gloating about their final scam— to sell Blackbriar House. Undoubtedly they had plans to leave as soon as the money was in their hands. How easily a regrettable accident could be arranged for Davie and me.

Davie touched my shoulder. "We go fishing?" he signed.

Thank heavens, he had not seen the swatch of red hair. I nodded, and quickly I put back the dirt and stones. My hands moved automatically while my mind raced. *Dear God, what am I going to do now?*

We started down the hill, and then I pulled Davie back behind a thicket of scrub oak. The woman was coming out of the back door. How could I ever have thought she resembled the girl in the photograph? She was older, and her bone structure was completely different. I had thought time had changed her, but she had never been the pretty, smiling girl in the photograph. The clue had been in my father's watch, but I had missed it.

I knew where the imposter was headed—to the whiskey still. Her face was drawn in an ugly grimace as she made her way up the hillside. Yes, she would have shot me that day on the stairs if they hadn't needed me alive. And she would have carried out Erskine's instructions to kill Davie if I managed to get away. My belief that Aunt Minna would never let harm come to us was a hollow mockery now that I knew they had killed my aunt and buried her body in the rock sepulchre.

As soon as the woman was out of sight, I put my finger to my lips in a quieting motion and gestured to Davie to go on down the hill. Once out of sight of the house, I began to breathe more easily, but new terror was sending my thoughts into a wild fury.

Davie bounded down to the lake, skirting the edge, and throwing sticks for Rags. The puppy looked like a mud ball after our hike, but he tumbled into the water repeatedly in his clumsy exuberance and came out clean, but soaked. He seemed to love the water as much as my brother. I didn't say anything when Davie splashed ankle high along the lake's edge getting rid of the cake of mud on his shoes. The matter of wet feet scarcely entered my consciousness.

Water lapped high on the rocky bank where we usually fished, and I had to warn Davie about losing his balance. He put a bug on his hook and threw his line out into the water. Then he sat on a rock and waited. His bright hair shone copper in the sun. McKenzie red!

My stomach turned queasy. I wondered how they had killed Aunt Minna. Had she trusted Erskine, her caretaker for ten years, or had she been his prisoner for that long? The vile man must have carefully planned her death . . . and arranged for the woman to impersonate her just long enough to sell all the property and then disappear. Since my aunt had been a recluse, all he had to do was keep people who might know her away from the house.

I had been a bonanza falling into his lap. A golden goose, as he had laughingly admitted, and how cleverly he had used me to gather his golden eggs. He had brought the judge here, then sent me to Tahoe City to sign legal documents. He had forced me to go to Chimney Canyon when he salted the gully with ore, and now he was using me to lure Lyle to reach his final goal of selling Blackbriar. Every step of the way, I had been helpless because of Davie. Using my brother as hostage, Erskine had made me the perfect pawn in his diabolical game.

Davie squealed as he pulled in a trout. The fish flapped on the rocks, and Rags gave an excited "Woof," shaking his tail so furiously it seemed ready to fall off. I made the expected approving responses. Inside I felt anxiety building to a point of explosion. As my brother settled down to catch another fish, my eyes scanned the bay, the small island, and the narrow opening into the lake. We had to get away!

Erskine would not be back for a few hours. It was usually late afternoon when he returned from Tahoe City. My eyes swept back to the boathouse. The rowboat must be locked inside. I remembered how Erskine's arms had strained to propel the boat through the water. The rhythm of his oars had been sure and practiced, but the movement had etched itself in my mind. I might be clumsy at first, but I was certain I could manage to copy the way he pulled the oars to move the boat. If I could just get us out into the lake, surely we could reach a settlement along the bank. I would take my chances on a lumbering camp or any other gathering of men. Nothing could be worse than remaining in the clutches of the master of Blackbriar and the woman who was ready to kill us when our usefulness was over.

I stomped on the ground. Davie looked back at me.

"Come on. We're going," I signed.

A mutinous look came in his eyes.

"Now!" I said with a slice of my hand.

With infuriating slowness, he rewound the line

around his stick. He started to pick up the fish.

I touched his shoulder. "No. Leave it here . . . for the birds."

He made a motion of protest but I ignored it. My thoughts raced ahead, formulating a desperate plan that had a slight chance of success. We rounded a curve in the bay, in front of the house. I know Davie was surprised when I motioned him to follow me as I walked out on the long pier to the boathouse. I knew that we could be seen clearly from any window in the house. I wished now that I had not been so zealous in destroying all the whiskey bottles. If the woman was in a drunken stupor, she would have little interest in what we were doing at the boathouse. If not—I shoved the anxious thought away.

The side door to the boathouse was locked. The heavy padlock and chain would have required a crowbar and someone ten times my strength to pry it open. The front doors that opened to allow passage of a boat were bolted from the inside. The small high window where I had seen lantern light was the only other opening into the tiny building. High above my head, the window was too small for me to crawl through.

I looked back at the house and wondered how long it would take my false aunt to get a gun and come after us. I looked up at the boathouse window again—and made my decision.

With a firm hand I pulled Davie over to the side of the building and pointed upward. "The window." I signed and mouthed the words. "You go through the window."

Glancing up and then back to me, Davie looked absolutely bewildered. "What?" he questioned with his fingers as if he thought he had misunderstood what I was trying to tell him.

"I'm going to lift you up . . . on my shoulders. You take this rock and break the window. Understand?"

His eyes were rounded and perplexed.

I was praying that there would be something stacked against the wall on the inside so he wouldn't have a long drop to the floor.

"Why?" The question was accompanied by a frown.

I took a deep breath and forced patience. "There's a rowboat inside. Understand?"

He nodded.

"We have to get away. You have to get inside and open the front door so we can get the boat out." My fingers flew. "Do you think you can do it?"

He swallowed, and I knew his mouth was as dry as mine. In spite of the urgency building up in me, I went through the instructions once more. "Ready?" I signed to him.

He nodded.

I bent my knees and motioned for him to mount my shoulders. An eight-year-old boy wasn't as heavy as I had expected. He was agile and sure-footed. I held his legs and forced strength into mine as I straightened up as close to the wall of the boathouse as I could get.

Were we being watched from the house? I couldn't tell. I closed my eyes for a second in a silent prayer. *Hurry, Davie, hurry.* There was no way to talk to him now. *Break the window. Break the window,* I ordered silently. Had Davie understood my instructions? He seemed to be standing motionless on my shoulders, looking in the window. Maybe he thought I just wanted him to look in and see if the boat was there. I couldn't let go of his legs to sign. My heart thumped loudly in my ears. We didn't have much time, exposed as we were to every window in the house. Maybe the woman was still looking for whiskey, but maybe she wasn't.

The sound of breaking glass was music to my ears as Davie finally whacked away at the glass. It seemed to take forever before all the jagged pieces were cleared away and he peered inside.

He looked down and gave me a motion to lift him higher. Like a scrambling squirrel, he stuck his head, arm, and leg through the opening as I lifted, and in the next instant he was gone.

He was inside. Would he open up the door that would allow us to float the rowboat out into the lake? I ran around to the front, watching and praying that the inside lock was something he could manage. If the woman had heard the glass breaking, she would be on us in a minute.

My frantic gaze searched the waters of the bay, and I squinted my eyes to see far out on the lake. Just because Erskine had taken longer for the trip other times didn't mean he couldn't come back earlier. I feared that he could return at any time. He seemed to have an uncanny sense about my thoughts and actions—as if he were truly in league with the devil.

"Davie, hurry," I screamed, even though I knew he couldn't hear me. Maybe he had hurt himself when he scooted through the window. Maybe he was lying inside with a broken leg. Maybe—

The sound of a bolt scraping on the inside cut off the rest of the self-torturing "maybes." Slowly the wide door floated open. I don't know what I would have done if the rowboat hadn't been there, but it was. I motioned Davie into it as I untied the rope. The puppy nearly tripped me, threading my legs in the excitement. Davie grabbed Rags and held him as he sat down in the bow.

Sitting down on the wooden seat, I awkwardly shoved the boat with an oar and clumsily managed to get the boat beyond the door of the boathouse. With frantic sweeps of the oars, I tried to imitate Erskine's pattern of rowing.

We barely moved.

Desperation was like a whip at my back. The oars were heavy and awkward, and at first I couldn't get them in the water deep enough to push the boat forward. We bobbed like sitting ducks only a few feet from the pier. Any moment the woman might have a rifle leveled at us.

Pure panic rushed a reserve of strength into my arms. I attacked the water again, dipping the oars deeper into the water and pulling back on them with renewed effort that nearly pulled the muscles from my back. The pain went unnoticed as we slowly began to move forward.

I was beginning to think I had the hang of it when my uneven pull on the oars started to send us in a circle. Oh, no! We were turned halfway back toward the boathouse! How much longer would our luck hold out? We were only a few feet from the pier. If the woman came with a gun we would be helpless. I tried not to think of anything but managing the unwieldly oars. It took several minutes before I finally got the bow headed back toward the opening of the bay.

What if Erskine suddenly appeared now, meeting us in the middle of the bay? What a laugh he would have at my clumsy efforts to outmaneuver him. But our luck was holding. No sign of our jailer—or his skiff.

With steady sweeps of the oars I moved the boat over the water—but the mouth of the bay was not getting much closer. The snail's pace was exacting all the strength I could muster. How would I ever be able to keep up the rowing long enough to reach any safe place along the lake?

Suddenly Davie threw up his arm to catch my attention.

"What is it?" I mouthed.

He pointed to the bottom of the boat.

I blinked, praying that my eyesight was faulty. Water was seeping up through several cracks at an alarming rate. The caulked seams had taken a beating in the rainstorm.

Dear God, no! We were sinking.

Chapter Twenty-One

There was no way to stop the water from coming in, nothing in the boat to bail it out. Three or four minutes was all we had to remain afloat. The sides of the bay were too far to reach before the boat would go under, even if I had been a proficient rower, instead of a clumsy, ineffectual paddler. All of this came to me like a bombardment of arrows. I reeled from the impact, and at the same time, some detached part of my brain took command.

I flung a look over my shoulder. Better to go back than to drown—but we had come farther than I had thought! I couldn't do it. No time to get the boat turned around and row back to the pier. Cold water swished around my feet in an ever-growing puddle in the bottom of the boat. We would go down in the middle of the bay.

There was only one place, one chance . . . the small outcropping of rocks that formed the small island in the center of the bay. Could we make it? Even as the question roared in my head, I was rowing toward it. Keeping my eyes on the ugly pile of granite rocks and sparse vegetation, I dipped the oars frantically into the water and pulled.

The crack in the bottom of the boat was allowing water to rush in faster. Davie was sitting in the water, his eyes growing wider as the boat sank deeper into the lake. The puppy was wet up to his rounded stomach. He splashed about indignantly before Davie lifted him out of the water and held him against his breast. Now they huddled together in the watery boat while I gasped and pulled and nearly jerked my arms out of their sockets.

We weren't going to make it!

Despite my valiant efforts, the island was still a terrifying distance away. Every sweep of the oars only moved the waterlogged craft a short distance. The weight of the water made the boat even more clumsy and unmanageable than before. A competent rower might have been able to bring it to beach, but I was being taxed beyond my strength and ability. Only a stubborn, unrealistic hope that somehow I could bring off a miracle kept me straining at the oars.

The boat was sinking.

Davie sliced the air with his hands. "Hurry! Hurry!"

There was nothing I could do. Water was claiming the craft—and us in it. We had made gains but were still a frightening distance from the island. Neither Davie nor I could swim. I looked over the side of the boat. Through the clear water I saw rocks not far below the surface. The bottom didn't look terribly deep, but was it an illusion? I remembered the time Erskine had showed me the sheer rock buttress that went hundreds of feet down into the water to a terrifying depth, even though it appeared to be just beneath the surface. What if the same deception was

302

occurring here? Could I believe my eyes? Maybe the rocky lake bottom was not a few feet under the water, as it seemed, but a depth that would make it impossible to struggle to shore.

No time to weigh the gamble . . . the stern of the boat sank behind me, tipping the craft up at an angle. I dropped the oars. I pointed to the island and signaled to Davie. "Go!"

We had just enough time to jump free of the boat before it turned over and slowly sank. As I went over the side, I heard Davie hit the water and the high-pitched squeak from the puppy. Then the water folded over my head.

I went down. My eyes and ears filled with water, and trapped air burned in my chest as I floundered. Without the clinging cloth of my skirts wrapping my legs I might have touched rocky bottom in my first descent, but I felt nothing but water around me as I thrashed my arms and legs and came to the surface again. Davie! I glimpsed his head bobbing above the water before I went down for a second time. I couldn't get to him. The weight of my garments dragged me under. I was sinking to the bottom of the lake with little chance of ever rising to the surface again. Suddenly my feet touched a hard surface, and I pushed hard against it and shot up again.

My head thrust out of the water. Frantically I splashed my arms, trying to stay afloat. I could see Davie in the water. He was almost to the island! He was going to make it! Thank God for his natural affinity for handling himself in the water.

I went down again, but this time my legs were under me as my feet hit a rocky shelf that slanted away from the

303

island in a gradual slope. The next moment I was standing tiptoe in the water. I arched my head to keep my nose above the waterline. My drenched skirts pulled me off balance as I bobbed forward. It was a miracle! I was walking out of the water with each step.

Davie was already on the bank, waving encouragement as I struggled forward, rising out of the water like a drowned rag doll. My brother's eyes were glistening with excitement. It was obvious that the ducking had held more fun than terror for him. Rivulets of water streamed down his face. Wet hair was plastered around his face, and wet clothes molded his childish body, but he was grinning.

Rags shook himself furiously and woofed indignantly as if someone had played an unwelcome trick on him by dunking him. He ran back and forth, ready to greet me when I stumbled out of the water. For a moment I couldn't do anything more than stagger to a dry spot and drop on the ground. The solid earth under me was something too precious to put into words. For a long moment, relief dominated my thoughts, then reality shattered the moment of bliss.

What were we going to do now? The horror of it struck home—stranded on a piece of rocky outcropping in the middle of the bay! Trapped as securely as prisoners sentenced to imprisonment on an island. We couldn't go anywhere.

There wasn't a ripple in the water where the boat had been, but I knew it must rest on the underwater shelf, not far from the surface. This realization was like a crack of summer lightning. It would mark the spot where we had overturned if anyone looked into the water and saw it

304

resting on the rock bed.

I squinted my eyes against the late afternoon sun, looking back toward the house. Not more than a few minutes had passed since the boat sank beneath us, but it seemed an eternity. The boathouse door stood open. The long pier was empty. No sign of Aunt Minna's imposter. If she had found a bottle, she might be back at the house. Had she watched the whole thing and was she now holding her sides with drunken laughter, delighting in the news she would have for Erskine when he returned?

"Your pigeons have flown the coop," she would say with a drunken sneer. "But they didn't get far." I could imagine Erskine's satisfied growl when she told him that we were stranded on the island. He might decide to leave us here for God-knows-how-long to teach us a lesson.

I touched Davie's shoulder. "Come on!" I signed quickly. We had to get out of sight. No telling when Erskine would return in the skiff. If Aunt Minna hadn't seen us, I didn't want to reveal our whereabouts any sooner than I had to.

And then I froze, not believing my eyes. Far out on the lake was the black silhouette of a skiff heading toward the mouth of the bay. Erskine was returning. We had to find a hiding place. If the woman hadn't seen the boat sink under us, perhaps he would think that we had made it all the way to the lake before he returned.

Davie pulled at my arm and pointed. I followed his pointing finger to the place where the rowboat had sunk. Somehow one of the oars had gotten free of its oarlock, and it was floating in the water, pointing toward the island as boldly as an arrow.

305

Oh, no! Erskine couldn't miss seeing it as he passed. We had to get it. My eyes swung back to the lake. The skiff was coming fast.

Before I could react, Davie had darted away from my side and back into the water.

"Come back!" I screamed at him, my orders literally falling on deaf ears. He had always used any excuse to splash about in water. I could have paddled him. The level of the lake rose on him as he headed out toward the floating oar. Above his knees . . . above his waist . . . to his chest . . . and now up to his chin. He kept bouncing, shoving upward as his feet touched the rock bottom, going under and then up again until the water was over his head.

He was going to drown. I lurched out into the water after him. The water was up to my waist when I saw him lunge at the oar and grab it with both hands. Kicking his feet, he propelled it back toward the bank.

When it came close enough, I reached out and grabbed it, pulling him and the oar back to shore. Relief took my breath away for a moment. Then, I sent a frantic look toward the head of the bay. Had we been seen? The skiff was almost ready to slip through the outstretched arms of the bay. If Erskine was looking toward the island, he could see us.

I quickly dragged the oar into some rocks. I motioned to Davie to follow me as I bounded upward over tumbled boulders. There were few trees on this mammoth rock pile set out in the middle of the water. Through the years some tenacious grass and twisted shrubs had found root space in shallow crevices between the rocks. No flat places invited meadow flowers or stands of conifers.

Stark and exposed to sky and water, the island was pitifully inadequate as a hiding place. The only tree cover was at the crown of the giant rock pile, and as we climbed toward it, I was afraid that we could be seen in all directions.

There wasn't enough time to reach the trees.

"Down!"

Davie followed my hand order and flattened himself against a slab of granite rock. I did the same, grabbing Rags in a desperate effort to keep him from running about and betraying us. Our only hope was not to draw Erskine's attention to the island. If he scanned it as he passed it on the way to the house, we were lost. Any movement would center his attention on the rocks—and we could be seen!

The rock felt warm under my cheek. Chilled by the lake water, I couldn't keep from shivering as I lay there, holding my breath, straining to hear the swish of water that would tell me whether or not Erskine was coming to the island or heading past us to the pier. The smell of Rags' wet fur filled my nostrils and he wiggled in my arms, stirring up dirt.

Like lizards motionless in the bright sunlight, we lay against the rocks and waited. Now that I knew my aunt lay dead on the hillside, undoubtedly a victim of Erskine's murderous hands, the belief that somehow Aunt Minna would protect us was ludicrous. From the beginning the woman I called aunt had been an impostor, ready to strike me, curse me, and shoot me without hesitation. If she'd had her way, both Davie and I would have been disposed of by now. Erskine had forced her to accept us because it was expedient to have me signing all

307

the bills of sale. At one time she seemed to be jealous of me, but he must have reassured her, because she had fallen back into her old patterns, waiting for him to decide when my usefulness was over.

My ears caught the sound of rippling water. I warned Davie with my eyes. In his silent world, he couldn't know that the man who held us in his deadly grip was guiding his boat through the water with a flap of sail and swish of rudder. The sounds floated over the water, closer and closer. Was he coming? Had he seen us in the water? Were we visible as colorful banners stretched out in the sun to dry?

I dared not raise my head to look. I gave Davie a reassuring smile but warned him with my eyes to stay motionless. After a long moment, I no longer heard the sound of disturbed water. No sound of a boat pulling to shore. No footsteps. Nothing.

I slowly lifted my head. Erskine's skiff was almost to the pier. He could see the open doors of the empty boathouse, the rowboat gone.

What would he do?

I flattened out again, fearful that he might look back and search the island with his eyes. Could he see us from the pier? I didn't think so—not unless we moved. The distance was too far.

I heard the sound of a door slamming and I guessed that he had rushed up to the house. I could imagine him yelling at the woman. "Where in the hell is the rowboat? Did ye let 'em get away, ye blasted fool?"

I prayed she was so far gone in drink, she wouldn't know what he was talking about. We would only have a few minutes until Erskine was on the hunt. He would know we had taken the boat.

I jerked to my feet, dropped the dog, and motioned to Davie. We had to make it to some cover before Erskine came back in his skiff a second time. He nodded and darted ahead.

We scrambled upward. The island was a mass of craggy rocks. Huge, round boulders from years ago blocked our way and we were forced to hunt for passage between them, only to slip backward or scramble upward on hands and knees. The pinnacle of the island ended in a sheer high cliff on the far end. A band of trees heralded a small stretch of level land at the highest point, and this was our target. When we reached it, we bounded into the center of the scraggy evergreens that had been whipped by the wind and winter storms. They sagged with thick branches that offered blessed concealment.

We couldn't be seen from any direction. Like a crow's nest, we were high above the lake. For a moment an exhilaration that defined our dire situation spilled through me. Quickly it was gone. The beauty of the scenery could not still a rising panic that we might end up pleading with Erskine to take us off the barren island. We could end up as food for eagles and only our bleached bones tumbled in the rocks would be discovered at some distant point in time.

No, we would hide out until someone sailed by the island. Maybe the *Tahoe Queen* would make a stop at Blackbriar Bay. It was about time for its run. From our vantage point I could see a great distance out onto the lake. My eyes raked the horizon. What if we waved? Would someone aboard the vessel see us and come steaming toward the island?

I positioned myself in the trees so I could watch the lake. Davie amused himself with a collection of pine cones scattered on the ground where we sat. He tossed one to Rags like a ball, and the two of them played as if on a holiday outing.

About a half-hour later I saw the steamer far out on the lake as it made its afternoon run and then disappeared. Any idea of leaving our cover and waving was pure idiocy. Any help we would get from the *Tahoe Queen* would depend upon her entering Blackbriar Bay, and I knew from past experience that it might be weeks before that happened.

We would starve to death before then.

Chapter Twenty-Two

We prepared to spend the night in the bower of trees at the highest point of the island. The two pieces of leftover chicken which I had wrapped and put in my apron pocket were soggy, but Davie and I ate them for supper with satisfaction, and Rags chomped on the bones. I was glad I had something to put into our stomachs. Rags took off on his own to find more to eat in the rock crevices. I decided that he must not have had much luck, because he didn't come back until the middle of the night, flopping down next to Davie with a low whine and nudge of his nose. He had had to scavenge for himself when he was a puppy, but there had been trash and refuse piles, not barren rocks and dry grass.

We spent a cold night, shivering under the branches of the trees, listening to birds rustling about and flapping their wings as they settled in nests scattered among the rocks. Our clothes were still damp from our fall into the water, and by the time I decided that Erskine wasn't going to come looking for us, it was too late to stretch out in the sun and dry them.

Davie's hand automatically stroked the dog's head as the two of them snuggled closer to me, as if I could keep them warm and safe.

Safe! The word was like a knife stuck in my side. The discovery I had made at the sepulchre had devastated me to the point that I had allowed fear to override good judgment. I had given in to panic and fled without any preparation. Nothing had changed at Blackbriar House except my concept of the situation. My aunt had been dead upon our arrival. We had never been family to the woman I called Aunt Minna. She had always been the enemy. How completely vulnerable we were from the very beginning. I shuddered to think how completely I had been taken in by the woman's impersonation—even though some deep intuition had tried to warn me. I had been determined to love and help her. No wonder she laughed at me with such malicious glee! All that talk of family must have turned her stomach. And my attacks upon Erskine had riled her enough to slap me about. We were lucky to have been spared more of her brutality. I knew I could never face the woman again without giving away the fact that I knew she was not Aunt Minna.

In the safety of darkness, I walked out of our bower of trees and stood among the rocks like a night animal, filling my nostrils for a warning scent and sending a searching gaze across the water to Blackbriar House. The house was dark, but I thought I caught a faint glow of light coming from the boathouse. Erskine? Was he pondering our escape, searching for a clue that would send him to the island? Once he came close enough to see the submerged rowboat, he would know his captives were safely snared. Maybe he knew that already—if his woman had seen us. If only we had been able to get away! If

Erskine found us he would exact punishment for our thwarted escape. I shuddered to think what he might do to Davie—and to me. His rage was like that of an inflamed bull. He would batter us within an inch of our lives.

We had to get away!

Morning came, and like a giant mirror, the lake reflected clouds of rose and apricot, shimmering like satin cloth until the colors faded, and tiny white clouds like crumbs of bread moved quickly across the pale blue sky. Huddled in the trees, we felt the first shafts of warm sunlight coming through the branches. Soon the rocks would radiate heat, but we didn't dare expose ourselves.

I was afraid that even the puppy moving about might be seen, so I had Davie tie him up with a piece of fishing line he had in his pocket. I had nothing to offer for breakfast. Davie looked at me expectantly, as if I could conjure up another meal out of my apron pocket. Nothing grew on the island that might sustain us for a few days, not even wild berries. At least we had water, I thought, trying to ignore the inevitable: we had to give ourselves up.

The moment for surrender came more quickly than I had planned. From our high perch I saw Erskine shove his skiff away from the pier and set sail across the bay. I watched him from the concealment of the trees. Was he coming to the island? If he knew we were here, he had deliberately left us here all night. A helpless rage surged through me. Fright, fury, and an unreasonable determination not to give in kept me from running down to the edge of the water and signaling to him.

I watched the skiff moving swiftly through the water, holding my breath. For a few moments I couldn't tell whether or not Erskine was veering in the direction of the island or heading for the mouth of the bay. It wasn't until he was passing the island and going straight ahead that I knew he wasn't going to stop.

He didn't know we were here! The knowledge brought foolish relief, postponing for the moment the time when we would have to throw ourselves on his mercy. Not yet, I thought, clinging to an absurd hope for a miracle.

Then the matter was taken out of my hands!

At that tense moment, a saucy bluejay swooped down to the ground in front of Rags, intent upon a sliver of chicken bone that had been left there. The puppy gave a lurch that broke the brittle branch where he had been tied and with a victorious bark bounded after the bird. With a flurry of wings, the bluejay sailed out of the trees with the puppy bounding in pursuit. His high-pitched bark echoed among the rocks and vibrated across the water.

"Rags! Come back!" I hissed as loud as I dared.

I grabbed Davie's arm and held him back, praying that Erskine was far enough past the island not to hear the dog's incessant barking. It was not a morning for answered prayers. Even as I watched, the skiff's sail swung about and the bow of the boat headed toward the island like a homing pigeon.

There was no place to run. A steep drop-off was at our backs, a sloping rocky terrain fell away from the pinnacle of trees on the other three sides. Rags was still barking, sitting on his haunches, looking up into the crown of a tree where the bird was cawing indignantly. His puppy woofs heralded our presence as clearly as royal trumpets blaring across the water.

Davie's slender shoulders quivered as I pulled him

close. My mind raced with the best way to protect him as long as I could. At that moment a shot rang out!

"Git yerself down here!" Erskine shouted. "Or I'll blow yer brains out."

At the sound of the shot, Rags bounded back into the safety of the trees. Davie's expressive eyes asked, "What are we going to do?"

Erskine was coming after us. He had climbed out of the skiff and I could hear rocks spinning out from under his boots. His vile oaths filled the air. What should I do? If we showed ourselves, would he level his rifle at us? What would happen to Davie if I stepped out and he killed me first? What would happen if I didn't?

"Come down here!"

The angry snarl in his voice was like that of an animal who had his fangs bared. "I'm warning ye," he shouted. A bullet whizzed through the trees just above our heads.

"Wait!" I shouted. "We're coming!" If we stayed penned up, we would have no chance at all. I shoved Davie behind me and stepped out.

He was standing on top of a large boulder, a short distance below. His mammoth legs were set apart, in a hunter's stance. An expression of eager cruelty shone in his eyes and twisted his moist lips. Like someone driven by a host of devils, evil radiated from him. *He's going to kill us.* I heard his diabolical laughter as he aimed his rifle at us.

"Drop the gun, Erskine!"

At the sound of his name, Erskine swung around. Below him, Lyle Delany stood with a revolver in his hand. I shoved a fist against my mouth to keep from crying out. For a frozen moment, neither man moved. Then Erskine swung his rifle into shooting position and fired. A chip of rock flew off a boulder just past Lyle's head. The next instant a responding crack from Lyle's revolver met its target.

Erskine wavered on the rock, his large body slowly losing its balance. Like Lucifer falling from heaven, he plunged off the rock, crashing down the steep incline and then dropping into the clear water and disappearing from view.

I ran down the slope into Lyle's arms. I couldn't believe that he was there, holding me tight and soothing my hysterical sobs. "How—?" I blubbered.

"I was coming to have a talk with you . . . I heard the shots and beached my boat by Erskine's. I heard his threats and . . . well, you know the rest. What a fool I've been to let him poison my mind about you. I should have known better." Lyle's voice broke. "I've been going through hell trying to sort out my feelings and come to terms with the horrid little schemer you seemed to be. I couldn't sleep, and this morning, I thought, facts be damned. I had to see you. Good God, will you ever forgive me?" He groaned as he pressed his lips against my cheek.

"I thought you were in it . . . with Erskine," I confessed. "Aunt Minna is dead," I sobbed. "Buried up on the hill. The woman who's been living there is an impostor. Erskine was using me to get my aunt's property. He was going to kill Davie if I didn't cooperate. That's why . . . I couldn't tell you the truth."

"Darling . . . it's all right . . . it's all right. It's over now." And from the way his soft blue eyes caressed my face, I believed the most wonderful of miracles. "I love you . . . want you with me always," he said. "I'll never let you out of my sight again."

"Never?" I managed a weak smile. "And will you walk

with me along the water's edge? . . . and kiss me in the moonlight?" My dream came back, and this time I was the one sitting in front of the huge fireplace, greeting guests in the beautiful dining room, and lying in my lover's arms in one of the lovely bedrooms overlooking the Lake of the Sky.

All the suspicions that had lain between us were gone, dissipated like early mist upon the water. As if to verify my most wonderful fantasy, he said, "I want to marry you, Annie. Let's go home."

Home! Tears filled my eyes. "What about . . ." I nodded toward Blackbriar House.

"We'll let the authorities take care of her. There'll be time enough later to decide what you want to do with the house." He turned and smiled at Davie, who had followed my mad rush down the hill. In a clumsy attempt at sign language, Lyle rubbed his tummy.

Davie grinned and nodded. I laughed at the two of them. Some understandings are beyond the need for words.

REGENCIES BY JANICE BENNETT

TANGLED WEB   (2281, $3.95)

Miss Celia Marcombe's dark eyes flashed with righteous indignation. She was not a commodity to be traded or bartered to a man
as insufferably arrogant as Trevor Ryde, despite what her high-
handed grandfather decreed! If Lord Ryde thought she would let
herself be married for any reason other than true love, he was
sadly mistaken. He'd never get his hands on her fortune — let
alone her person — no matter how disturbingly handsome he
was . . .

MIDNIGHT MASQUE   (2512, $3.95)

It was nothing unusual for Lady Ashton to transport government
documents to her father from the Home Office. But on this par-
ticular afternoon a gust of wind scattered the papers, and suddenly an important page was lost. A document desperately
wanted by more than one determined gentleman — one of whom
would murder to get his way . . .

AN INTRIGUING DESIRE*   (2579, $3.95)

The British secret agent, Charles Marcombe, had done his bit
against that blasted Bonaparte. Now it was time to nurse his
wounds and come to terms with the fact that that part of his life
was over. He certainly did not need the likes of Mademoiselle
Therese de Bourgerre darkening his door, warning of dire emer-
gencies and dread consequences, forcing him to remember things
best forgotten. She was a delightful minx, to be sure, but it would
take more than a pair of pleading emerald eyes and a woebegone
smile to drag him back into the fray!

HISTORICAL ROMANCES BY VICTORIA THOMPSON

BOLD TEXAS EMBRACE (2835, $4.50)

Art teacher Catherine Eaton could hardly believe how stubborn Sam Connors was! Even though the rancher's young stepbrother was an exceptionally talented painter, Sam forbade Catherine to instruct him, fearing that art would make a sissy out of him. Spunky and determined, the blond schoolmarm confronted the muleheaded cowboy . . . only to find that he was as handsome as he was hard-headed and as desirable as he was dictatorial. Before long she had nearly forgotten what she'd come for, as Sam's brash, breathless embrace drove from her mind all thought of anything save wanting him . . .

TEXAS BLONDE (2183, $3.95)

When dashing Josh Logan resuced her from death by exposure, petite Felicity Morrow realized she'd never survive rugged frontier life without a man by her side. And when she gazed at the Texas rancher's lean hard frame and strong rippling muscles, the determined beauty decided he was the one for her. To reach her goal, feisty Felicity pretended to be meek and mild: the only kind of gal Josh proclaimed he'd wed. But after she'd won his hand, the blue-eyed temptress swore she'd quit playing his game — and still win his heart!

ANGEL HEART (2426, $3.95)

Ever since Angelica's father died, Harlan Snyder had been angling to get his hands on her ranch, the Diamond R. And now, just when she had an important government contract to fulfill, she couldn't find a single cowhand to hire on — all because of Snyder's threats. It was only a matter of time before she lost the ranch. . . . That is, until the legendary gunfighter Kid Collins turned up on her doorstep, badly wounded. Angelica assessed his firmly muscled physique and stared into his startling blue eyes. Beneath all that blood and dirt he was the handsomest man she had ever seen, and the one person who could help her beat Snyder at his own game — if the price were not too high. . . .

Available wherever paperbacks are sold, or order direct from the Publisher. Send cover price plus 50¢ per copy for mailing and handling to Zebra Books, Dept. 3319, 475 Park Avenue South, New York, N.Y. 10016. Residents of New York, New Jersey and Pennsylvania must include sales tax. DO NOT SEND CASH.